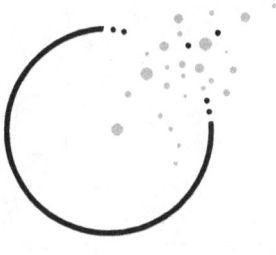

PRAISE FOR *PLENUM: THE FIRST BOOK OF DEO*

"Vanu is one of those rare characters who stays with us, pushing up against our waking dreams. Hir exquisite curiosity mobilizes worlds we can't quite fathom even as we live them. This is the power of *Plenum: The First Book of Deo*. The first of *The Ido Chronicles'* braided quintet of trilogies, it launches us into a compelling tale that weaves between story and history, troubling the cleave. We enter with abandon, launched into a realm of complex spirituality and sexuality, our worlds alive with the sound of resonant creatures singing life, and we emerge knowing, in the deepest recesses of our collective being, that any life worth living is born of the most unanswerable of questions. Vanu is a conduit for this learning. We can't help but follow her lead toward modes of existence yet to be invented. I was deeply moved. What an extraordinary book."

> **Erin Manning** is a philosopher and artist. She teaches at Concordia University, Montreal, Canada. Recent books include *The Minor Gesture* and *For a Pragmatics of the Useless*. 3E is the direction her current research takes—an exploration of the transversality of the three ecologies: the social, the environmental, and the conceptual (3ecologies.org)

"Like the far off song of the jonahs, Geoffreyjen's creation is luminous, keening, and strange. The author is at once warm and wise on the page—fearlessly plunging the reader into re-imagined theologies, ambitious political systems, and new sexual landscapes that verge on the poetic. In the world of this book, gender identity can be understood more like a musical scale. Geoffreyjen guides us with intelligence, scientific rigor, and mystical grace into the first chronicle, where we enter a stream of stories so deep and vast that they span universes and eons. We find ourselves far removed from our own planet and time, yet the struggles Vanu and the other characters endure echo our own."

> **Heather Fester** is a poet, essayist, and author of the forthcoming chapbook *Ghosts of Things Unsaid*. She was an Allen Ginsberg Fellow at Naropa University and directed the Center for Writing & Scholarship at the California Institute of Integral Studies; she now teaches creative writing, rhetoric, and composition courses at the University of Colorado, Colorado Springs.

"A young star gardener embarks on a religious pilgrimage in this debut space opera.

In a distant, seven-gendered future, where time can move fast or slow depending on one's position, Vanu Francoeur lives where stars are born. Vanu, who uses zhe/hir pronouns, is a Novice member of the Kinship of the Suffering God, a religious community. The Kinship inhabits the Annex, a space station floating in the Plenum Star Nursery. Vanu is right on the cusp of adulthood and, as such, will soon be a full member of the Kinship, though zhe still doesn't quite understand the nature of God or the complexities of tending to the Star Nursery. Two strange occurrences arise to shake up Vanu's world. The first is a sexual encounter with a female visitor to the Annex that proves controversial among the other members of Vanu's community. The second is a dream vision of darkness that excites and awakens hir spiritual self. The two may in fact be related: According to one of Vanu's superiors, people are more receptive to visions after a sexual encounter. The Kinship's reaction to Vanu's relationship causes hir to question if zhe will find what zhe needs in its teachings—like the mystery of the song sung by a space-inhabiting descendant of Old Earth's whales. In this novel, Edwards not only creates a rich world, but renders it in vivid, lyrical prose as well. Vanu looks at a nebula "as a creature of the deep might stare towards the distant lights of the surface. The pastel ceiling was intercut with dark bands and splashes of varicoloured luminosity, violets, pinks and yellows, shapes that echoed hir inner turmoil, the fires of space frozen in time." The vocabulary takes some getting used to, though there is a certain logic to much of it (the descendants of whales are known as jonahs), and the author helpfully includes a glossary in the back. This is only the first installment of a 15-volume SF series following five far-future subcultures. While that may seem like an intimidating prospect, Edwards demonstrates an imagination befitting an epic on that scale.

A poetic and wondrous SF tale that grapples with gender and faith."

Kirkus Reviews

PLENUM

THE FIRST BOOK OF DEO

Geoffreyjen Edwards

Volume 1, Book 1 of *The Ido Chronicles*
(A Braided Quintet of Trilogies)

Untimely Books

Untimely Books

untimelybooks.com

An imprint of Cosmos Cooperative
PO Box 3, Longmont, Colorado 80502
info@untimelybooks.com

Book design by Kayla Morelli
Cover Art by Jonathan Proulx Guimond

Publisher Cataloging-in-Publication Data
Edwards, Geoffreyjen.
Plenum : the first book of Deo ; a coming-of-age space opera / Geoffreyjen Edwards. — Longmont, CO : Untimely Books, 2022. — p.cm. — (The Ido chronicles : a science fiction far future saga ; 1)
Gender identity - Fiction. — Religious communities - Fiction. — Science fiction.
PR9354.D88 P54 2022 — 819.13
ISBN: 978-0-9716635-6-5 (pbk.) 978-0-9716635-5-8 (ebook)

"From fulfillment into grace, from the inner heart to divine transformation, we surrender ourselves to God's path of suffering, sacrifice and awakening."

—*Motto of the Kinship of the Suffering God*

"This meaning of events is the supreme meaning, that is not in events, and not in the soul, but is the God standing between events and the soul, the mediator of life, the way, the bridge and the going across."

—C.G. Jung, *The Red Book*

"All history is the history of ensoulments."

—Peter Sloterdijk, *Globes*

CONTENTS

PROLOGUE

Commentary from the working notes of Doric, Co-Scribe of the Sentiat, Ido Era 1538

An understanding of the creation of the Sentiat from the embers that emerged from the Crucium Crisis requires a multiple, some might even say, fragmented, perspective, within which five strands, or colours, can be picked out, one for each pre-crisis faction. The Books of Deo concern one of these strands, the story of Vanu Francoeur, hardly the least significant personage, in spite of hir humble origins. It also examines part of the history of DeoFax, and the role that faction played in the larger organization of the Humanitat, the civilization that preceded the Sentiat. Here is the first act of Vanu's story.

I

HOW BIG IS GOD?

"Does not everything depend on our interpretation of the silence around us?"

—Lawrence Durrell, *Justine*, Accessed from the
All-Human Compendium, Literature, Ido Era 1537

Vanu looked up from the platform on which zhe was anchored with a mix of reverence and frustration. The airless environment was only a mild inconvenience. Hir bren, no more than a few molecules thick, protected hir from the worst of the interstellar vacuum. Tempo took care of the rest. Particularly the cold. The time slippage gave hir gestures a viscous quality. Zhe moved through a sea of sludge. *Tempo slows the heart's own flows*, went the saying. If only that were true. Hir heart flows were entirely too turbulent for any sense of pleasure.

Vanu welcomed the solitude. Zhe used to get it in the water tanks lining the skin of the Annex; these served as shielding from the high energy cosmic particles of the interstellar medium. But zhe had had an accident in there once when zhe got caught between one of the machines that monitored the fluid and its recharging station embedded in the bulwark, and since then zhe had spent less time there, and more enjoying the outside environment with its distractions. Either way, zhe never got enough time on hir own.

Hir mind teemed with questions. But without answers, no matter how much zhe dwelt on them. Zhe kept hoping God would intervene, and save hir from the throngs within, but God didn't seem to be listening. Of course, didn't the doctrine of the Suffering God mean zhe was meant to suffer? Wasn't suffering an integral part of hir spiritual journey? There were times zhe thought zhe understood what that might mean. Unfortunately, such moments turned and fled when noticed, minnows flashing into the dark.

Vanu was looking up, away from the platform and towards the nebula itself, as a creature of the deep might stare towards the distant lights of the surface. The pastel ceiling was intercut with dark bands and splashes of varicoloured luminosity, violets, pinks and yellows, shapes that echoed hir inner turmoil, the fires of space frozen in time. Lashed to the extended, flat platform, on both sides of where hir magsoles clamped hir in place, were machines. Behemoths from an antique era. Hir magsoles soundlessly clamped and unclamped from the metallic surface in a timed dance as zhe shifted hir feet in place, restless as usual. Depending on how zhe stood, zhe could view the platform itself as floor or roof, or simply an oblique wall.

The entire habitat occupied by the Kinship of the Suffering God was called the Annex. Vanu had often wondered why. Something was usually annexed to something else, but no one seemed to know what that might be. Despite its use of wide, flat surfaces, the Annex exhibited no privileged sense of direction, for gravity was absent. Two puck-like cylinders were under spin, providing pseudo-gravity, but these were mostly hidden from where zhe was currently situated. The platform gave the appearance of a vast institute lying on the floor of some sea, but of course the Annex was free floating in space, a different kind of ocean. Vanu had investigated studies of underwater environments once when this similarity had been pointed out to hir. Hir experience inside the shielding tank left hir sensitive to marine environments.

Vanu was on a work detail, an assignment given hir as part of hir training as a Novice. Zhe was inspecting the efforts of the dotes, the tiny flickering machines dedicated to environmental cleanup. The Kinch, like other spiritual communities across the millennia, valued cleanliness. They assigned their youngest members the task of ensuring its maintenance. Whether human inspection was really necessary, Vanu wasn't certain, but it wasn't difficult and it carried its own rewards. Spending time outside, surrounded by the strange splendour of the star nursery, was exhilarating.

There was a sense of expansion, of the immensity of the spaces humans inhabited. Vanu always increased hir oxygen intake when zhe was out here, enhancing hir feeling of well-being. The upwelling tide thrummed through hir, rushing to fill the dips and crannies of hir unsteady moods. The rising current pulled other flotsam into its wake, however, darker thoughts that clung to the undersides of hir emotional landscape.

None of the Kinch seemed aware that one could drown in too many thoughts. They were exemplars of calm waters, a state

Vanu desired with all hir heart. Zhe was certain such beatitude was beyond hir reach. Or was it simply a matter of aging? The older you became, the more empty? The other Novices weren't calm, which would confirm the hypothesis. They just didn't seem to suffer as much from their inner lives. Why was zhe so different, even from hir crib siblings?

The Kinla who inspired Vanu the most was Val Yatsen, a young Kinch recently arrived at Plenum. So the age theory didn't hold up. And Kinla Eugaine, for all hir great age, hardly seemed at peace. Zhe was in a state of constant worry as a result of the myriad problems that arose in hir area of responsibility, that of raising the Novices from crib to maturation.

Vanu was only a few months away from mat status hirself, hir official acceptance into the rights and privileges of adult life. Nonetheless, zhe couldn't imagine being ready for full immersion into the Kinship. Zhe still had far too many questions.

And where would zhe find any meaningful answers? The databanks were useless, the neuws even worse. Hir questions weren't of the type that had factual answers. Zhe didn't want to know how big the Humanitat was (the question was rather more complex than at first appeared), nor did zhe want to know the energy needs of the Crucium Matrix, questions that Kinla Eugaine considered appropriate. The Kinch had a job to do within the Plenum Star Nursery, and understanding how they fulfilled the terms of their contract was an important lesson for Novices. Still, Vanu didn't understand why those kinds of questions were legitimate, but not questions about the nature of God. What was the point of being a member of a spiritual, or *mycs*, community, if you couldn't ask questions about God?

Oftentimes, hir questions were so far reaching, there was no easy way to articulate them. Zhe wanted to know, for example, how big God was. When zhe asked, they either made fun of hir or scolded hir, but zhe was serious. Being told that God was infinite, omniscient, or even all loving, told hir nothing at all. Later, zhe came to believe zhe needed to know not how big God was, but how big God was in relation to hirself. But that wasn't it either. When the adults made any attempt to answer, or when zhe looked up answers in the Book of Doctrine, they spoke of God as a loving Parent. But Vanu didn't know how a parent behaved. Kinla Eugaine was the only parent Vanu had ever known, and zhe was more stern than loving.

Did it come back to the question of calmness? In order to convert hir inner turmoil into some kind of emptiness, how big did God need to be? That was better. But it still wasn't right. Vanu didn't mean to imply that God should be anything other than Zhe was. The questions were merely hir way of deepening hir understanding of, and relation to God. Zhe had an inkling that these musings brought hir closer to an answer that would serve, even if no one else seemed able to understand.

Another question: how could a Suffering God be both in continuous emergence, the goal towards which they were moving, and the ground from which humanity developed? Vanu could understand God as both Creator and Destroyer, that made sense. It was a paradox, but there was a tradition for paradox within the Humanitat. Weren't members of IdoFax devoted to paradox? Indeed, those two aspects of God seemed bound together. But there appeared to be no necessity, in the same way, for a God understood to be "emergent" to be both source and destination, as well. That wasn't a paradox so much as it was functional impossibility. Although was "ground" the same thing as "source"? Was that where zhe had it wrong?

Vanu unclamped her left magsole from the platform, allowing hir to turn to peer around. Zhe was looking for hir friends, the multi-tentacled oggies. Vanu enjoyed their playful and intelligent company, often more than that of hir crib siblings. The oggies could even express themselves in limited ways in conversation. But although they were social among their own kind, they were shy around humans. Vanu had become friends with a young oggie zhe called, affectionately, Jetsu. All the oggies used jet propulsion to get around, so the name could have applied to any of them, but zhe needed a name for hir friend, and Jetsu suited.

The oggies were descendants of a genus from Old Earth's seas called octopus. They had been adapted to function in a hard vacuum environment. Vanu had been studying the history of co-adapted species, along with the development of the different technologies that everyone today took for granted. The oggies had eight highly motile tentacles they used to hold themselves in place or to push away from stable surfaces. Also, they jetted gas, enabling rapid movement across short distances. Indeed, they were better suited to weightless environments than were humans. Even the binach used by humans did not offset this advantage. The oggies acquired gas from the motes that served humans, but supplemented this with gases harvested from the ubiquitous greenbak, the kelp-like growth that clung to the outer hull of the habitat.

Motes and dotes and little lambs eat ivee. It was a part of a nonsense rhyme that played in Vanu's mind when zhe thought about the motes. Lambs, zhe knew, were an animal on Old Earth, long since extinct, but what ivee was zhe had no idea. Whereas humans absorbed oxygen from the swarms of motes that moved through their habitats, via receptor sites built into their brens, the oggies had receptor sites directly on their skin surfaces.

Years ago, Vanu had been told, there had been efforts to remove the oggie population. The ecosystem adaptations introduced to space platforms in the early days of humanity's exodus from Old Sol had fallen into disfavor. Yet both the flora and the fauna had proven themselves robust and adaptable, proliferating throughout the Humanitat, including around the Annex. Some viewed them as a kind of infestation that required cleansing. Along these lines, several among the Kinch argued the oggies in particular were a major nuisance. They were constantly building nests onto the hull, often around the places where water vapour leaked out from the shielding water tanks and formed clouds of frozen droplets. There had been efforts to catch and move the oggies elsewhere. However, the Annex exterior surface was both huge and complex, despite the geometric simplicity of its internal arrangements. There were many places to hide. The oggies were also highly intelligent. They knew the locations of the external sensors and were able to stay out of view. They also learned how to obtain oxygen and carbon dioxide from the gas-filled pods formed by the greenbak. The attempts to control the oggies via their access to the oxygen-carrying motes therefore failed. After a time, all such efforts were abandoned, and the creatures became an accepted part of the external Annex ecology.

Today, however, Vanu had no luck finding Jetsu. Zhe tried locating him via hir binup interface, but the link was inactive, as was sometimes the case. Although the oggies had no sophisti-cated control interface in the same way humans did, they had a rudimentary link. But this was not as reliable as that embedded in humans.

Zhe turned back to hir work. It would be time to go in soon, and zhe needed to finish the job.

II

STAR NURSERY

"What are stars but points in the body of God where we insert the healing needles of our terror and longing?"

—Thomas Pynchon, *Gravity's Rainbow*, Accessed from the *All-Human Compendium, Literature*, Ido Era 1537

The Plenum Star Nursery was a natural star formation region about sixty light years in diameter. Originally, it consisted of a dense patch of interstellar medium (that is, of gas) containing the matter equivalent of some 2500 solar masses. From this cloud, 200 of an eventual 500 stars had come into being. A few of these were hot blue stars, but the majority were smaller yellow and red suns, and a sizeable number were tiny brown dwarfs, mere embers. This cluster, even shrouded within the cloud material, lit up the nebula in a kaleidoscope of colours which changed over time, albeit with stately grace even to tempo-slowed eyes. In addition, several dense black spheres dotted the expanse. These were Bok globules, dark molecular clouds hiding the final stages of the star formation process. The region emitted in the infrared, optical, and ultraviolet, as well as via microwaves, radio and x-rays. Indeed, by using hir zoomer, Vanu could view the expanse at any frequency, not just those available directly to hir eyes. Zhe didn't need to be outside to see the nebula, either. Hir binup interface provided access whenever zhe wished. But it wasn't the same as anchoring hirself to the exterior shell of the hull and looking out, and up.

Viewed directly, at optical wavelengths, the scene was heart-rendingly beautiful. It wasn't just its appearance, but also its size. The nebula dwarfed the Annex, filling half the spherical sky. And at a tempo reduction of 800, one hour of viewing time corresponding to a month of realtime, the changes in the nebula's appearance, although small, were discernible. But its beauty was also tied to its function. This was where the cycle of life started, where stars were born, and stellar winds whipped up the spaces around them, casting elements out into the cosmos.

It was hard not to see God in this unspeakable beauty. Of one thing, Vanu was certain. God, and the communion with Hir one experienced living here, exceeded any literature we might have. It was no accident that led the Kinch to settle Plenum.

The task of the Kinch, as Vanu understood it, was to enrich the molecular clouds with an additional thousand solar masses of material in such a way that the nursery would yield twice as many stars. They would achieve this, in part, by using the brown dwarfs as source material, although Vanu didn't understand how. Zhe knew that some of the machines zhe was inspecting were designed for this task. There were magnetic gravity generators, and quantum phase generators, among other devices, all of them massive. The new stars that were to be molded in this way would serve as anchors to the Crucium Matrix, the data-bearing interstellar field which supported the oracular functions of the Ido. The role of the Kinch, therefore, was that of a stellar gardener, weeding out unwanted brown dwarfs so that other stars could better develop. Carrying out this work under contract with the Humanitat assured their community many of the benefits of the extant civilization, while retaining control over their own destiny.

Vanu also knew that the heart of the task was difficult in the extreme. On the periphery of the nebula, life moved ahead in a normal progression, albeit at the tempo characteristic of the Humanitat, 800 times as slow as realtime. But those who occupied the Core faced huge challenges. They were called upon to coordinate the adjustment of stellar energies across a major part of the star nursery, and first and foremost this required that they select a high value of tempo. For each hour spent in the Core, years went by in the Kinship, even though this already operated at a tempo far from realtime. Hence those who worked in the Core were unable to maintain long term relationships with other Kinch. Even tracking the other Core workers was difficult, as they came onto slowtime and then off at different times. Hence Core work meant accepting a life of utmost solitude. Only a few were able to undertake those activities, even within the framework of the Kinship. Vanu was drawn to that challenge, considered to be the highest work of God, although hir heart quaked when zhe thought about it too. This was why hir questions mattered.

Hir mind cast back over recent exchanges zhe had had with hir sibs, Ranee and Joh. One, in particular, stood out.

<Do you ever stop to wonder what our lives would be like if we lived elsewhere?> Ranee had asked.

<You mean, not at Plenum?> Joh replied, in hir tentative way.

<I mean, not within the Kinship,> Ranee said.

Vanu shrugged hir shoulders. They were in their private lounge, the one that served their crib. Among hir eight crib siblings, Vanu was particularly close to these two. Ranee was a child with a certain roundness to hir appearance. It wasn't so much hir shape, since binach checked any natural tendency to gain flab. Zhe was a little rounder than hir sibs, true, but zhe also had a dark, oily complexion, a soft appearance to hir joints and limbs, a rumbling voice and a way of moving under pseudo-gravity as of a larger body, with a slight tendency to curl forward. And when zhe got excited, zhe would flail hir arms, as if trying to swim. In an airless environment, few actions were as ineffectual as that one.

In addition, zhe tended towards bossiness. Not all the other children allowed hir to order them around, but many did. Vanu appreciated hir sib's other qualities, hir fierce loyalty towards hir friends, hir inclination towards fairness and hir wherewithal to defend those weaker than zhe. Ranee also knew how to laugh, something Vanu appreciated.

Joh, on the other hand, was both small and slender, as well as being lighter in colour, at the lower limit of the variation in body morphology allowed by binach. Indeed, sometimes Vanu wondered if hir binach wasn't defective, as Joh seemed too small and weak for an acceptable level of health. Binach came in a whole slew of different cocktails, each combination characterized by distinct and unique properties. It was remotely possible that the modules administered to Joh were defective in some way. Vanu had questioned Kinla Eugaine about it once, but was told to mind hir own business. Later, Kinla Eugaine had taken Vanu aside and told hir that zhe had checked, and Joh's ecology of nanoparticles, hir binach, was fine. This was typical behaviour for Kinla Eugaine, who seemed dismissive and inattentive to begin with, but took time out of hir schedule to follow through on concerns zhe judged to be legitimate.

<I can't imagine life outside the Kinship,> Vanu said. <Why would you even think about such a thing?>

<Oh, I dunno, boredom maybe?> Ranee replied, but Vanu could see hir face had that crinkly look zhe got when zhe was teasing. <No, seriously, are things so perfect here? Don't you ever think about other places?>

<I don't want to be anywhere other than here with you two,> Joh said.

<Don't worry, little sib, we're not going anywhere.> Ranee was quick to reassure Joh.

But Ranee's question had lingered in Vanu's mind, long after the three of them had left the lounge to follow their separate pursuits. The Humanitat occupied a huge area of interstellar space, billions of star systems and trillions of habitats. Why assume that the Kinship had the last word on the nature of things? It was a good question, Vanu thought, despite what zhe had said to Ranee. The Humanitat included vast numbers of cultures and ways of life. If you had the least spirit of adventure, you could wander for a lifetime and never discover more than a fraction of the secrets that followed humans around wherever they went. Not to mention the half dozen alien civilizations they had also encountered. The Humanitat was an immense sea with myriad islands and shoals, some little larger than villages, others harbouring mini-civilizations of their own. It was perhaps worth thinking about, after all.

Vanu sighed. It was time to go back inside. Zhe had a tutoring session coming up, and it would be better if zhe was on time. Vanu liked learning new things, that wasn't the problem. It was the other Novices who created issues for hir. One in particular. With a last glance backwards at the vast panorama behind hir, Vanu slipped in through an airlock. This part of the Annex, near the children's nursery, maintained an atmosphere. Zhe turned down hir bren's temperature, to avoid overheating. There was no point increasing the discomfort zhe would already be feeling.

III

THRAILPARD

"A talent is formed in stillness;
a character, in the world's torrent."

—Johann Wolfgang von Goethe, *Torquato Tasso*, Accessed from
the *All-Human Compendium, Literature*, Ido Era 1537

The thrailpard was full by the time Vanu got there, even though zhe was a few minutes ahead of schedule. Hir designated place was still available, of course, but the others were all there. The pard wasn't large. The roughly cubic space had room for only eight Novices. Each occupied a corner of the chamber, all peering inwards towards the murky centre. None of Vanu's sibs were here. This was intentional. Cribs were encouraged to move within broader social circles.

Vanu floated over to hir designated parflot, using the conveniently placed tethers to adjust hir movement. Zhe allowed the oscillating particles that made up the parflot's support field to accommodate hir presence and fix hir in place. Today, the particles felt damp, although that must be an illusion. Parflots worked at any tempo, although the device's behaviour changed at different settings. Novices were expected to avoid using tempo most of the time. Indeed, there was a widespread belief that the tempo field could inhibit brain development in the young. The databanks denied that any such effect existed, but many assumed that the official information was wrong. A strict interdiction was not, however, enforced, as tempo could be life-saving, as on this occasion, when Vanu was outside. A reduced tempo value took the edge off the cold that seeped in from the vacuum, making the whole experience a lot more comfortable. And if for any reason zhe got into trouble, tempoing down could save hir life, until zhe could be reached by others. The rule was being relaxed as they approached maturity, but out of habit Vanu avoided using tempo when not outside. Here in the thrailpard, however, at realtime tempo, the parflot particles clung together, forming a thick dough. If you moved around a lot, long periods in the parflot would lead to discomfort. Vanu had a habit of fidgeting.

The first thirty minutes of the teach session were private study. The lesson dealt with the committee structure of adult Kinship tasks. Vanu, however, used the time to find out more about the communities that made up the Humanitat, following hir earlier thoughts. It was another area the Kinch discouraged Novices to explore, but Vanu was now curious and wanted to know more about other places and other ways of living. According to the binup, there were four types of communities—*glov, grat, mycs* and *primes*. These distinctions dated to the First Exodus. *Glov* communities were planet-based. They dominated human history in the First Exodus, but had declined in popularity during the Second and especially the Third Exodus. *Grat* communities were nomadic. According to the binup, they operated outside the purview of the Ido. Not unlike the Kinch, Vanu noted. *Mycs* communities were religious or spiritual communities, like that of the Kinship. *Primes* were not a community, but rather a group of people who opted out of all communal structures.

What about spaceborne communities that weren't *mycs, grat* or *primes?* Vanu wondered. Most of humanity lived in such communities today. Did they not have a name for them? Zhe also had a passing thought about the terms themselves. Zhe had looked up "thrailpard" recently. It was an odd name. Pard, of course, was normal—it just referred to the room itself along with its personal support functions. But thrail? Zhe had struggled to come up with an answer. None of hir first efforts revealed anything useful. Then zhe broadened the search parameters to include ancient sources, and finally, got a result. It was a pre-binach term that referred to following in the path of another. That made sense, zhe thought, for a pard devoted to teaching, and to learning.

What about the origins of other terms though—*glov, grat* and *mycs,* for example? *Mycs* zhe knew, it was a shortened form of mystics. Did that mean the other terms were also contractions? *Glov* turned out to be precisely that. It meant "global village." But *grat?* The binup had little to say about it, and Vanu's efforts were brought short by the chime that announced the end of the private study session.

The next period was to be a guided discussion. The tutor did the prompting via their binups. Vanu now had no choice but to face hir companions. Most of these were friendly, but staring directly across from hir was the Novice called Dev.

Dev was from an infolded crib, born a year before Vanu's exfolded crib. Infolding meant cloning, whereas exfolding meant that an external gamete donor was involved. Stocks of gametes were updated on a regular basis to ensure they were available for reproduction. In principle, infolded cribs looked more or less alike and shared similar behaviour patterns, whereas exfolded cribs were characterized by greater variation. Dev, however, was an exception. Zhe was part of an infolded crib, and yet expressed behaviours that were different from hir sibs. Zhe even looked different, although you had to be attuned to hir personality traits to really notice. It wasn't so much hir facial or body features, as the energy and movement hir body expressed; for example, how zhe often formed hir hands into fists. Vanu could pick Dev out from hir cribmates without difficulty.

Dev's cribmates were all built larger than Vanu's, with big bones and pale, squarish faces. Furthermore, they tended to dominate the spaces within which they moved. They were more competitive and aggressive than were Vanu and hir sibs, but Dev had a mean streak that went beyond just being competitive. Vanu had had many occasions to witness Dev's devilry. At first, zhe hirself had fallen victim to some of these acts. Over time, however, Dev had come to realize that Vanu was not a good target. Zhe defended hirself vigorously, and so for the most part Dev avoided interfering with hir. It was with Vanu's smaller sib, Joh, that the trouble arose.

Dev seemed to have decided that Joh represented the perfect victim for hir taunts and actions. If it were only verbal abuse, Vanu might have let it slide. They were increasingly using tempo as they neared adult status, and that meant they communicated more and more using pseudo-voice and the binup rather than direct vocalizations. This meant subvocalizing what they had to say. The binup interface picked up the subvocalizations and these were transmitted electronically, broadcast, in fact, to one's audience. Although one selected who could hear, the adults sometimes monitored binup-mediated communications. Vanu was certain that if the insults became too virulent, these would be picked up by the adults. Dev had obviously come to the same conclusion. Hir verbal abuse of Joh had declined of late. Zhe made nasty insinuations, but stopped delivering so many blatant insults.

Instead, Dev had become more active with hir tricks, and what zhe called jokes, which zhe and hir sibs laughed at but which weren't funny. Like the time zhe managed to get cleaning fluid connected up to Joh's favorite elpac flav. The seal on the flav packets was broken only when loaded into the liquid dispenser, or elpac, that snapped onto the bren, and which served as the body's main source of nutrients. It shouldn't have been possible to contaminate one, but Dev was imaginative. Joh had been sick for hours until hir binach cleaned the toxins out of hir system, and zhe never touched that flav again. Another time, Dev interfered with hir dotes, which provided waste management for the body. The perturbed dotes had left trails of brown, odorous slime on Joh's bren. Vanu wished Dev would use hir creativity more constructively, but although zhe had tried several times to intervene, often the backlash had been worse. There was something crooked about Dev, but Vanu didn't know how to change hir behaviour.

The tutor was explaining the conditions necessary to attain mat status. Although the evenly modulated voice sounded human, it was not. It was an intelligent machine. Rumour had it that at one time, machine intelligences had been ubiquitous, until it was discovered that an over-reliance on these could be devastating to human relationships. In the modern era, they only carried out certain well-defined tasks. Monitoring learning was one of those, and thrailpards were where this was done.

Dev signalled a question. The tutor stopped in mid-sentence. <Yes, Dev? You have a comment or question?>

<When we achieve mat status, we can do what we want, right?>

<Within reason, yes,> the disembodied pseudo-voice of the tutor replied. <To attain mat status, you have to demonstrate that you can be responsible for your own actions.>

<Sure, I understand that. But we won't have to follow so many rules.>

<I'm not sure I agree with that sentiment,> said the tutor. <Kinship membership requires following many rules, even among adults.>

<Then what's the point of attaining mat status?>

The tutor hesitated. <Attaining the official designation of an adult means accessing the rights and privileges of full Kinship membership. And should you decide to do so, you may choose to leave the Kinship. All adults are free to make such decisions. The Ido also confers rights and privileges, independently of the Kinship. But any society, whether the Kinship, the Ido, or another, has rules that need to be followed.>

<We'll be able to temp down any time we want,> one of the other children remarked, a child from a younger crib than Vanu's. Unlimited tempo control was one of the privileges most of the Novices coveted. Vanu wasn't sure why. You could skip over

boring situations, but even among adults there was an etiquette about when you could do so and when you could not. It was not considered acceptable to temp down during sermons, for example. Beyond boring situations or periods spent outside, zhe failed to see the interest. Why delay living? You still had to live through each moment. Tempo didn't change the total number of moments you had available to live. It just slowed down the speed at which you lived them. Of course, most Kinch didn't function in realtime. Like folk throughout the Humanitat, they set tempo to the human normal, or humorn, value of 800. So the free use of tempo meant living in synch with the adult Kinch. Useful, no doubt, Vanu mused, but desirable?

<Why do some people get mat status earlier than others?> Paolo said again.

<I mentioned earlier that you have to demonstrate that you can be responsible for your actions. Your binup monitors your cognitive development, and an assessment is made continually. This assessment alerts the relevant adults concerning the readiness of a given child to be awarded mat status. Cognitive abilities mature at different rates in different indivs. Hence for some children, mat status arrives earlier, and for others, the process may take more time. Also, the child must not only be cognitively ready, but must understand the import of mat status before it can be awarded. For this, it is necessary to give formal consent.>

<The adults seem to have a lot of power over the Novices,> Dev commented. <So mat status does confer something. It confers power.>

<I disagree,> Vanu found hirself replying. <That is, the adults do have a form of power, but so do Novices. Power is more about strength of character than about some arbitrary kind of authority.>

<Well, that lets you out of the game,> Dev replied.

<Vanu is right,> the tutor said, interrupting. <We haven't talked about power before. What, in your opinion, determines power? Anyone?>

<It's like Dev says,> Paolo replied. <It's when someone can tell other people what to do.>

<Perhaps,> the tutor replied. <But why would those people comply? Why does anyone follow someone else's command?>

There were several moments of silence. <Vanu, would you like to try to answer?> the tutor asked.

<I'll try,> Vanu said. <What you're trying to tell us is that power is the ability to convince other people to do something. So it's about motivating, not ordering.>

<Very good, Vanu. So your comment about strength of character is pertinent, because people are motivated when they encounter the right kind of character.>

<But what if there is a threat behind the command?> Dev tried again. <That's a kind of motivation, too. If non-compliance means punishment, then one is motivated to follow the order. Or else!>

<Vanu? How would you reply to that?> the tutor asked.

<I don't know. I suppose that if you resisted punishment, or allowed yourself to be punished, then you still wouldn't have to comply. It would depend on who else agreed with you.>

<But attaining mat status is not just about having power over others,> Paolo, the child who had spoken earlier about controlling

tempo, added. <It is also about having the power to decide for ourselves what to do.>

<Technically, that is correct,> the teach said. <In practice, as you approach mat status, you will find you are given more control over your life choices. Mat status consolidates the ability to choose while also reaffirming the responsibilities that go with that ability. The more you accept your own responsibility, the more freedom and control you will be awarded. It's a process.>

Good in theory, Vanu thought. But it all depended on how it was done in practice.

IV

CHILDHOOD

"...mystery, something which would lose its very nature if it lost its mysterious character. 'Mystery,' in this proper sense, is derived from muein, 'closing the eyes' or 'closing the mouth.'"

—Paul Tillich, *Systematic Theology I*, Accessed from the *All-Human Compendium, Theology*, Ido Era 1537

A life is like a large, sprawling edifice with a great many chambers, some of which are no longer used and others still undiscovered. Over a long life, we can expect to live, at different times, in entirely different wings of the structure. Our inner lives are often richer than most people credit. Indeed, we may never notice how much is going on within, so much do we spend our time peering beyond the confines of our home. Dormant sections are no less influential than lived-in sections. Indeed, they may sometimes be more important. The closet we hide from ourselves is far more potent than the one we know about but keep hidden from others. However, maintaining awareness of all the dimensions of our inner home can, in and of itself, pose a challenge. The longer we live, the more of a challenge it becomes. In this sense, immortality may be a psychological impossibility.

In our childhood, we are seldom aware of the immensity of our inner chambers. The rooms we inhabit are often barred to us even a few years into our teen years. These in turn will become difficult to enter once we take on adult responsibilities. This is not so much because of the small stature of children. We may be physically small, but our inner lives as children and adolescents can be enormous. It is rather the immensity of these spaces that makes them difficult to access. We learn to compartmentalize our lives, creating large numbers of small, hollowed-out spaces like the chambers of a nautilus shell. And then we discover that large spaces are not only uncomfortable, they have become unbearable. Indeed, much of the movement we undergo, over the course of our lives, seeks to keep the unbearable at bay. This is why we compartmentalize. Children do so too, but the process is different, given the large internal spaces in which they live. It is during the often troubled period of our adolescence that we learn to compartmentalize the way adults do.

Vanu was already in hir mid adolescence. In some respects, zhe had led a quiet, uneventful life. From the point of view of the ancient, pre-binach civilization, confined to the surface of one planet, the setting of this life was so extraordinary that it would have been difficult to convince them that this life was, in any acceptable sense, ordinary. It is hard to imagine what life must have been like for people before binach became so ubiquitous.

As Vanu was leaving the thrailpard, a pair of sibs joined Dev. The three were laughing about something. Vanu had a sudden premonition that it might involve Joh. Zhe had caught a sly look on the part of one of Dev's sibs. What new torment had Dev developed for Joh? And was there nothing Vanu could do about it but wait until the trap was sprung?

Vanu could go and see Kinla Eugaine. Zhe had, in fact, considered doing so on several occasions. Vanu's crib had grown up under hir care. The latter was not given to much expression of sentiment or feeling. Zhe occupied hirself with the practical requirements of hir vocation, perhaps excessively so. Zhe truly cared for hir charges, and that was, at least in part, the reason for hir preoccupation, but zhe may have lost sight of the points of view of those charges, in hir efforts to meet their outer needs. Furthermore, hir responsibilities were large. There were more than 150 children under hir care, although zhe did have some help from other adult Kinch. Admittedly, with binach, the care of one child was greatly reduced compared to earlier epochs. However, Kinla Eugaine still had to oversee their education, their binach upgrades as appropriate to the tasks assigned, their community prayer and participation in religious services, their contributions to communal life, the occasional health issue, and, if there was time left over, their emotional needs.

But Vanu wasn't sure hir remarks would be treated with seriousness, and zhe didn't have any real idea what even an adult could do under the circumstances. Although there was lots of discussion in the religious services about the challenges life posed, about leading a life of spiritual wholeness, about awakening to one's inner light, there was, in fact, very little in the way of concrete examples of what constituted a spiritual shoal and how one might deal with wrongdoing. Such implicit issues were rarely addressed directly. Instead, a person was expected to "suffer" in silence, to be a passive receptor for the pain and suffering that came with life. This left Vanu confused about finding a solution to what had become a serious problem. Zhe could see that doing nothing might lead to serious harm to hir sib, even perhaps outright death.

Vanu remembered discovering Joh crying in one of the passageways near the storage platform where Vanu carried out hir inspections. Joh had been wearing a bren for outdoor tasks, but the bren was in tatters. The bren had come apart as Joh entered the airlock to go outside. Zhe could have died from direct exposure to the hard vacuum of space. In fact, if it weren't for the protective qualities of binach, Dev would have killed Joh on more than one occasion.

<I don't understand why zhe torments me,> sniffled the smaller child after Vanu comforted hir and programmed a new bren into a nearby dresser unit.

Vanu didn't know how to answer. Zhe also didn't understand. How was it that this kind of behaviour was tolerated? Wasn't one supposed to act for the greater good of the community, and express caring for others? Zhe resolved to raise the issue with Kinla Val, the new Kinla, in whom zhe had more confidence of being understood than with Kinla Eugaine.

Vanu contacted Kinla Val by binup and asked for an appointment. Zhe was on hir way to hir appointment when something else perturbed hir, bringing to the surface yet another area of turbulent questioning.

As zhe moved along one of the more crowded corridors towards Kinla Val's office, Vanu caught a momentary glimpse of an unusual figure being shepherded along by a cohort of adult

Kinch. It was, apparently, a young woman, or "findiv," without doubt a visitor. That glimpse, however, had generated a torrent of contradictory reactions.

Despite her surroundings, the young findiv had been wearing a tunable bren. These were almost never seen in the Annex. Bright colours were frowned upon if not outright banned, regardless of where in the environment they were found. And dynamically changing bright colours, that was unheard of. Despite the distraction of her clothes, Vanu had also glimpsed her face and body morphology.

She was very pretty, with a small, round elfin face and finely demarcated features, a deep brown skin colour, and a slender torso with long legs, so that she would be taller when standing than one would have expected from examining her face. She wore her dark hair short. Long hair was often a liability in extreme environments so short hair or a shaved scalp were the predominant fashions in most human habitats. Furthermore, in the split second they had crossed glances, she had grinned across the corridor at Vanu as zhe turned to watch her, a smile that passed beyond her mouth and was in her eyes. She also arched her neck slightly, exposing it to Vanu's gaze, a gesture with a subtle eroticism that Vanu received with a jolt. It was but a glimpse, yet Vanu knew they had connected, that the findiv would be receptive if zhe made an effort to contact her.

In the moments that followed the encounter, Vanu queried hir binup to find out who it was. Her name was Shosee, and she was a trainee from the Yard who was staying at the Annex as part of her preparation for the School. That meant, Vanu guessed, she would be staying in the sequestered guest quarters.

Zhe didn't dare try to reach her by binup, however. Zhe was sure Shosee's binup communications were monitored, even if zhe was unsure whether hir own were. Zhe needed to meet with the young woman face to face and find a way to talk with her discreetly. These were hir rebellious thoughts when zhe arrived at the small office where Kinla Val waited.

The office was located on the outermost level of the Main Section, off one of the secondary corridors that branched from the central corridor. The central location of the office within the business level indicated that Kinla Val had significant status within the community. The residence pards were spread across the middle levels. The innermost levels were given over to laboratories and workshops. Prayer pards were located throughout the Annex, with a large cathedral space lodged against a side wall of the Main Section, offering a view of the backsky, away from the nebula. Kinla Val's office was, however, little more than a cubbyhole, although it was pressurized as were most of the official spaces in this part of the Annex. The chamber felt humid, which was odd. Most environmental spaces at the Annex were dry.

Kinla Val was a long-limbed ebony figure with a flat cap headpiece. In repose, zhe looked relaxed and comfortable, but when zhe moved, hir long limbs seemed angular and pointy, as if zhe were more beetle than human. This ungainliness actually made Kinla Val more likable. There were no pretensions about hir. Zhe wore a loose overbren that tended to balloon outwards over hir body-fitting bren. This was also an odd choice and not one that followed Kinch fashions, or any other with which Vanu was familiar.

<Sit yourself in, my friend,> Kinla Val broadcast in private binup-to-binup mode, pointing to a second parflot, similar to the one zhe was using. Parflots were not used everywhere in the Annex—most common spaces lacked them and many private pards also. This one was more yielding than most, more responsive to Vanu's efforts to adjust it. <It's a real pleasure to see you again, Novice Vanu. How are things in the crib, and with Maestre Eugaine?>

<Kinla Eugaine is as well as ever,> Vanu replied. <As for the crib, well, that's, at least in part, the reason I asked to see you.>

<Tell me, my young friend. I can see that it is a weighty affair.>

<I'm worried about my friend, my crib sibling, Joh.>

<Indeed. That's very commendable. It is part of the Suffering Way to be concerned about others.>

Vanu shook hir head. <No, I'm not... I don't mean it that way. There's an infolded Novice who, well, who teases hir, who makes hir life miserable. Who *bullies* hir, is that the word? Well, if it was just teasing, zhe, we, would suffer through it, but lately this older child's actions have been getting out of hand. One day, I'm afraid zhe'll kill Joh if zhe keeps this up.>

<I see. That is a serious accusation. You say this Novice is infolded? Are hir siblings also part of this hazing?>

Vanu hesitated. <Not directly, no. They just don't seem to intervene in any way. They don't try to stop hir.>

<So, it is not just Joh we should be worried about?>

For a moment, Vanu didn't understand what Kinla Val meant. Then hir perspective shifted and zhe realized that the older Kinch was referring to Dev and hir sibs. <I hadn't thought about it that way. I was focused on the plight of my friend.>

<We all carry a dark self within us, Vanu. How we gain hir ear and give hir voice often defines how we live with God. Our dark self is one of God's gifts to us, to set us on the Suffering path. This child, Novice...?>

<Dev. Novice Dev.>

<This Novice Dev is already well down the Suffering path. We should be as concerned about hir welfare as about that of your friend Joh. Hir path won't be an easy one. Nor, I suspect, will yours.>

Vanu felt the charged intensity of this Kinch's regard spiral through hir outer shell and enter hir inner holds, leaving hir soft centre exposed, just for a moment. Then a moment of turbulence muddied the waters and zhe trembled.

<You've said nothing about this to Kinla Eugaine?> Kinla Val went on.

Vanu recovered hir equilibrium with an effort. <I didn't know... We're told that suffering is the way to... salvation. I didn't know if it was appropriate to say anything. But I do know that this can't continue without... harming Joh, Novice Joh. And not only hir...>

<I understand. You realize, Vanu, that this is a delicate matter. Although incidents of hazing do occur from time to time, there is no.... How shall I say it?... there are no defined procedures to follow. The problem is not just yours, or even Joh's, but it is as much a problem for... Dev, or for any of us. If mishandled, we could condemn any one of you to a lifetime of futility. That is my experience. We don't seek to cause suffering for its own sake. Suffering leads to transformation, and it is through our continual transformation that we find God. Suffering without

the knowledge of transformation is, ultimately, meaningless. Anyway, I will act on this, you can be sure of that, but you must trust me to do this in my own way.>

Vanu nodded. Of course zhe trusted Kinla Val. That's why zhe had come to see hir, and not Kinla Eugaine. But what zhe had heard shook hir, as well. Not shook hir, exactly. Stirred hir would be a better term. Nobody had ever explained this about suffering, that it served another purpose, an intermediate goal. Transformation!

<I did the right thing to come to you, then?> zhe asked, looking for confirmation.

But Kinla Val said nothing for a moment. <There is no way to tell what is right and what is wrong in any ultimate sense,> zhe replied, finally. <I know you want me to reassure you, but I have no oracular powers. And here, in the Kinship, we don't follow the practices of the Ido, for good reason. But I think you needed to come and see me, and really, that is more important than any arbitrary sense of right or wrong.>

Vanu tried to make sense of this, but the argument was subtle. And the reference to the oracular functions of the Ido? This wasn't the first time Vanu had heard something similar. What, exactly, did zhe know about the Ido? It was a service available to most people across the Humanitat. As zhe understood it, the binup, the interface that gave humans and a few other species control over the ubiquitous bio and nano technologies, or binach, that inhabited the body, had a built-in connection to the Crucium Matrix, the star-spanning field that provided the computational substrate for the Ido. So all humans had the ability to access the Ido from birth, or rather from the moment the binup was implanted shortly after birth. But you had to undergo a procedure in an argeet, a medical unit, to activate the link to use it. The binup, of course, provided access to basic communication functions via the matrix, but these were different from the Ido itself. You could access the Forums, the databanks and the knowledge repositories as well as the neuws services without needing to go through the Ido.

The Ido was, originally, a gaming environment. Apparently, playing games became one of the primary activities of humans after the arrival of binach. But over time, one of its most popular games became the dominant function of the Ido, the oracular game. The idea was, you asked it questions—about your life, your proposed decisions, your plans—and it gave you feedback in return. This could be confirmation, public approval, even agreement under the best of circumstances, but also criticism, disapproval, or disagreement if things went less well. In essence, each person's questions incorporated values or issues that were analyzed, extracted and harnessed to generate answers to other people's questions. Over time the procedures had become more and more sophisticated, and more reliable.

Vanu knew some of the Kinch were members, although it was generally viewed as a morally suspect practice. However, Kinla Val seemed to have something more specific in mind in hir criticism of the Ido. And, presumably, since zhe was a recent arrival who hadn't been born at Plenum, zhe had some basis to be critical of the Ido as a practice.

<Is there anything else, then?>

Vanu wanted to ask the older Kinch about hir growing inner turmoil, but didn't know how to talk about it. Zhe felt unsettled by hir feelings, such as those aroused by hir encounter with the findiv, Shosee. Zhe didn't know where the discussion would lead if zhe opened that particular quandary, and zhe wasn't sure how much zhe could lean on Kinla Val, so zhe shook hir head.

<Well, if you need someone to confide in, you'll come back and see me again? Promise?>

Could Kinla Val really see right through hir shell, into hir soft centre? Vanu wondered. Zhe nodded. <I will. I promise.> Zhe left, in some ways more troubled than when zhe arrived, although not by the same questions.

Kinla Val had left Vanu with a lot to think about. Vanu had never thought about how Dev's nastiness could be hurting Dev hirself. Was it even possible? Based on Vanu's limited experience, and combined with what zhe knew from the Scriptures, zhe had assumed there were basically good people, like Kinla Val, and hir friends Ranee and Joh, and basically bad people, like Dev, as well as a lot of other people in a kind of neutral camp. People like Kinla Eugaine and Dev's siblings. But Kinla Eugaine was really basically good, wasn't zhe? Not perfectly so, but that's what the word "basic" implied, that you could be basically good and still not be perfectly good. And zhe would then have assumed that Dev's siblings were basically bad, just not perfectly bad. So maybe there were just two camps, and a group of "undecideds"?

But Kinla Val's comments challenged this view, and not innocuously. In this new view, everyone carried good and bad inside themselves, and the difference between people was how they expressed both sides of their nature. So there was only one camp. When Vanu thought hard about this, zhe realized this was actually in line with the Kinship teachings. They reproached the older Scriptures for having too much of a polarized perspective.

Vanu had never truly understood this criticism of the Bible and its first Testament, even the first two Testaments.

So from this perspective, Dev wasn't in a different camp at all. Zhe wasn't basically bad, just as Kinla Val, or Ranee, or even hirself (although zhe was uncomfortable putting hirself into any of these categories), weren't basically good. Instead, Dev was just like they were, just like zhe hirself, but zhe had given hir dark side more rein; zhe had invested hir dark half with more power than the others had.

That made Vanu wonder. What was hir own dark side? Were these subterranean feelings zhe had been struggling with part of hir dark side? What if zhe invested them with power? What would zhe do? How would that change hir behaviour?

V

THE PLENUM HABITATS

"The opposite of a fact is a falsehood,
but the opposite of one profound truth
may very well be another profound truth."

—Niels Bohr, *Max Delbrück: Mind from Matter: An Essay on
Evolutionary Epistemology*, Accessed from the *All-Human
Compendium, Science*, Ido Era 1537

*Additional commentary from the working notes of Doric,
Co-Scribe of the Sentiat, Ido Era 1538*

The job of a scribe, or a co-scribe in our case, is always a challenge. One has to find a balance between telling the story, and commenting upon it. One is also tempted to provide numerous background details in the service of historical accuracy, while the reader interested in understanding the confluence of forces that gave rise to such important events may prefer not to wade through such intricacies.

First, it is necessary to lay down a rough sketch for the Annex, Vanu's home environment. The Annex was the space platform occupied by the people we know as the Kinch. It was ten kilometers in width, just over one kilometer in depth and some 50 kilometers long, and harboured a population not much more than 50,000. The Kinch spent most of their time in limited parts of the Annex, the rest being given over to autonomous machines or simply left unused. The platform had been designed for a much larger population than had ended up occupying it. Furthermore, the Annex wasn't in orbit around any particular star, as were most space platforms. Instead, it orbited the centre of gravity of the star nursery as a whole.

Although not completely symmetrical about its longitudinal and central plane, the Annex was generally understood as having a ship-like geometry. Aft were the docks, while forward was the bulky box-like shape of the Nursery, housing the children's residence pards, sandwiched between two cylinders that spun on either side to create pseudo-gravity environments. Amidships was the Main Section, another block-like volume that extruded from the base layers, larger overall than the Nursery Block, while between the Main Section and the Nursery stretched a flat area called the Machine Platform. The Main Section housed the offices as well as the residences of the more senior Kinch. Bowed outwards from the middle of this, but flush against the Machine Platform on its edge, was the curved outline of an Observation Portal with its transparent shell. The Observation Portal was used as a meditation space to view the nebula as a whole.

Sizes were deceptive within the Annex. What looked like it might be a walkable distance across the Machine Platform from the Nursery Block to the Main Section was actually ten kilometers. Even using auggies, that is, binach-based muscle enhancements, it would be a hike. The platform was big.

Several other habitats within the Plenum region of space harboured important populations. The whole nebula was classified as predominantly DeoFax, that is, within the governance of the Ido, although its politics were largely determined by the community called the Kinship of the Suffering God. Aside from the Core, the Annex, and some satellite outposts maintained by the Kinch, there were three main habitats, each of them *mycs* communities operating within the broad mandate associated with DeoFax.

The largest habitat was called the Yard, or, sometimes, the Churchyard, a small moon that had been placed into orbit around one of the numerous brown dwarfs within the nebula. This was the home of the community called the Emergence Christian Church, or ECC. The population of the Yard exceeded half a million people. Like the Kinship, the ECC believed in an emergent God, although the ECC also folded in doctrine from pre-binach eras. Unlike the Kinship, the ECC maintained a gender-mixed community where all seven contemporary genders were accepted. Membership in the Kinship, on the other hand, was limited to lindivs, and sexuality, when expressed at all, was confined to homogender relationships. The whole issue of sexual expression among the Kinship was largely a taboo subject.

The third major habitat was the transport station called, more often than not, the Station. The Station was operated by yet another *mycs* community, the New Pantheist Church, with a population of about 100,000. Like the ECC, the New Pantheist

Church was a gender-integrated community. From a doctrinal perspective, the pantheists viewed God as both immanent and emergent. They made much of the paradoxical relationship between these two ideas. The Kinship, of course, was also organized around the notion of an immanent and emergent God, yet made little or no fuss over the first of these two aspects of God. The ECC, by way of contrast, were explicitly Christian, and reconciled ancient teachings of the Christ figure with modern views of the emergent God through recourse to the *Third Testament*.

Finally, in a completely separate habitat, there was a DeoFax School for advanced studies called, in the same spirit as the other habitats, the School, which in principle served all three *mycs* communities. However, the Kinship, which kept itself separate from the other *mycs* communities within the nebula, snubbed the School.

The Plenum Nebula region as a whole was unusual in other respects as well. The presence of the Kinship community both illumined the other populations that inhabited the region but also cast its shadow across them. Furthermore, the Ido had only a muted influence there, even though the purpose of the entire area was to support the Ido's functions for the Humanitat as a whole. It was an island within the larger Humanitat with its own distinct modes of exchange and commerce. Its internal paradoxes acted as a kind of exemplar for the paradoxes of the wider human project, where faith and religion also exerted an influence beyond the numbers of individuals nominally associated with DeoFax.

VI

CHOICES

"The way to make people trustworthy is to trust them."

—Ernest Hemingway, *Carlos Baker: Ernest Hemingway, Selected Letters 1917-1961*, Accessed from the *All-Human Compendium, Literature*, Ido Era 1537

Following hir meeting with Kinla Val, Vanu was spurting back towards hir residence pard, just past the hub area where zhe had caught sight earlier of Shosee, and zhe was moving at a high velocity when zhe encountered a group of older Novices, more than a dozen of them. In null gravity, it took time to pick up speed by tugging on successive tethers, but it was common practice among the Novices, although frowned upon by the older Kinch. Indeed, one could get into unfortunate accidents. Collisions sometimes occurred, and they could be messy. Vanu did hir best to move along the side of the corridor, but the group of Novices filled the space, almost from edge to edge. Zhe tried to avoid contact, but it wasn't possible.

In the melee that resulted, Vanu noticed Dev and hir siblings at the back of the group, unaffected by the collision. Zhe apologized profusely, and made attempts to help the Novices zhe had bowled into realign themselves and find stable anchors. It was fortunate there had been no adults in the group. Vanu might have had to face more serious consequences were that the case. The Novices were fortunately much more tolerant of such incidents. Zhe finally moved to the side to let the group move forward again, pulling on the tethers that were attached to the corridor walls. As they passed, Vanu waved at Dev and hir siblings, and gave them a big, spontaneous grin. To hir satisfaction, Vanu caught a look of startled surprise on their faces.

Somehow, Vanu knew that Dev would not be the problem in the future zhe had been in the past, even if the incidents didn't cease right away. As long as zhe was Other, a demon, zhe seemed invincible, but the moment zhe became human, and a rather sorry and sad human being at that, Dev had no more power to hurt Vanu nor, zhe would see to it, hir friends.

But even if Dev was not the figure of destruction zhe'd always supposed hir to be, the problem of Vanu's own dark self remained. The one realization went with the other. It was so easy to... hate another person when you thought they were all bad, but so much more difficult to find your way within your soul when you came to see your own ambiguity.

For example, what was zhe to do about hir unruly emotional states that threatened to overwhelm what equilibrium zhe had been able to achieve? The reaction to that girl, for instance? It had begun innocently enough, a shared smile, but had mutated into something much more powerful and turbulent. And acting on those sensations would mean stepping into forbidden areas of conduct. Not that there were any real opportunities for that in the Annex.

The experience of pleasure seemed to be relegated to a kind of limbo within the Kinship, even though there were any number of active sexual relationships among the Kinch. In fact, it was tacitly assumed that such relationships contributed to the cohesiveness of the community. Sometimes these relationships developed naturally between crib siblings. Those who chose to remain celibate, or single, however, were also respected.

Vanu felt ambiguous about hir emerging sexual feelings. Zhe had experimented with sex, but had found little desire for other Kinch, even among those with whom zhe was closest. As for self-pleasure, lindiv sexuality could reward individuals dramatically. Although one of the neutral genders, lindivs had replaced genitalia with a sensitive skin layer, called a shoud, that covered the whole body. The sensitivity of the shoud could be heightened via conscious volition—hence it offered enormous potential for self-stimulation. That said, Vanu felt little motivation for this. Instead, zhe found hirself drawn to stories about other genders and communities outside the Kinship. This interest worried hir. It seemed to be yet another example of how zhe was different from the other Kinch. Nothing was explicitly expressed by the adult Kinch concerning sexual relations outside the Kinship. Vanu nonetheless sensed that this was not a choice that would be tolerated.

So on the one hand zhe had hir anger over Dev, whose actions zhe had successfully dealt with without resorting to more coercive behaviour, while on the other hand she had hir misbehaving libido. Where did that leave hir? Zhe should attend to Joh. Hir sib would be needing hir. As for the questions about hir future, they would have to wait until zhe understood what hir choices truly were, as distinct from how zhe imagined them to be. Telling the difference clearly posed a challenge.

VII

OVERGAME

"You seem to me, Socrates, to be quite like a prophet newly inspired, and to be uttering oracles."

—Plato, *Cratylus*, Accessed from the *All-Human Compendium, Literature*, Ido Era 1537

It worked out as Vanu had predicted. Dev didn't know how to react to Vanu's new way of interacting. Vanu greeted hir in a friendly manner whenever their orbits crossed, as if there was no bad blood between them at all. At first, Dev continued to cause trouble, but the number of incidents began to drop off, as if Dev needed Vanu's outrage to goad hir into harassing the younger children.

<I'm not sure why,> Joh commented one day, <but Dev has stopped bothering me. Was it something you did, Vanu?>

Vanu tried to hide hir reaction, but the younger child was too sensitive to miss it. <So it was you,> zhe affirmed, a quizzical smile on hir face. <How...?>

Vanu shook hir head. <I'm not sure exactly. It was pointed out to me that Dev was a real person, not a monster. The day I started treating hir as a person was the day zhe stopped acting like an idiot. It was a valuable lesson.>

The younger child looked at hir with awe, making Vanu squirm. Zhe didn't deserve such admiration. Zhe had only meant to explain enough to hir friend so that Joh could also learn the importance of humility. Instead, zhe seemed to have had the opposite effect.

<There's a new overgame the other sibs are playing,> Vanu said, to distract Joh. Zhe meant by this the older sibs in their crib. Vanu, Ranee and Joh were the next to final cohort of sibs within a much larger crib—all children that resulted from the same gene mix, but whose births were offset in time across several years. <Do you want to go in together?> Vanu said.

Overgames weren't accepted by all the Kinch. Indeed, many adult Kinch expressed outright disdain towards such activities, but certain of the more spiritual-styled overgames were tolerated in the nursery and cribs. Maestre Eugaine Mosche turned hir eye away from such activity. Vanu rarely participated in such things, but zhe wanted to celebrate with Joh hir new freedom from Dev's bullying actions.

The particular overgame Vanu had heard about took place in a historical context. The events portrayed were those undertaken by the legend known as Ionian Nazari, who wrote and popularized what became known throughout the Humanitat as the Third Testament. Vanu had read the Third Testament of course. Along with the Old and the New, it was required reading in school, so zhe had some basis for at least situating ECC doctrine. The game scenario focused on the turbulent events that led to the siege of Old Ascent Station by a team of volunteers, in their successful bid to take back control of the Crucium Matrix from the dissident Emergentists. Most of the players took on roles such as those of the volunteers or the dissidents under the leadership of Shom Rudik, but Vanu was more interested in Nazari and hir entourage.

Gender morphing was only just beginning at the end of the Second Exodus, and Nazari's role in this remained speculative. Little was known about hir actual life, but it was widely believed that zhe was one of the first individuals to adopt the neutral gender. This almost certainly implicated the mi-gender, with the *moelen* genitalia, instead of the la-gender that characterized the contemporary Kinch with the *shoud*, which hadn't been introduced until later. The moelen was a membrane that could fold either to act as penis or vagina, and hence replaced both. The fact that Nazari took on the neutral gender helped explain why zhe remained in the shadows hir whole life. The neutral genders were still controversial at the time. In the overgame, Nazari presented as a *mindiv*, or mi-gendered individual.

Rather than play Nazari hirself, Vanu chose the role of Ugo Spinetti, Nazari's personal assistant. Furthermore, Vanu created a fictional younger sib for Ugo, which zhe proposed to Joh. The game allowed such variations. Joh chose the name Boris, and the two of them entered the game.

It had been running for weeks, but had now entered the final interval before the assault. It was played in near realtime for a variety of reasons. Although it was an overgame, and hence played itself out within a virtual environment, parts of Old Ascent Station had been recreated within the Annex and these had been synched to the game itself, allowing one to physically engage within the game, and not just virtually.

Vanu explained the setup to Joh. <Nazari and Spinetti are occupying two out-of-the-way pards in the outer section of the Station, near its hull. Rudik and the other Emergentists are in the inner region, well away from the vulnerable hull area, although they have left observers and guards behind. That whole section of the Station has been recreated and integrated with the Annex. Come on, it's at the back of the Crib Nursery!>

<What are we going to do?> asked Joh, excited now, but also fearful.

<Oh I just want to talk to Nazari!> Vanu replied as zhe pulled hirself along the corridor towards the Nursery, leaving Joh trailing behind.

Overgame characters followed prewritten scripts, so technically Vanu wouldn't be able to freely speak with Nazari as if the character were alive. However, the scripts were usually extensive and covered many different eventualities. They were also emotionally cued, so as long as you stayed within the overgame scenario, you wouldn't notice the limitations. Vanu had few doubts that a character as important as Nazari would have a wide variety of script options including the ability to discuss hir theological ideas.

They found the relevant station section without difficulty. Once they entered the gaming area, their binups synchronized with the game, updating their visuals, audio and tactile sensations to correspond to the overgame environment. This became a lot darker—none of the usual adjustments to the binup visuals seemed to be able to produce more light, and they progressed almost by feel along the final section of corridor.

<It should be around here somewhere.> Vanu sounded hesitant.

<Wh...at should?>

<The spaces occupied by Nazari and hir followers. Ah, this must be it.>

They drifted into a new intersection, and off to the right they could see the code-sign of an inhabited pard, whereas all the others they had passed had been lifeless, unoccupied. Vanu drew up to the code-sign and pressed hir finger against it. If their binups had been fully functional, they would have signalled directly, but the binup seemed to have reduced functionality, no doubt simulating life in the late period of the Second Exodus.

At first, there was no reaction, but after a minute or so, the door irised open and Vanu, followed by a still hesitant Joh, pulled hirself through into the space beyond.

<Ugo, is that you?> The pseudo-voice sounded feeble.

Vanu had forgotten in the excitement of finding the pard that zhe had taken on the role of Nazari's assistant. Now, with a jolt, zhe realized that Nazari needed a response "in character."

<Yes, I've spent most of the day with Shom. They think that an attack is imminent. They asked me to convince you to move deeper into the station. You're vulnerable to attack here. Oh, by the way, this is Boris, a young man intrigued by what you are trying to do. He wants to help.>

<You are welcome to join our lost cause, Boris, for the time that remains to us. But you know as well as I do, Ugo, that a move is impossible. I suppose you told them you would try anyway.>

Vanu nodded, nonplussed. Why was Nazari unable to move further in? Vanu drifted further into the pard, towards the figure still half hidden in liquid shadow. If Vanu made an effort to see past the binup overlay, zhe would be able to make out which of hir sibs was playing the role, but zhe was enjoying the fantasy and didn't want to spoil it. The indiv was unusual in appearance, remarkably so. Hir face was broken into the ten thousand wrinkles one associated with great age. In Vanu's own era, age did not manifest itself in this way. The skin repaired itself over time. But in the time of the Second Exodus, the auto-repair mechanisms were less effective. Yet despite the mottled appearance, Nazari's face still showed strength. A powerful personality animated the desiccated mask.

<You're feeling tired, maestre. You should rest. Do you want me to set up a cradle for you?> Parflots were not common in this period of history, but Vanu's overgame-adjusted binup provided the right word instead. A cradle, Vanu discovered upon querying hir binup, was a net arrangement used as a sleep berth in null gravity, not so different from their own sleepnets.

<Please, Ugo, I've told you before no honorifics, not even "maestre." And yes, I'm tired, I had another vision while you were gone. They have been getting more demanding recently, more draining. And more frequent. I sometimes find myself wishing the divine had chosen someone else for these intimations.>

Vanu started to protest but Nazari waved hir hands. <Don't worry, I'm not serious. I'm not sure another would have known how to respond properly. I am almost finished recording this segment. And no doubt you are right, sleep would help. I hesitate to sleep too much, though, as I don't want to miss any revelations.> Zhe paused, and dropped hir head; then, as if making an effort, went on. <They have been getting weaker—maybe that's why I find them more draining. I have to be so present to catch it all.

But I must pay attention to my own health as well, or I will not be able to serve as their instrument. Did you pass the last set of texts on to Shom?>

Nazari was positioned with hir back to Vanu, and appeared to be too weak to turn around. <Yes, maes... Ionian. I could tell she wasn't as happy with them, though, as she used to be.> Vanu followed the scripted impulse to speak those particular words, discovering them for hirself as zhe offered them to Nazari. The visions reminded Vanu of hir own dreams, which could also be disconcerting.

Nazari nodded in turn. <I'm not surprised. At first, the visions seemed to reinforce and confirm the messages of the Emergentists, but lately they have begun to diverge from Shom's script. Not enough to cause a serious rift yet, but I can see a day coming when our presence here may become a source of conflict. Another reason to stay here, near the station's skin, not just because it is here than I can best hear the voices from the folding.>

<Voices? I thought they were visions.> The comment slipped out, unscripted, but it nonetheless seemed to find resonance within the game interplay.

<Always wanting to know more, eh, my lovely Ugo? For your notes, no doubt. I've told you before, they are both voices and visions, the one merges into the other. More states imposed upon my mind than images per se. But they draw upon my own resources to find form. My memories and heart states. They are burning through me, slowly, the fires of my sacrifice. No wonder I am tired all the time. Now, let's find my cradle, shall we?>

The binup, although limited, did provide Vanu with a modicum of information about Nazari's statements. The folding was some kind of psychic environment that caused images to form in Nazari's mind. These seemed to fade as Nazari moved away from the hull of the station, almost as if zhe were picking up messages sent to hir from the interstellar void. After each vision, Nazari translated the images into the text that would eventually become known as the *Third Testament*. Vanu was fascinated by the idea that visions could be used in this way, and also that the famous *Third Testament* had emerged through such a process. Nazari had called it 'translation'—meaning, in its original form, it had been nonverbal. Was that another reason why the text was so powerful?

<Zhe seems to have gone to sleep,> Vanu commented later to Joh. <Do you want to temp forward until zhe awakens, or go back to our pard?>

Joh shrugged. <Maybe we could come back another time?> zhe suggested timidly.

Vanu acquiesced, and they left the simulation area. Joh hadn't seemed impressed, but Vanu knew that for hirself, zhe would be back.

VIII

IDENTITY ISSUES

"This isn't who I am."
"You don't know who you are.
No one knows who they are."

—Dialogue from a pre-binach mass media drama, *The Good Wife*,
Accessed from the *All-Human Compendium, Popular Culture*,
Ido Era 1538

Additional commentary from the working notes of Doric,
Co-Scribe of the Sentiat, Ido Era 1538

With reference to the story of Nazari, it is of interest to reflect on
the role that gender identity played within the unfolding events at
the time of the Crucium Crisis. This is especially so given the fact
that in our current situation, our relationship to identity is shifting yet again as we experiment with merged identities. It could
be argued that the Emergentist Rebellion progressed as far as it
did, before its collapse, in part because it provided opportunities
for expressing new and emergent identities that were enabled by

advances in the binach technologies of that time. The new binach capabilities allowed for vastly more effective transformations of the human body. Maestre Nazari hirself provided a good example of this, as one of the earliest gender morphs.

Before that period, gender identity was considered a social norm, a negotiated relationship between a person and the others with whom one interacted, and was still largely structured around the original biological pairing of pre-history. On the other hand, historical records suggest many groups broke out of the strait-jacket of a strictly cis-gendered understanding of the world. Gender fluidity appears to have been much more natural and normal to the human condition than was generally believed during earlier times. With the development of binach capability, however, it became a great deal easier to change the physical body to align with different forms of identity, and after considerable experimentation, the system of seven genders stabilized, for which the musical scale was used as a descriptive language.

Four of the genders were still polarized: the do- and re- genders were considered masculine, and fa- and sol- genders were considered feminine. Mi- and ti- genders, on the other hand, were considered bi-gender, and the la-gendered were treated as neutral. Each of these genders involved one or more of the four types of genitalia. The penis with testicles, the vagina with the uterus, the moelen and the shoud. Only the four polarized genders were fertile. With the explosion in the number of genders, sexual orientation became highly complex, as did the relationship between gender and sex.

This was the dawn of collective sentience, a definitive turn away from the individual as the agent of change. Indeed, part of the raison d'être for this extensive history of the Crucium Crisis is to trace out the change in consciousness that gave rise to these new forms of identity. Our role in this, as Co-Scribe, is a result of these transformations.

The Fax system came into being during the same period that the genders emerged. Each faction grouped people with similar ideas about how to deal with the future, which had become the primary concern of humans once binach settled the problem of survival. Initially there were three, UmaFax, EngFax, and EcoFax. UmaFax grouped the artists and humanists, EngFax, the engineers and technologists, and EcoFax, the ecologists. Together, these represented 85% of the extant population of the Humanitat. DeoFax also emerged in the same period, that is, over the course of the First Exodus, but it was restricted to a minority of people. More may have felt some affinity to spiritual matters, but those who identified themselves as DeoFax viewed spiritual considerations as the most important in determining humanity's future. By the time of the Crucium Crisis, DeoFax included roughly 10% of the population across the Humanitat. Finally, IdoFax, with its emphasis on the resolution of paradoxes, became the de facto faction for dreamers, visionaries, mythmakers and the like. These have never been abundant within the human sphere of activities but have always had an impact far outweighing their numbers. The organization of the Ido explicitly recognized their contributions to the whole. Membership in IdoFax, however, was never larger than a few percent.

The development of these stable forms of bio- and socially engineered identity led to a restructuring of social forms during the Second Exodus and leading up to the early period of the Third

Exodus. Indeed, even the success of Nazari's *Third Testament* may be traced to this phenomenon. Religion took on new forms that were grounded in the changing relationships humans were developing with the cosmos, and the wildly popular *Third Testament* encapsulated and gave form to such novel understandings of the divine.

Gender identity underpinned most aspects of early binach civilization, including spiritual matters. Hence societies which were more gender fluid were, overall, more creative and more tolerant of difference, while those which retained gender rigidities were more restrictive societies overall. In the old understanding, God had been viewed as masculine, and even religions which were not strictly monotheistic tended to be organized around a paternal center. Others, in rebellion, adopted a maternal center, but often remained as polarized. It took several hundreds of years for humanity to wean itself from this gendered mentality and thereby support these different embodied understandings of the world.

The Kinship inherited this revised, fluid understanding of the universe. Indeed, they upheld the Emergent view of God, itself a radical departure from earlier eras that focused on the unchanging nature of God. The Emergent God as described in the *Third Testament* was grounded upon the change in gendered understanding of the cosmos. In a polarized universe, things tend to adopt one state or its opposite, and this reinforces a perception of stability. In a post-gendered worldview, fluidity meant change, and so even God conformed to these ideas. In other ways, however, the Kinship was a throwback to the past. This is often the way of human societies; they encapsulate ideas from different eras and mentalities, like a mountain stream that consists of interacting currents, with gradations of temperature, sedimentation, and quality of light.

Binach was also a kind of post-gendered technology, allowing enhanced mutability in identity as well as supporting new functionalities. It consisted primarily of modules or cocktails that were injected into or ingested by the body. Each cocktail would contain a mix of active ingredients that mutually supported each other to achieve a particular range of target behaviours—for example, the binach modules devoted to innervating muscle groups in lieu of exercise, or those that allowed the body to absorb oxygen through receptors in the skin and release carbon dioxide in parallel mechanisms. Despite the powerful functionalities of such cocktails, there was also danger that different modules could interfere with each other. So there was a trial period following application during which these effects were assessed within an argeet. If severe interference effects were observed, then the cocktail would be removed and adjusted before reapplication could occur. All indivs within the Humanitat, and most of the co-adapted species that accompanied them, incorporated multiple cocktails of binach. As a result, each person had their own internal ecology. In fact, this was why pards were generally assigned to only one individual. Pards had active functions for monitoring the upkeep of an indiv's internal ecology.

The binup also played a role in the formation of identity. Binach and binup were complementary, even symbiotic technologies. Each relied on the other to function effectively. The binup was organized, like its counterpart, to function within the homeostatic system of the body. It was, first and foremost, a regulator. Of course, it also acted as an interface between humans and their cybernetic extensions, including their expanded senses. It was physically composed of specialized organic elements that actively impinged on the brain. Among other items, small conductive antennae were implanted into the upper shoulder and neck region of the body, extending up into the brain stem. These antennae were enervated by specialized binach. The binup, along with its complementary binach, were implanted shortly after birth, and grew along with the body, although some adjustments needed to be made as the child grew.

There are arguments among some historians that the presence of the binup may have been one of the reasons why formal religion went into decline. The privileged link that was created between humans and the oracular functions of the Ido via the binup may indeed have reduced the attraction of divine intercession. However, the advantages of the technology appeared to so outweigh such considerations that virtually no one eschewed using it, not even the Kinch.

Relationships were, in addition, affected by these technologies. The histories reveal examples of friendships breaking up because of binach incompatibilities. The binup, however, generally enhanced the many modalities that supported communications between both humans and the half dozen alien species they had encountered. It provided access to extensive enhancements of the body and modulated other functions using organic means. As a result, human identity shifted in ways that took a long time to work themselves out.

However, at the time of the events that led to the Crucium Crisis, a thousand Ido Era years after Nazari's time, gender identity had long been stable. The *Third Testament* had become canon; indeed, it constituted one of the basic tools that facilitated communication between the diverse *mycs* groups organized within the Ido faction called DeoFax.

Nonetheless, the system as a whole was experiencing stress. The source of this stress was, as one might expect, a complex checkerboard of different factors, but among the most pressing problems was the fact that the region of space occupied by humanity, often called the Humanitat, had become so large that even with the enabling technologies of tempo and the Crucium Matrix, there was a growing number of pockets that no longer functioned in any uniform way within the whole.

This breakup of uniformity found its most direct expression in the ways by which identity, including gender identity, were called into question. Whereas for generations, centuries even, binach-enabled identities had been a given, there were pockets where the status quo was breaking down. This, in turn exacerbated the stresses beginning to show up in diverse groups, and exacerbated the problems that precipitated the Crisis.

IX

MAT CEREMONY

"Tradition is not only a protective, conservative principle;
it is, primarily, the principle of growth and regeneration…
Tradition is the constant abiding of the Spirit and not only
the memory of words."

—Kallistos Ware, *The Orthodox Church*, Accessed from the
All-Human Compendium, Theology, Ido Era 1537

<Ranee reminded me yesterday that hir mat ceremony is coming up,> Vanu mentioned to Joh a few days later. <We need to get hir party organized. As hir friends, that's our responsibility. Have you any ideas where we should hold it?> Zhe was actually of two minds about Ranee's maturation. Ranee didn't seem to be any more mature than any of hir other crib siblings. Zhe was always larking around instead of focusing on hir class work. Vanu wondered if the process for determining maturation status was as infallible as claimed.

<What about holding it in the ball pit?> Joh asked, timidly. There weren't all that many locales that would be appropriate, but

Vanu hadn't thought of the ball pit. The Kinch valued exercise and sports as part of keeping a healthy body. Although they frowned on other games, especially overgames, team sports with a physical edge were encouraged.

The ball pit was a large dodecahedron volume used for playing a range of microgravity sports, as well as some spin sports. The twelve pentagonal walls created a fascinating set of rebound surfaces. Under spin, the ball trajectory curved in ways that were very hard to predict, even for those with years of experience. Vanu's favorite game was a kind of netterball, using a ball the size of a person's head, although with a smaller mass, enmeshed in a long trailing net. Although netterball could be played under spin, Vanu preferred playing it in true microgravity. Usually the game was played among three teams with three equidistant goals. For this, three of the twelve walls were sensitized to record collisions of the ball. The game was most interesting with at least three players on each team—zhe, Ranee and Joh often formed such a threesome, and, unlike other cribs, their nine person crib was just numerous enough to form a full game.

<That's a great idea, Joh! Let's reserve it right away—oh good, it's still available. Who should we invite, do you think?>

They couldn't invite any of the adult Kinch. It wasn't part of the tradition. But aside from their own crib, they interacted often enough with three other cribs. Also, Vanu knew that Ranee had been forming other associations due to hir work shifts with the habitat Liaison Committee. Ranee's contacts included older Kinch, but also several candidates from other cribs. Vanu and Joh made sure invitations were sent out to those people as well.

The mat ceremony itself was highly formal. It was held in the Kinship Hall, within the Outward Rotator. There were two other celebrants present, neither of whom Vanu knew well, although they were both in several of hir classes. There were also several dozen adult Kinch, most of whom Vanu didn't recognize. Some, zhe assumed, were members of the Hospitality Council on which Ranee served. Others must have had similar links to the other two candidates. Everyone wore formal robes over their brens, dark for the most part, with the exception of the candidates and the other youths present. The Hall was pressurized, and pseudo-gravity was present, but was relatively low, as was usual in the Outward Rotator, so the capes tended to billow in the air. A sweet, slightly spicy, scent also wafted through the space—frangipani according to hir binup, a homage to Ionian Nazari.

The Kinship Hall had been embellished at numerous locations with the field of stars that was the DeoFax sigil, including on the capes worn by the candidates. The Kinship's distinctive ripple design was displayed more discreetly. A careful examination would show that the Hall itself incorporated elements of the ripple design in its architectural scope. In addition to the senior Kinch in attendance, there were two members of the regional DeoFax Board who were not members of the Kinship.

Held within the broader traditions of DeoFax, the mat ceremony accorded citizenship status that was valid throughout the Humanitat. Kinla Chou-foc, head of the Kinship Council, presided. The ceremony began, following the identification of the candidates with the reading of the two report summaries for the first candidate, which wasn't Ranee. Vanu only half listened. The first text was the summary from the cognome, the cognitive monitor built into the binup which was used to assist in evaluating queries to the Ido, and for youths had the legally mandated role to monitor their everyday cognitive functioning. The second text was the summary of the report of the designated supervisors.

Following the reports, passages were read from the Humanitat Concordance, the document that laid out the rights and responsibilities of sentients throughout the Humanitat. To Vanu's relief, they weren't reading the whole document, but only the most relevant clauses, the one dealing with choosing one's legal status along with the one concerning mat status.

> <Article 6. Everyone has the right to recognition everywhere as a sentient before the law, regardless of legal regime, whether within the Ido Convention, whereby law is determined by that convention, or without the Ido Convention, whereby law is determined by the OutFax statutes. The choice of legal regime is also guaranteed by these statutes, and may be changed at any time.>

> <Article 16b.2. Youths are also granted adult status, called mat status by convention, when their cognitive monitor considers them to have achieved the capabilities to assume full adult life, under consultation with designated adult supervisors.>

The prior article essentially dealt with deciding whether or not to join the Ido. It was said that over 99% of humans chose to be bound by the Ido Convention. However, fewer than half the Kinch opted for that regime. Vanu remained confused about the benefits of membership in the Ido. Various sources treated the matter differently. Some spoke of governance, others of the Ido as a game, and still others proclaimed its oracular possibilities. None of these were enticing to Vanu. Hir sentiments seemed to be shared by all three of the celebrants—none of them expressed any interest in the overtures regarding Ido membership.

Following this, the first candidate repeated the formal words indicating hir assent to be granted mat status, in a rather desultory fashion, Vanu thought. Kinla Chou-Foc then declared, naming the candidate directly, that the indiv was hereby given mat status and had attained all the rights and privileges of an adult within the Humanitat Concordance. This formal declaration, recorded by the cognome, would terminate its legally mandated monitoring function. Henceforth, only the basic cognitive functions necessary to ensure survival would be monitored, and no action would be taken by the cognome without the indiv's consent.

The whole procedure up to this point was then repeated for the other two candidates. Ranee clearly enunciated each word of the formal phrases zhe was asked to repeat, something not always easy to do in pseudo-voice. Vanu experienced a fierce sense of pride in hir sib.

Finally, once all three candidates had been processed, Kinla Chou-Foc read the articles concerning responsibility towards the community.

<Article 29

<1. Everyone has duties to the community in which alone the free and full development of hir personality is possible.>

<2. In the exercise of hir rights and freedoms, everyone shall be subject only to such limitations as are determined by the Ido solely for the purpose of securing due recognition and respect for the rights and freedoms of others and of meeting the just

requirements of morality, public order and the general welfare in the post-binach society.>

<3. These rights and freedoms may in no case be exercised contrary to the purposes and principles of the Humanitat and the Ido Statutes.>

Vanu followed the repetition of phrases with interest. The syntax was very like that used within the Kinship, but there were subtle differences. Some of these locutions, zhe knew from hir historical studies, bespoke a text of great age, although other phrasings suggested traditions that were different from those held by the Kinship. Zhe wished zhe knew more about these alternative traditions—perhaps they would help hir with hir endless series of questions.

Finally, the ceremony was over, and Ranee was being congratulated by many well-wishers, a number of whom had arrived late. There were far more than Vanu had expected to see. Kinla Eugaine was there, several of their teachers, and also, Vanu noted, Kinla Val. Finally, the numbers dwindled and Ranee turned around to find Joh standing there. Vanu and Joh approached their friend. The ball pit was waiting.

There was already a netterball game in full swing when they arrived. However, it was being played between two groups, not the traditional three, so it was a simple matter for the three of them to join as the third team. Vanu didn't recognize everyone on the other teams, although Ranee clearly knew them well enough. Vanu moved into position as the person who defended their home pentagon, using conveniently located tethers to hold hirself in place, while Joh and Ranee pushed off towards the central zone where the others players were tussling with each other and with the ball.

Maneuvering across the middle space was a challenge. There were several cables that crossed the space, providing opportunities to catch hold and redirect one's flight, but otherwise the only means for doing so was via other players and the ball itself. The ball had sufficient mass that it could significantly alter one's flight path if one flung it away at a good speed. It also required attention when one was on the receiving end—its heft meant that it could deliver a significant punch if one was inattentive. Serious accidents, however, were rare; you just needed to give yourself over to the game and not allow distractions to cause attention to lag. And if anything more substantive did occur, the repair functions provided by binach would take care of these, although not always instantaneously.

Ranee was an aggressive player. Systematically, zhe would push off towards another player and grapple with them, whether or not the ball was nearby, using the other players to re-orient and push off again. Furthermore, Ranee had an uncanny ability to anticipate where the ball would be sent, often arriving first before anyone else even had timed their arrival. The ball could move fast; anticipation was an important skill to master, since if you headed where the ball was at any time, you would almost certainly arrive too late to be of any use. Vanu didn't understand how Ranee was so successful at guessing where the ball would be—its netting meant that it could be flung in almost any direction by its wielder. Also, Ranee was known to use hir own teammates sometimes to provide the extra push zhe needed to re-orient hir motion. Both Vanu and Joh had learned to go passive when Ranee was setting up such a rebound path.

Joh, although much more timid than either Vanu or Ranee, managed to hold hir own overall, although generally more in an assistive role. The three of them often did well in competitive matches. Vanu had developed an ability to defend their home turf, which required a different set of skills from those used so successfully by Ranee in the central zone. Zhe relied heavily on the tethers to adjust hir position and provide leverage to cast the ball away from the turf. Joh would pass the ball towards Ranee when zhe acquired it, and sometimes would locate hirself strategically so that Ranee could use hir body mass to redirect hir own motion.

The game was fast and boisterous, and required vigorous muscular effort to do well. Although the ball pit was not currently under spin, it was pressurized, and so sounds splashed across the space—yells, grunts, and thuds when the ball collided either with a person or with one of the walls. The ball game was run in realtime, like all activities that drew function from the physics of interactions, since tempo slowing would have changed the activity in drastic ways.

This game was particularly unruly, surprisingly so. Ranee was acting as the provocateur, as if hir exit from the world of the novitiates must be heralded by an unchaining of the inhibitions that the Novices were expected to enforce. Vanu found this absence of the usual limitations around play both exhilarating and unnerving. Ranee's thrusts and pushes often exceeded what Vanu considered acceptable, putting other players into jeopardy, although they always seemed to recover in time before any actual injury resulted.

Furthermore, although Vanu usually acted as an anchor, a source of stability in the dynamics of the game, on this occasion zhe found hir traditional arena encroached upon. Normally, the space in front of the home pentagon remained free of bodies. Only the netter ball would cross that space. Now, however, Ranee frequently passed within that space, transversally, and even used Vanu's tethered body as a springboard for achieving trajectories that were unexpected by the opposing teams. Some of Ranee's rebounds left Vanu tumbling without access to a support tether for long minutes. If the ball had come hir way, zhe would have been unable to stop it.

Finally, the game drew to a close. Their team had won, and not because the opposing teams had withheld their own efforts. Although it had been a good workout, Vanu was frustrated by Ranee's excesses. Zhe expected Ranee to want to linger, but both hir sibs were ready to head back to their pard. They thanked the other players, and left just as a new game was starting.

X

RANEE

"Nothing resembles selfishness more closely than
self-respect."

—George Sand, *Indiana*, Accessed from the *All-Human
Compendium, Literature*, Ido Era 1537

Ranee's pard was right next to Vanu's and across from Joh's, so
it really was home territory for all three of them. All nine crib
siblings had their own pards, arranged in a three-dimensional
cluster organized around their common lounge. They had left the
Crib Nursery some three Ido Years previously to join their pard
cluster. Movement between pards was open and free, as it had
always been within the Nursery, but it was possible for each crib
sibling to declare a privacy zone around their individual pard,
something not possible within the Nursery. It was rarely used,
but its availability changed the relationships between the crib
siblings. Now, once the three of them entered Ranee's pard, zhe
turned on the privacy zone so that they would not be disturbed
by their other crib siblings—or anyone else.

<I've got something I want to share with you,> Ranee told them, with a conspiratorial smirk. Zhe pulled a small box free from the wall net which prevented it from floating in the micro-gravity environment and showed it to Vanu and Joh. Vanu had wanted a quick word with Ranee after the game, but was now having second thoughts. It was Ranee's mat party, so maybe not the time to raise such concerns. Also, zhe was intrigued. The box looked like some kind of control surface, but such devices were rare, since almost all environmental controls were accessed via binup.

<What is it?> zhe asked, finally, hir curiosity overcoming hir reluctance to show hir ignorance.

<Let me show you.> Ranee pulled both Vanu and Joh towards hir, then activated the controller. The pard walls disappeared, and, along with them, the vabrens they wore at all times. The vacuum-adapted Kinch were equipped with an ultra-thin bren that protected them against the harsher aspects of living and working in a vacuum. The vabren was also equipped with receptor sites for oxygen-carrying motes, so that they were able to obtain the oxygen they needed to survive from the mobile particles. The environment they were now in had removed their vabrens. Instead, they were connected to a central node via umbilicals.

<It's an *s-bren*,> Vanu exclaimed, both awed and worried.

Ranee nodded. <Because its controller isn't binup-mediated, it doesn't show on the monitors,> zhe explained.

Although s-brens or social brens had an innocent sounding name, they were, in fact, primarily used for sexual encounters, and particularly those involving lindivs. They generated a bren-free bubble in which several people could interact. Sexual encounters among other genders, involving the penis, vagina or moelen, were not strongly affected by the vabren. The thin membrane barely modified sexual response. However, the vabren reduced the sensitivity of the shoud severely. The use of an s-bren, therefore, was a common adjunct to sexual encounters involving those genders. Vanu had heard rumours that these devices were in circulation among the Kinch, but zhe had never before encountered one.

S-brens, like sexual encounters more generally, weren't banned in the Kinship. There was nothing illegal about their use. Nonetheless, they were rarely mentioned or discussed. Sexual abstinence was considered to be part of the way of suffering, part of the basic doctrine of their order, a given. Those who indulged sexually were considered by many to have left, or deviated from, the noblest path. That said, rumours were rampant and very few Kinch actually seemed completely exempt from suggestions of mild impropriety.

<I'm not sure we should...> Vanu couldn't help saying to hir friend, trying to find the right words.

<Come on, aren't you the least bit curious?> Ranee replied. <I thought for my mat celebration, we could at least try one out. And who better than with my two cribmates, the two people most important to me in the whole world? My colleagues at the Liaison Committee all swear by the experience. From time to time. You don't need to use one all that frequently. Although there really is no harm in it. We've all indulged in sex a little, in any case!>

What Ranee said was true. Even in the presence of the vabren, their shoud response could be heightened voluntarily. Self-stimulation was just about impossible to avoid. Vanu, although zhe had tried to abstain, felt in hir moments of shoud-induced pleasure, that zhe was closer to God than at other times. It was part of hir confusion about sex and faith—why should an experience that appeared to bring one closer to God be considered a step away from the moral path?

<Where did you get it?> Joh asked, eyes wide.

<From a friend,> Ranee told them, evasively. <I don't want to say more, I don't want to get anyone in trouble. Well, what about it?>

Ranee was always taking them into new experiences. Zhe was the initiator, had been from their early days together in the Nursery. Zhe took them outside before they even knew there was an outside. There was the day they had jetted away from the Annex and had had to call for help when they ran out of jetting gas. Zhe also took them into the heavy spaces, the wheels with high rotation rates. They had collapsed and needed help to get out, then, too. Ranee had ferreted out an aberrant teach, one of the machine intelligences that coached their learning. They had sequestered it in their crib for several weeks before it was discovered. The teach had allowed them to outperform the other students in school. So, at least on the surface, this was just another of Ranee's adventures. All hir adventures had a troublesome side, but that had never stopped them before.

Vanu could see that Joh would follow Ranee, no matter where zhe led hir. Into hell if zhe were asked to go along. But Vanu had reasons not to follow this time. Zhe was physically uncomfortable with what Ranee was suggesting. Even repulsed by it, but for reasons zhe couldn't clearly articulate to hirself. Intellectually, there was nothing wrong with Ranee's proposal. Sex between lindivs was simply an attentive form of touch, a kind of caress.

And of course zhe loved Ranee and Joh, but in hir understanding, sex wasn't about love. Zhe could see why some people thought it was, but, for hir, sex was something else. Not pleasure, or rather, not just pleasure. Rather it was a kind of connecting to something inside hirself zhe didn't understand. Something that frightened hir, although why, zhe didn't know that either.

Zhe would trust Ranee, and Joh, with hir life, but zhe couldn't trust them within a sexual encounter. Vanu was convinced, without understanding why, that this could, would, do harm. To them? To hirself? Zhe didn't know. But zhe couldn't go there.

<I can't,> zhe finally stated. <I'm going back to my own pard.>

Zhe could see the uncomprehending hurt in hir friends' eyes, as zhe unhooked hir umbilical from the central node and pushed hirself free of the strange binach bubble that encased them, hir own vabren reforming around hir. From the outside, it looked like they were simply floating together in a parflot. Zhe felt relieved, relieved that zhe had had the strength to say no to hir friends, even though zhe couldn't explain hir reaction to them. Zhe pushed off through the entrance and back into the common area, then on to hir own pard.

They would forgive hir, zhe was certain. Eventually.

XI

THE POET

"The world... is impossible to measure."

—Guy Gavriel Kay, *Under Heaven*, Accessed from the
All-Human Compendium, Literature, Ido Era 1537

Vanu did hir best to keep clear of hir two sibs over the next few tendays. Zhe did this because zhe hirself was uneasy about hir own behaviour. Zhe wished zhe could be more open with them, but wishing did not make it so.

Staying out of their way wasn't easy. They all shared the same pard cluster. Vanu arranged to sleep at other locations within the Annex, but couldn't stay away altogether because their shared cluster was the only space programmed directly to maintain hir personal binach ecology. So zhe went back from time to time, but tried to choose odd moments when neither of hir sibs were likely to be present.

This behaviour led hir into a wandering mode, and zhe found hirself in parts of the Annex zhe had rarely if ever visited. One of these areas was the Outward Rotator. The Annex included two spun cylinders, one on each side of the Nursery Block, and both poked out beyond the water tanks that shielded most of the platform from random cosmic particles. These were called the Outward and Inward Rotators, depending on whether they were on the side of the Annex turned towards the nebula or away from it. The Inward Rotator contained the main exercise gymnasium, which Vanu, like most of the Novices, used regularly. It provided spectacular views of the nebula in realtime. The heavy weight wheels were also located there. The Inward Rotator maintained an atmosphere, but the Outward one did not systematically do so. Its portals looked out into the deep, away from the shifting colours of the nebula. The Outward Rotator was maintained at a more sedate spin rate, since it was not used to support exercise activities.

In the Outward Rotator, zhe stumbled into the garden. Zhe'd known there was one, but had never actually been there. This was an inverted space with views into the deep dark, although the blackness was sliced into two sections by the diffuse band of the Milky Way. The space was inverted in the sense that upwards was towards the centre of spin, as in all rotating habitats, but here the floor was perceptibly curved, giving it a claustrophobic feel. The garden did not circumnavigate the cylinder, but the floor did curve across about a forty degree arc. And unlike the rest of the Outward Rotator, this chamber had an atmosphere. This was necessary for the biological sustenance of the plants. The light, which came from large disks near the ceiling, had the yellow character of Sol, humanity's birthstar, artificially generated here with the right spectrum to favour plant growth.

The garden was organized into neat rows of well-tended plants, in a patchwork arrangement like some vast handcrafted quilt. Hir binup informed hir, in response to hir query, that this was a herb garden. Each zone had a distinctive shade, texture, and odor, once Vanu remembered to activate hir natural smell sense. Milkweed, poppies, rosemary, several kinds of mint, mother-wort, passion flower, meadowsweet. So many different colours and evocations. There were several adults crouched at locations across the space, but they paid no notice to Vanu as zhe strolled along one of the carefully marked pathways. In fact, these figures were fixed in place, as Vanu was using near realtime tempo, and they were using a much slower tempo. Vanu sometimes liked to wander at tempos closer to realtime. The Annex was vast, and there were many small nooks that one might not encounter if one didn't go looking. And moving at near realtime meant zhe would be left alone to hir thoughts.

Zhe stopped beside a flat shelf on the side of the path, and sat tentatively upon it, wondering if it would support hir weight. It seemed solid enough. Zhe sipped on hir elpac, filling hir mouth with a splash of lime. Across from hir, the spinning image of the galactic disk held hir attention. The wall of the cylinder was almost completely transparent at eye level, whereas it fogged as one raised one's eyes towards the ceiling.

Zhe wondered if zhe should be polite and reset tempo to that of the others. But nobody expected that of hir, and they were all busy working anyway. Better to just sit here and enjoy the kaleidoscope. The scents that wafted past were also fascinating. Vanu particularly liked the spicy, almost prickly odor of mint.

Then zhe noticed that one of the figures was visibly moving towards hir. As zhe watched, the figure's pace of movement increased fluidly until zhe came to a stop beside the place where Vanu was seated. Surprised, zhe realised that it was Kinla Val Yatsen.

<Vanu! How lovely to find you here. How are you doing?>

<Well,> Vanu replied, even if that wasn't entirely true.

<Do you often come here?> Kinla Val asked. <I haven't seen you here before, and it is one of my favourite locations.>

<I didn't even know the garden was here,> Vanu confessed. <I just stumbled across it.>

<Tell me, how is your younger sib making out? I did talk to hir bully...>

Vanu was grateful for the change of subject. <The problem seems to have gone away, at least for the moment,> Vanu replied. <I have been wanting to thank you, so I'm actually glad to have run into you today.>

<Good. Good. I had something to suggest to you, but I didn't want to take you away if the problem was still an issue.>

<A suggestion?>

Kinla Val nodded, and sat down beside Vanu. <Your apprenticeship period is coming up, if I'm not mistaken. I was thinking you might like to go to the Hospitality House at the Yard. It would offer you a change of scenery, and encounters with other ideas as well. I thought it might help you broaden your understanding of Kinship matters.>

A chance to get away, zhe told hirself. Relief flooded hir body. <That sounds intriguing,> Vanu said. <How kind of you to think of me for this, Kinla Val.>

<I can easily arrange it.> Zhe must have picked up on Vanu's body language, the sense of worry zhe had been radiating, because she added, <And I'll keep an eye on things with your sib while you're gone, too.>

They sat in companionable silence for a time. <May I ask you a question, Kinla?> Vanu finally ventured.

<Of course, my young friend.>

<You said this was one of your favourite places within the Annex. Is that because of the view?>

Kinla Val smiled. <No. Usually I work here at humorn tempo. And at that tempo, the view is simply a whirl, you can't look at it for very long or you'll get dizzy! This,> zhe said, pointing out at the slowly turning panorama of the nebula, <is a discovery for me. I will set tempo to realtime again, now that I know about this. No, it is the quiet work of tending the garden I come for.> Zhe paused for a moment, thinking. <And it has such a long history, too. Religious communities have been tending gardens from the early days of life on Old Earth. In fact, I believe old Mendel invented genetics in just such a garden. I love that about this place, that its roots drink the centuries.>

<You are a poet, too?> Vanu dared to say.

Kinla Val merely smiled, and they went on looking at the view.

XII

THE YARD

"If my mind's modest
I walk the great way.
Arrogance
Is all I fear."

—Lao Tzu, *Tao Te Ching*, Accessed from the *All-Human Compendium*, *Theology*, Ido Era 1537

Sometime after the encounter with Kinla Val in the herb garden, the offer to spend time at the Yard found its way to Vanu. The Yard was the largest of the *mycs* communities in the Plenum Nursery system. Hir apprenticeship was with the Hospitality Group. All Novice candidates were given appropriate service duties within the community in the period leading up to their mat ceremonies, usually as a result of assessing their strengths and also, to some extent, their natural inclinations. These assignments oriented them towards their adult contributions to the community, all except for those who chose to undertake Core tasks since the latter choice was only permitted after a candidate had been accepted fully into the Kinship.

The Hospitality Group was responsible, not for hospitality offered to visitors at the Annex—this was part of the Liaison Committee's mandate—but rather for the offering of hospitality services within the other *mycs* communities outside of the Annex. Vanu found this confusing. Zhe would have switched the names of the two groups, but traditions among the Kinch were highly valued, and even though the confusion was widely acknowledged, there was no serious initiative to change things. The Liaison Committee resided primarily at the Annex, and undertook visits to the other habitats within the Plenum neighborhood in order to facilitate exchanges between the communities, while the Hospitality Group was divided into sections, and members rotated through the different Hospitality Houses, one at the Yard, one at the Station, and one at the School, with time also spent at home in the Annex. By rotating the Group members in this way, the process of Hospitality was kept dynamic and the sense of community with regard to the main Kinship group at the Annex was maintained.

Like all young people across the Humanitat, Vanu was fascinated by the interstellar voyage, short as it was in duration. The trip was undertaken in the small arship that the Kinch maintained for ferrying Kinship members between habitats within the nebula. Unlike the large intersystem arships, there was no true Observation Deck, only a few portals, access to which required that you be seated at the right locations. You could always use your zoomer, of course, the zoom capability built into the binup interface, but that defeated the interest as far as Vanu was concerned. Zhe had jockeyed for one of the portal access seats, but that had been reserved for adult Kinch. Vanu had to make do with a seat a little farther back. This meant zhe had to crane hir head forward to see outwards.

The seats onboard were not the more comfortable parflots, but rather hard surfaces such as those used extensively throughout Kinship habitats. Comfort was a lesser priority among the Kinch, and hard surface seating was judged adequate for most in the community. Within microgravity environments, contact with a seat was minimal in any case. You needed a tether to stay in one place. The Yard was only five light years from the Annex, but even so, the arship would attain a speed about 90% lightspeed for most of the trip. Acceleration would remain low, however. Within the nebula, the ramjet had access to a high density of particles to support acceleration and deceleration—indeed, there were if anything too many particles rather than too few. With a time dilation of 50%, the trip took a little over 30 hours at a tempo of 800. Although that corresponded to slightly more than six years realtime. Many passengers set their tempo to a much higher value, but Vanu left hirs at humorn, that is, 800, at least at the start of the trip. Although zhe had looked at this view all hir life, zhe found the idea that they were actually moving, even such a short distance within the star cluster, to be exciting!

Vanu was intrigued by the physics of interstellar travel. Across the five light years that separated the Yard from the Annex, the arship spent half a realtime year in rapid acceleration and the same time in rapid deceleration at the other end. On the main leg of the trip, the ship would be travelling at about 90% light speed, which accounted for the 50% time dilation. This was only a moderate speed; many arships could travel much faster than this, engendering time dilations as great as a factor of 10 (corresponding to 99.5% light speed) or, in some cases, even as much as 100 (corresponding to 99.99% lightspeed). This meant that, aside from the acceleration and deceleration stages, the ship would arrive only slightly behind any messages sent out at its departure. Vanu had speculated at times what this might mean if a ship needed to be intercepted, or a warning sent about a ship in transit. Carrying out such tasks in a timely manner would be tricky.

After thinking about such scenarios for a while, Vanu finally tired of the scenery, and so set hir tempo to the recommended 10000. This actually turned out to be as interesting, because now the nebula became a swirling basin of movement. The time whizzed by, and zhe had to act quickly to reset hir tempo upwards after the arrival warning sounded so as not to miss out on the docking procedures.

The Yard was not a space platform like the Annex, but rather an extensive architecture constructed around a small moonlet. The Rock, as its residents named it, was some fifty kilometres in diameter. This was commensurate in size to the Annex, but, of course, the surface area of the Rock was actually much larger, and the folding architectural structures that embraced it extended the surface area by many orders of magnitude. Naively, one would have expected vertical structures pinned onto the Rock, but the Yard was structured horizontally rather than vertically. Instead of spires, it consisted of folded sheets through which poked a large rounded section of the Rock. It had slightly more gravity than a true microgravity environment, but at humorn tempo, objects still settled quickly enough to notice. If you left things floating, they floated downwards at a stately pace, but the oblique angle of the sheets often made the downwards direction something other than the apparent vertical!

The Hospitality House was a low-slung structure standing upon one of the rocky extrusions, but very near its edge. The area behind the House actually pulled drunkenly away at an angle along one of the oblique folds. The juxtaposition was a shock to the eye, especially one trained by the flat and unambitious structures used within the Annex. It was, on the other hand, a normal sight within the Yard. The House itself had the same conservative organization as the Annex—Vanu wondered if part of the hospitality offered to the Yard inhabitants might not be access to a more "normal" environment. Inside, the House felt like a small part of the Annex, with its rectangular rooms, rounded edges, tethers and surfaces of diverse orientations. Untethered objects, however, were usually located on surfaces parallel to the floor, making these rooms somewhat different in how they were organized compared to their counterparts in the Annex, which had no gravity to speak of, and hence no privileged direction of motion.

Furthermore, the Yard and its structures were not equipped with an atmosphere. Vanu needed to wear a full vabren at all times, and all communication occurred via binup as there was no ambient gas to carry sound. Vanu was used to wearing the vabren, but it did add another layer of discomfort to the general level zhe was already feeling. Because the vabren supported breathing via binach-modified skin pores, one had to be at least aware of oxygen/carbon dioxide levels, whether these vital gases were transported to and from the body via motes or via a direct linkup to an oteat.

There were some two dozen Kinch residing within the House. Hospitality consisted of hosting events both within the House itself and in the space around the House, including the ceremony of Mass. In addition, some of the Kinch participated in administrative functions for the Yard. After several days of adjusting to the environment, and getting to know the other Kinch, Vanu became aware that one of these—Kinla Pater—tended to keep to hirself. Zhe even slept apart from the House. Zhe occupied, instead, a small building located at the boundary between the Rock and the oblique floor of the Fold. This building, unlike the House itself, was not organized as a set of flats, but rather as a chaotic set of oblique surfaces, a topsy turvy building with no untethered objects.

Vanu felt drawn to Kinla Pater, although zhe couldn't say why. Pater had the soft looking figure of someone who stayed away from physical exercise and also turned off hir muscle-toning binach. Zhe was neither tall nor small, nor particularly thick or big boned, simply a little softer and rounder than most of the Kinch. Zhe had, however, bright blue eyes that darted around and seemed to catch everything in their net. Zhe went about the business of the House as silently, and as diligently, as the other Kinch, but zhe seemed to carry a small bubble around hirself, a zone of avoidance, and the other Kinch kept clear of this zone. It was strange. Almost unconsciously, Vanu started to shadow Kinla Pater, finding hirself often in hir company. It was as if the same bubble that the others avoided acted as an attractor to hir alone.

After several days, Kinla Pater took Vanu to one side at the end of the shift, when the other Kinch were preparing to withdraw for sleep, and Vanu was getting ready to retire to hir own assigned pard. <If you'd like to share my pard for sleep, you are welcome to come along,> Kinla Pater said via binup, making a small gesture of invitation with hir hands.

Vanu was wary, after hir experience with Ranee. Zhe was not looking for another encounter of a sexual nature, but zhe didn't think that was what the older Kinch had in mind. <The other Kinch won't protest?> zhe asked.

Kinla Pater smiled and shook hir head. <They are used to my ways, and you are not the first to find me better company. Please, I have no ulterior motives—only sharing and good company.>

<Then I accept,> Vanu replied. Zhe followed as Kinla Pater drifted across from the main building to the small shelter at the back. <Why do you live apart from the others, if you don't mind me asking?>

<Not at all. No reason, really. I was here first, though—this is the original site of this Hospitality House. The larger building was constructed much more recently. When the new building was completed, I elected to stay on here.>

<So you don't rotate through the other Houses?>

Kinla Pater shook hir head. <That is also a more recent practice. When the Houses were first set up, there was no rotation roster. As one of the oldest living Kinlas, I am allowed my ways. Also, I wasn't here all my life. I spent many years working in the Core.>

That suggested Kinla Pater was a lot older than Vanu had initially assumed. The ability of humans to function inside stellar atmospheres was a consequence of tempo control. Tempo was a self-sustaining field. Once it was changed, it maintained itself without requiring further adjustment. Tempo control slowed down particle interactions at the quantum level. As wave phenomena entered the field, these lost energy and hence were redshifted. Because of the way neurons were also modified by tempo control, as well as the manner in which the human brain worked, this redshift was barely perceptible. The higher the tempo rating, the more extreme the redshift. Since redshifting also meant a reduction in energy, hot, radiation-intense environments could become comfortable for appropriately equipped and protected humans. Gravity was locally affected as well.

However, despite the use of tempo to soften the harsh energies of this extreme environment, particulate matter remained a problem. Human cell structures were sensitive to alpha particles, which could cause damage of a kind that binach couldn't keep up with. To protect against particulate matter, therefore, humans were encased within artificial boxes of degenerate matter called qubes. And to insert these qubes down into the star, an elevator system was used. Tempo ratings to work in stellar interiors needed to be high. A rating near 20,000 was a lower limit. As a result, those Kinch who worked in the Core, quickly outlived their friends and family who did not work there.

So even if Kinla Pater was what zhe appeared to be, roughly two centuries old, subjective time, if zhe had spent time in the Core zhe could be five hundred Ido Years or more in age, which would agree with hir statements about being present when the Hospitality Houses were established.

As they entered the shelter, Kinla Pater pointed out a cabinet that contained some nutritional elpacs, as well as several branch points for oteats, direct connections to the oxygen/carbon dioxide gas system that obviated the need to rely so completely on the ever present and almost invisible motes. The habitat was also much more organic than Vanu was used to at the Annex, with many vacuum-adapted plants and animal species unfamiliar to hir. The only ones Vanu recognized were the patches of greenbak that grew here and there. The inside space was not, as zhe had expected, open, but rather a honeycomb of chambers criss-crossed by spiner strands ranging in diameter from finger-sized to half-body sized. It looked nothing at all like the geometric structures that were habitual on the Annex and present also in the main Hospitality House. This abundant chaos contrasted even with the order of the herb garden zhe had encountered.

Vanu oriented hir body to one of the larger spiner strands, seeking to provide hirself with a reference. <It's like one of my dream spaces,> zhe commented, awestruck. Spiners were used within the Annex, but in limited ways. They were descended from another Old Earth creature called a spider, but spiners ranged in size from a dozen centimeters across to several meters in size. They 'spun' threads in accordance with their size, and these threads, of high tensile strength, were used as construction materials, sometimes hollowed out into tubes. Vanu was, as always, fascinated by the diverse ecosystems that had been adapted to support human activities away from Old Earth.

<Do you like it? I'm afraid the organics have gotten out of hand since I've been on my own here. I much prefer them to the usual Kinch spaces. I believe God meant us to live in equilibrium

with other species, not to pass our lives separated from natural biotes. I'm afraid few among the Kinship share my feelings on this.>

Vanu wasn't sure zhe agreed with Kinla Pater about the lack of other Kinch sharing hir views. Although the interior environment of most of the Annex tended to be geometrically organized, there were several gardens that were cared for and maintained, plus the external environment with which Vanu was so familiar. It seemed to hir that Kinla Pater painted an image that was more caricature than real. On the other hand, they did tend to use machine-made structures rather than the more organic spiner threads.

However, zhe hid hir misgivings from the elder Kinch. <It's great! Do they all serve a function? I mean, the organics outside the Annex are all both co-adapted and functionally targeted at particular tasks. Even the oggies serve a function. Is that the same here?>

<All God's creatures have a right to their own existence, independent of the function they may serve for humankind. Originally, these were functionally targeted, but over time the ecosystem has drifted and I'm no longer sure exactly what they all do now. That's partly what I meant about the organics getting out of hand. But I like it this way. Sometimes they surprise me! Like those cabrali over there in the corner. The lanky plants with the omnidirectional spines? They were designed to harvest and store water from the ambient environment. Variants of an ancient Earth plant family called cacti. They are more effective in an atmosphere than in vacuum, but they do manage to pick up some moisture here, perhaps from their neighbours. I sometimes

use their water instead of elpacs, as it has a subtle flavour. Here, try some if you like!> Zhe guided Vanu's hands towards the moisture that clung to one of the leaves. Vanu caused the pores in the vabren around hir tongue to relax enough to let the moisture pass through. <You see how sweet that is? I suspect they use it to attract water-bearing insects.>

Vanu agreed. It was not just sweet, but tangy.

<If you go through to the next few chambers, you'll find several nemos that have a very soft outer skin and a set of tendrils that can hold you in place for your sleep cycle. They're actually more comfortable than a parflot, and much better than the hard beds the other Kinch prefer. Another reason I prefer living here than over at the House!>

Vanu examined the intricacies of the environment, and only half listened to Kinla Pater as the latter rambled on. Each time Vanu was able to isolate a plant species from the tangle, zhe sent a query to hir binup which returned a detailed description of its genus, its function, and its usual habitat. Also, zhe turned on hir vabren's vacsmell unit and enjoyed the subtle interplay of perfumes hir brain picked up. One could get lost for days or weeks, exploring this environment.

Later, Vanu went in search of Kinla Pater—zhe had lost track of the Kinch's location. It took hir several false tries, following twisting and turning passages that led to dead ends. Finally, zhe found Kinla Pater in a more open space near what must be the rear of the building. The alcove was actually filled with large, cup-like blue flowers, that gave off a subtle, spicy scent for hir vacsmell unit. Kinla Pater was transferring small, round insects—they looked like some kind of ant—from one area and plant species to another.

<Do you mind if I ask you a question?> Vanu queried.

<Ah, there you are, my young friend. Not at all. I sometimes like to facilitate the interactions between different organics. This particular variety of ant leaves a sticky trail that helps these delicate flowers stay open a day or two longer than they might otherwise do. I'm not sure why it works—although their tempo rates appear to be slightly different, so it may have something to do with that... Sorry, I do go on, don't I? You had a question?>

<It will seem silly to you, I'm afraid. The other Kinch always think my questions are silly. It's this—why do you keep yourself so busy? When I need to talk to God, I find I need to slow down, even stop what I'm doing, but you always seem to be occupied, and a lot of the other Kinch also seem to keep themselves busy. I'm sorry if my question sounds so trivial...>

Kinla Pater turned to look at Vanu, a look of chagrin on hir face. <Actually,> zhe replied, <your question is not trivial at all. Indeed, it speaks of a sensitive and questing soul. Would that all we Kinch stopped to ask such questions from time to time. Let me answer by asking you another question. What do you know about the value of prayer?>

Vanu reflected for several minutes before replying. <It is a complicated question,> zhe finally admitted. <The notion of prayer, although it has a millennial basis, has evolved, especially in relation to the *Third Testament*. Once it was considered a kind of communion with the Living God, but in today's understanding of the spiritual journey, prayer is more an accompaniment, a sense of Walking with God, more dynamic. As I understand

it, this emphasizes the Emergent nature of the modern concept of God, since walking is a form of becoming.>

<You're a very good student, Vanu. Walking with God, that is a near perfect description. So, what does that tell you about what I have been doing here, with my gardening?>

<You were... gardening with God? Oh, I see. Walking is a metaphor. There are many different kinds of walking.>

<Yes, Vanu. When you slow down, or stop, you are doing something a little different. You are thinking about God, or maybe just feeling for God. You are looking inwards. That is good, because God is within us. But when you move forward, when you undertake tasks, you are matching your inner self to the outer world. God is also part of the world. So Walking with God is actually a more inclusive approach than Being with God. God is in my hands, my movements, my every step and every becoming. Yes, in my silences also, but not only there. That is the sense of the Emergent God. I do not need to think about God every moment for this to happen. It's not about thinking, it's about letting God pass through us as we walk and work. Does that help?>

Vanu nodded, humbled. <But...?>

<Yes?>

<But, isn't there still a danger that by being too busy, there is no space for God to come to us?>

<Of course. But it is a question of attitude, the attitude of prayer. If you are open to prayer, then God will Walk with you. But if you are not open, then you will shut Hir out—whether you are motionless or busy doing things. The difference is not what you do, but how you do it.>

That sleep cycle, as Vanu lay thinking over the exchange, zhe noticed the old questions pressing up from the seas within. Where to fit them into the vision? If only zhe had asked Kinla Pater about the Suffering God. But really, zhe didn't even know how to frame the question. Vanu felt, intuitively, that somehow hir body held the answer, but the body was not an aspect of God that Kinship doctrine addressed. The body of Christ, maybe, or the body as a vessel, but not the body as a source of suffering and torment, and especially not as a source of luminosity and plenitude.

XIII

SHOSEE

"Sex is a handshake."

—John D. Macdonald, *The Long Lavender Look*, Accessed from the *All-Human Compendium, Literature*, Ido Era 1537

Vanu had been at the Hospitality House at the Yard for three Ido Era months when zhe encountered Shosee. For most of the first nine weeks, Vanu was kept busy at the House itself and gave little thought to exploring the wider expanses of the Yard. This was the House's most intense period in the year. There were several large gatherings to organize, for events such as Advent and the Celebration of Emergence, the latter ceremony held across all the *mycs* communities, not just within the Kinship. There followed a more quiescent period. Vanu finally had the opportunity and the available time to explore further afield.

Zhe knew the local Rock neighbourhood pretty well, but zhe had not ventured much up onto the Fold, nor within its underground layers. It was a more challenging environment to navigate. It was fully three dimensional rather than what was commonly called two-and-a-half for planet-bound environments, surfaces which could move to different heights but retained no thickness. The helter-skelter neighbourhood near the Hospitality House consisted mostly of residence pards, but further out there was a transition to more communal spaces as well as some artists' pards open for public viewing. There were also several churches in this section, a large ECC church and several smaller spaces for mixed congregations.

The neighbourhood was busy. Vanu saw more people just spending an hour in the central court than zhe believed zhe had seen in hir entire life up to that point. Furthermore, the people were of all genders, colours, and forms. Zhe saw many mastodons sail by, a bear-like body modification Vanu had read about but never actually seen. Vanu wandered into a drinking space. Zhe realized it was a perflav bar, another environment zhe had read about but never seen. Zhe wondered if there were any ceethrees, the kind of perflav bar given over to sexual encounters, but none was in evidence. Too bad—zhe had been curious to see one.

Vanu was looking into a thrailpard in the upper reaches of the court, containing numerous dedicated learning environments, when someone tapped hir on the arm, startling hir. Zhe had not expected to encounter anyone zhe knew, unless it was another Kinch.

It was Shosee. Her appearance was unmistakable, even within the rounded shape of the obren she wore. The same delicate face, the same body curves that set Vanu's blood racing, so different from the more neutral forms of most of the Kinch, the same enigmatic smile which Vanu now noticed had a slight tremor. The last time Vanu had seen Shosee, it had been a glimpse across a crowded and busy corridor. Now she could be examined at leisure.

Although tall and slender—in the corridor at the Annex, Shosee had seemed markedly different from the other figures—here she was in her element. Her stance radiated assurance as she held hirself beside Vanu, one hand holding herself steady via one of the ubiquitous support braces that had been placed for this purpose. Her bren was more subdued than the brightly coloured one she had worn at the Annex, but it was a pearly white, contrasting with her dark skin and drawing the eye towards her just as effectively. Her muscles had structure and tone, no doubt the result of working out. She was, however, an airbreather, unlike Vanu, whose body had been modified to breathe through hir skin via the oxygen-bearing motes that clung to hir bren like small suckerfish. Indeed, Shosee's bren lacked the extra pockets for storing oxygen and carbon dioxide required to support the vabren.

Vanu reoriented hir body to align with Shosee's, a smile breaking across hir face.

<I didn't expect to see you here,> Vanu told her. <I thought you were still at the Annex.>

<I needed a break,> Shosee said. <So I got my nana to send a message that I was needed at home.> Her eyes sparkled mischievously.

<Your nana?> Vanu asked. Zhe knew about parents, but had no idea what a nana was.

<It's complicated,> Shosee said. <Someone who took care of me while I was growing up, but who wasn't my mother or my father.>

<Oh, I see. Like Kinla Eugaine for me.>

<Ah, probably not, actually, although technically, zhe might be a kind of nana. Usually a nana has only one or two children to take care of, not hundreds like your Kinla Eugaine!>

<I'm so pleased to meet you, away from....> Vanu hesitated to finish hir sentence.

<Agreed,> Shosee replied, with emphasis. She arched her back slightly, emphasizing her body's contours and drawing Vanu's gaze downwards. <Your Kinch seem way too oversensitive about sexuality. It's very strange.>

Vanu flushed. This brash young woman excited hir, but zhe also felt daunted by her. Zhe took a sip from hir bren's elpac. It was a cranberry flavor zhe had adopted recently, with a touch of jalapeño, part of her experiments with less sugary mixtures than those zhe used to enjoy. Was zhe ready to open the whole issue of sexuality again, and with Shosee?

<We are a bit, well, set in our traditions,> Vanu finished by saying.

<I heard you had been sent here,> Shosee said. <I actually asked about you. I hope I didn't get you into any kind of trouble. Your Kinship Hospitality House is nearby, isn't it? I've never been there, but I have heard about it.>

<It's on the boundary between the Rock and the Fold, east of here.>

<Let's find a more private place to talk,> said Shosee. <I'm not worried about meeting anyone I know here, but it wouldn't do for you to get into trouble with the Kinch. There's a ceethree upFold from here that I know. Let's go there. We can book a private pard if we want to.>

Vanu nodded hir assent, although with a surge of panic at the root of hir spine.

XIV

ENCOUNTER

"...the closer you come, I think, to another human being, the more completely mysterious and unreachable that person becomes."

—Andre Gregory and Wallace Shawn, *My Dinner With Andre*, Accessed from the *All-Human Compendium, Cinema*, Ido Era 1537

Shosee booked them into a small pard at a large and rather boisterous ceethree. Vanu was uneasy. First because of the cee-three itself—although zhe had been curious, the crowded, noisy space put hir on edge. Pressurized to support airbreathers, it allowed Shosee to unseal her obren and free herself from its bulky layers, albeit with a certain amount of squirming in the low gravity environment.

The removal of the obren drew Vanu's eyes towards the graceful curves of her body like a koi fish drawn towards a bright light. Zhe couldn't look away from her. Hir whole skin tingled as hir shoud involuntarily engaged, sending tantalizing waves of pleasure shooting inwards. The shoud's nerve clusters swelled, as they did when aroused. Vanu felt the sharp edge of hir being seep outwards so that zhe lost hir sense of being bound to one location.

Instead of the discomfort zhe had experienced with Ranee and Joh, Vanu found that zhe did not want to fight this urgent yearning. The fear was still there, but now tempered by a subtle blend of other spices. A sense of shame, but also of adventure. The shame flowed from hir abrupt loss of self-control. As for adventure, was this not a whole new set of experiences? Finally, though, beyond the doubt and unexpected sensuality, what of this tumultuous undertow of passion? Zhe had never encountered anything like this, certainly not with such intensity. It both perturbed and innervated hir.

Without conscious thought, Vanu reached out and cupped hir hands around Shosee's head. Shosee moved into hir touch, as if expecting it, and drew her own hands up over Vanu's wrists. Like a blind person who touches the face of a lover, Vanu's hands traced out the features of her face. The shallow bowls of her eyes, the flaring nostrils, the tremulous lip, the cavities and bumps of her scalp, a tactile landscape that tingled against the pulpy softness of hir fingers. Instinctively, Vanu dampened the pleasure response of the nerve endings in hir palms as hir probing pressure became more intense and the codes zhe was reading through hir skin tumbled into the realm of pain.

Shosee's hands fluttered across hir wrists and along the undersides of hir arms, sending rivulets of superheated magma coursing through hir body. Pain was bound up with pleasure as the molten liquid seemed to merge into hir shoud. It was an intensity zhe could, in theory, dampen as zhe had a moment ago hir palms, but now zhe found hirself unable to do so. The molecular sheath of hir vabren should have interfered, but seemed to have no effect at all.

Now, Shosee shed her underbren, allowing it to flake off as Vanu pulled her close. They were free floating in the pard, well away from the walls, so they both moved together, tumbling and swiveling, body touching body, skin sliding against skin. Vanu's shoud was becoming wet. Its natural lubrication pulsed out through hir vabren, designed to let perspiration pass outwards. A mucous humidity transformed hir skin into a slippery envelope. Like some mer-creature of the ancient seas, hir body spiraled around Shosee's, the ecstasy growing with each successive spin.

Vanu, like all human children, knew basic human anatomy. Zhe knew what to do to stimulate hir partner, although zhe had no practice at all doing so. Zhe realized zhe had a tendency to rely on touch, skin to skin, because of hir own pleasure response. But Shosee needed hir mouth and hir tongue, not only hir fingers, to reach her own high plateau of pleasure.

Now, Vanu applied hirself as if to make up for lost time. As before zhe had been an organ of skin, now zhe became an organ of tongue, an organ of lips. Zhe discovered Shosee's fingers, the inside of the joints that seemed to curl in turn around hir tongue, the fingertips as responsive as hir shoud, the tongue of flesh between each pair of fingers, the insides of her wrists, her shoulders like sea anemones, the soft flanks of her breasts, her nipples that resisted even as Vanu passed hir tongue across them, her inner thighs, that set tremors racing throughout her body. Zhe discovered Shosee's tongue and lips, meeting thrust for thrust, nip for nip, passion for passion. Eventually, Vanu found her labia, the folds of her clitoris, the narrow slit of her vagina, with its tangy, salty, and honeyed taste. As Shosee shuddered her way into a series of orgasms, Vanu's own pores flooded with lubricants, signaling the long, tidal climax of a lindiv.

Vanu felt hirself tugged downwards into lightless regions of the deep as the pleasure subsided. More relaxed than zhe could ever remember being, zhe struggled against the downward pull, but this only made hir dizzy. Zhe was frightened again—of the dark that surged around hir, of the things zhe could discern swimming towards hir; shapes with malevolent intentions. Who knew what doom was to be found there? Zhe struggled again, panicking, trying to stop the downward motion, but the dark swelled up around hir, a flood filling the space in which zhe floated... and, finally, eventually, inevitably succumbed.

XV

A VISION OF DARKNESS

"...is it not a contradiction in terms to speak of the revelation of something which remains a mystery in its very revelation?"

—Paul Tillich, *Systematic Theology I*, Accessed from the *All-Human Compendium, Theology*, Ido Era 1537

All was quiet, a silence so absolute, so pure, it couldn't correspond to any reality Vanu knew. Where was zhe? Zhe was lost, cut off from the world zhe knew, disembodied. An intense plenum of darkness surrounded hir, stretching away in every direction, a black deeper than any zhe had ever experienced, thick and intrusive. Zhe reached out hir hands, trying to grab hold of its substance, but encountered only clammy cold. There was nothing tangible to grasp, despite its weight upon hir. This nether cloak filled every interstice of the space around hir. More disturbing, it was also inside hir. But it wasn't the black of negation, of absence, of emptiness. That, zhe would have been able to manage. No. This was a pregnant black, a moist black, a blackness filled with a restless power. It waited to surge out from the confines of hir soft center, to invade the outer universe, the real world of people and pards and oggies, of gravity and light and q-fields.

This blackness that filled hir inner universe shocked hir. If zhe let it free of the chains that bound it, would it not flood outwards? Would it not contaminate everything, overpowering the best intentions of the world at large? Might it not use its sinister force to destroy everything that was wonderful and magical about being alive and living in the company of others? Was this the Devil incarnate, the one of which the Old Testament warned? The serpent that swallowed its own tail, encircling the world with its deadly power?

This was a terrible idea, but an even worse one darted out from behind the other. What if this darkness wasn't the devil? What if it was the Suffering God instead? What if this ancient darkness, this humid rankness, rampant with ambiguity, was merely an expression of hir inability to understand God, an unspeakable response to all those nagging questions that nobody was ever able to answer? Vanu shuddered. Zhe wondered how zhe could experience such a thing and still go on day by day, still find hir way through the miasma of questions and half-guessed answers that somebody, some force (God?) was throwing back at hir?

Zhe heard a voice. It sounded as if it were coming from a great distance, through the dampening fluid, a tinny voice, calling hir name. <Vanu? What's wrong? Are you all right?> And suddenly, zhe was back in the ceethree, and Shosee was leaning over hir. The voice was in hir binup. Zhe reached out and grabbed a tether, and the world stabilized, settled, became normal again.

Normal?

Vanu reassured Shosee. Zhe promised they would meet again, and then, somehow, with no memory of hir movements, found hirself back at the Hospitality House. Begging off from the chores that were hir usual lot, zhe pleaded a need for solitude. Then zhe retired to Kinla Pater's house at the back, where zhe fell into a deep and dreamless sleep.

XVI

KINLA PATER

"The word "revelation" ("removing the veil") has been
used traditionally to mean the manifestation of something
hidden which cannot be approached through ordinary ways
of gaining knowledge."

—Paul Tillich, *Systematic Theology I*, Accessed from the
All-Human Compendium, Theology, Ido Era 1537

When Vanu awoke, zhe felt both listless and alive. It was a contradictory state with which zhe had no experience. Well, that
wasn't entirely true—many of hir emotional states recently had
had a paradoxical nature, but none so extreme as this. And it
wasn't the first time zhe had woken from an unruly dream. But
this hadn't been a dream, had it? It had been something else
altogether. Zhe wanted to stay where zhe was and not face the
day. But at the same time, hir body hummed with energy. The
result of the sex? Or of the vision?

The dream, vision, whatever it was, left hir in a state of near
panic, whenever hir thoughts orbited in too closely. Was zhe

possessed by the Devil? But the Devil was a figure out of legend, an androgynous creature associated with the Old Gods, gods of violence and power. Zhe was also associated with the God of the Old, or First Testament. There was no obvious place for hir within the idea of an Emergent God. Furthermore, historians disputed the role attributed to the devil in the so-called New, or Second Testament. Some claimed that the Christ figure replaced the notion of evil, of Satan, with a focus on benevolence and tolerance. Others denied this, citing the overturning of the moneychangers at the temple, and other biblical passages, to support the claim that Jesus understood and addressed the existence of evil.

Despite these theological arguments, the idea of the devil was still used to scare children into submission during the course of disciplinary action, even within the Kinship. As a result, Vanu, like many of the Kinch, grew up within the shadow of Lucifer, even if this was not part of standard Kinship doctrine.

But that left Vanu in a dilemma, a situation that was even more disruptive than the visceral idea that zhe was "possessed by the devil." Vanu had not the slightest doubt that the power-ful images that zhe had experienced were part of some kind of spiritual vision. Zhe just didn't know what to make of it. If there was no devil, then that creeping, tangible darkness, blackness, must be a manifestation of God. And what, then, did that mean? And what did that say about Vanu, that zhe could be susceptible to such a vision?

And yet. Despite the uncertainty of these reflections, energy and excitement swirled through hir body, like a battery topped to its maximal charge. A sense of well-being, of connection to the world, of opening new paths to spiritual discovery, had taken hold of hir.

Indeed, the excitement was not only the result of the sexual encounter, the meeting of minds and bodies with Shosee. The vision also played a role. The fear that had intervened in the encounter with Ranee and Joh had been well founded. Sex connected hir to something Other, something unknown, some mysterious force. How could it not be a manifestation of God? Vanu felt a new sympathy with the figure of Ionian Nazari whom zhe had encountered within the overgame before Ranee's mat party. It couldn't have been easy to be on the receiving end of a series of bizarre trance states.

<May I intrude on your thoughts?> It was Kinla Pater, floating outside the cocoon Vanu had made for hirself.

<Of course, maestre! I'm sorry, am I in trouble?.>

The older Kinch shook hir head, but it wasn't quite a denial. <The others are worried about you. You didn't present yourself for your duties this morning. I got them to leave you alone for a while, but I'm not sure how long that is going to work. You need to do something, at least to excuse yourself if not offer an explanation.>

Vanu hastened to untangle hirself from the long tendrils of the nemo that had held hir in place while sleeping. <I had no idea it was so late,> zhe said, shocked. <Something happened to me. I don't know how to deal with it.> But as zhe broadcast this to Kinla Pater, the panic receded and Vanu found a measure of control. Zhe had things to do. Zhe needed to push the feelings down and pass above them, at least long enough to fulfill hir responsibilities to the Kinch. <I'm all right,> zhe added, and, to hir surprise, found this to be true.

<All right,> said Kinla Pater. <Go and deal with the others right now. But later, if you feel up to it, you could talk to me, if you wish. I sense in you a need to talk to someone.>

So Vanu went over to the main House. Zhe excused hirself for hir earlier absence, and did hir chores for the rest of the afternoon, right up to the communal evening prayer. After the service was over, zhe slipped away to the smaller building and went in search of Kinla Pater.

Zhe found hir, unexpectedly, tethered above the roof of the structure, watching the dark sky with the vast red and gold nebula splashed across it. One of the things Vanu loved about being around Kinla Pater was hir calm. Many of the people Vanu knew had numerous nervous tics, hirself among them, but Kinla Pater was generally placid, and hir calm was contagious.

<I come up here to remind myself of the magic of Plenum. I spent much of my middle life in the Core. There the view is truly awe-inspiring. At tempo ratings of 20000 or more, the nebula pulsates like a heart, contracting to birth new stars and expanding via coronal winds. The balance between the two movements is always changing, and there's a variable movement to it, just like that of the human heart. Working in the Core has its challenges and difficulties, but there is nothing quite like it. Come and join me up here, if you'd like. This is a tether for two!>

The nebula was bright enough to paint the roof and its occupants with pale red and ochre shadows. Kinla Pater was floating in the ungainly, near horizontal position characteristic of relaxation in microgravity, the body folded slightly forward. Vanu attached the tether to hir own bren and allowed hirself to unfold into a similar position. The slight gravity meant their backs, legs, and feet slowly settled until they merely touched the rooftop.

After a long silence, Vanu began. <I had a vision,> zhe told the aged Kinch beside hir. <Well, I'll come to its origins in a moment. It was a very disturbing experience.> Zhe told Kinla Pater about it, in detail, about the invasive blackness that surged from within hir out into the world, like some massive tide, unstoppable and huge. When zhe had finished, uninterrupted, Kinla Pater was silent for several minutes.

<I don't know any more than you what it might mean,> the Kinch observed. <But it is clearly a *speaking*, a message from God, from the Cloud of Unknowing, as Zhe is sometimes called. Divine visions are not meant to be easy, despite what you may have heard. The visions you read about have usually been heavily edited and interpreted. They are simplified in the telling, stripped of the confusing micro-details characteristic of true vision. You must count yourself incredibly blessed to have received such a *speaking*, even though you may feel anything but blessed right now. Now, tell me what led you into this. You must have been in an unusually receptive state. I'm guessing you may have had some form of sexual encounter?>

As if the suggestion was the key to a lock Vanu didn't even realize was present, the whole story tumbled out, even though zhe had promised hirself not to tell it to anyone, least of all another Kinch. Kinla Pater had been quite right, zhe did need to talk about it to someone. And there was no one else zhe could say all this to. Even Ranee and Joh were off limits right now. And

Shosee wouldn't understand either. She would just be exasperated with the built-in limitations of Kinship doctrine and practice.

Vanu had no idea if Kinla Pater was the right person to talk to, if zhe could be trusted with these confidences. So far, the Kinch had been understanding and sympathetic, but that was before Vanu revealed that zhe was breaking the taboos of Kinship society. But zhe had to unburden hirself, and Kinla Pater was the only possible person with whom this could be done. Vanu was taking hir chances, but zhe was at least hopeful that confidentiality, at a minimum, would be respected.

<I don't know why I find her so interesting,> Vanu said. <I know I should be focusing on the Kinship, but... she, at least, takes my questions, and my doubts, seriously!>

Again, Kinla Pater listened without interrupting, and remained silent after Vanu ran out of things to say. Finally, the response began to take shape, for just as Vanu needed to talk, zhe also needed to hear some form of echo. <I will not say whether this was a wise course of action or a fatally flawed one. Certainly within Kinship precepts, it will be judged severely. If I appear to know something about these matters, you should know that the Kinship was not always so intolerant of other relationship, uh, modalities, let's say. When I was young, there was more room for, well, fluidity, between genders and between communities. I had experiences, perhaps not as deep as yours, but certainly encounters that would not be found acceptable by today's standards.

<But coming back to your situation, I do think it likely that it will be discovered, not because of anything I may say—you can be certain I will preserve your secret—but because these things tend to come out, one way or another. Not if it were limited to

the one incident, but I believe that unlikely. You will go back for more. It is in your nature, something you have to do. And over time, across several such encounters, it will be discovered.>

Vanu listened, hir feelings in turmoil. At first zhe had been jubilant. Kinla Pater would not report them. But then the bottom dropped out, as the realization of what Kinla Pater was saying struck home. Yes, zhe would go back to Shosee for more, assuming the young woman was willing, and, yes, discovery was likely, even if they took all the precautions in the world. But the experience of sex was too intense to ignore, too fulfilling to pass over. Yes, Vanu was part of a community that viewed suffering as important for one's spiritual journey, but it was not a community that enforced abstinence either. If others indulged, why shouldn't Vanu?

As if guessing these reactions, Kinla Pater went on. <You must not confuse the idea of the Suffering God with the principle that we Kinch must worship difficulty. That is not the intent of the doctrine. I know that many Kinch *do* confuse the issue, but you need not be among them. Human existence is filled with suffering, there is no need to go and create it artificially, nor to worship it either. The idea of the Suffering God is that God suffers along with us, so that, by sharing in our suffering, Zhe helps lighten the load.>

<Yes, Kinla Val said something like that to me,> Vanu replied.

Kinla Pater turned hir head to glance at Vanu.

<Indeed. Tell me this, then, do you think suffering is necessary?>

Vanu had half expected the question. <Isn't it how we grow and change?>

Kinla Pater turned hir head back to the variegated sky. <Yes, it is the motor of our evolution. Not only that, it is from within our suffering that God emerges. God is Emergent because of our suffering. If we didn't suffer, not only would there be no humanity, there would also be no God.>

<And none of this splendour?>

<And none of this splendour! Yes, indeed.> Kinla Pater smiled. <For although the universe has its own reasons for existing, its being is resonant with our own.> Zhe paused again, then went on. <This is the framework within which we feel, think, act, practice community, and worship. Now let's come back to your actions, and, perhaps, yes, also to your vision. I am not saying this is necessarily the case, you will need to find your own understanding of your vision, but the blackness you experienced could be this self-same suffering of which we have been speaking. Although generally understood negatively, suffering is actually a positive force, a tangible source of good in the universe. Perhaps your vision tells us something about the value of this tangible good. And the fact that the vision came out of a powerful, sexual experience is also important, even if this was taboo. A life of experience tells me that both the vision and the experience that preceded it are important, but I cannot tell you how, nor how to assimilate them into your life.>

<Still, your words are helpful. I have had difficulty seeing this experience in a positive light. I will need to think about what you have said.>

<Yes,> Kinla Pater said. <Although thinking is not always what is needed. I will say this, however. If you should come to a sense of having broken something, of a fracture within your

being or in your relationship with God, you will need to enter a process of penitence and redemption. These are not easy things to do, but they are necessary to ensure healing. Penitence means sacrificing something of yourself. It has to hurt to work. And redemption, although I call it a process, is not within your control at all. Redemption comes to you by the Grace of God. That word, Grace, is very important—it is not something young people know much about. Redemption is a "coming back," a "coming home" if you prefer, to a sense of contact, a union with God. But it is not something you do, nor is it something you take, or even call into being. Instead, it is something you must be given. Look up the term, "grace," and you will understand better what I am saying.>

They both fell silent after this lengthy exchange, and soaked up the empyrean swirls that held them in thrall. A more sober Vanu came down off the roof than the one who had gone up.

XVII

CRITICISM

"...the purpose of life is not to be happy at all. It is to be useful, to be honorable. It is to be compassionate. It is to matter, to have it make some difference that you lived."

—Leo Rosten, *The Rotarian: The Myths We Live By*, Accessed from the *All-Human Compendium, Popular Culture*, Ido Era 1537

On hir next free day, Vanu contacted Shosee by binup. It wasn't, perhaps, the wisest thing to do—binup broadcasts, even binup-to-binup, could be monitored, but zhe didn't know how else to reach her. Shosee had given hir no address aside from her binup idotag, and although Vanu had made a half-hearted attempt to find her by other means, these attempts had failed. If zhe wasn't willing to wait until they bumped into each other again, the only way to reach her was via binup.

Since they were no longer at the Annex, Vanu judged the chance the Kinch would be monitoring hir binup to be low. And following hir discussion with Kinla Pater, zhe was feeling fatalistic about the affair anyway. Zhe would take precautions, reasonable ones, but since discovery was likely inevitable, there seemed little point in being paranoid about the measures taken.

Shosee was as eager to meet again as zhe was. They arranged to go to the same ceethree as the first time. Both of them knew the location and it wasn't far for either of them. Trying to amend hir ignorance, Vanu inquired about where Shosee lived. This turned out to be a complex on the other side of the public court where they had met.

Vanu used hir binup to find a quick route to the ceethree, and Shosee was waiting for hir when zhe arrived.

She was as beautiful as the first time. In fact, Vanu was shocked by how beautiful she was. If anything, she was more desirable than before. She wore an obren which presented swirling smoke patterns to the eye, but within which bright embers glowed and flared into flame that licked along her arms, across her belly, or down her legs. The effect was galvanizing, even though Vanu had never actually seen fire. Fire and flame of the chemical, as opposed to the nuclear kind, required ambient oxygen to burn, and was also almost impossible to maintain within a tempo field. The flickering properties of flame were hence lost to modern humans, and even its ability to warm was muted by tempo, so fires were seldom used or referred to outside of legend. This made the effect of the obren she was wearing even more potent and magical.

<You like it?> she asked, archly. <A friend of mine is a bren designer. You might be interested to learn that the flames are mapped to my state of arousal. As you can see, you have a certain effect on me!> Even as she made this affirmation, the flames

curled around her belly and down towards her pelvis, as well as upward across the curve of her breasts.

Just as involuntarily, Vanu's own skin, hir shoud, burst into activity, sending thrills of pleasure in molten rivulets coursing across hir body surfaces. The sensitivity of the shoud, the skin surface of the re-, sol-, la- and ti- genders, was widely understood to be under voluntary control, and Vanu, in hir own experiments, had found that zhe could sensitize or desensitize different areas of hir skin at will. But with Shosee, the sensitivity shot up without any voluntary control at all, and zhe could do little to dampen the effect. Vanu was therefore more of an instrument played upon by Shosee than zhe was the musician. The fire-programmed obren that Shosee wore, however, enabled Vanu to read Shosee in a parallel and similar way, to see the effects the barest trace of a touch would generate on Shosee, even though she had no shoud, only the normal skin that humans had evolved within their environment of origin.

The sex was even more intense than it had been the first time. The experience went deeper, since they each knew more about the specific responsiveness of the other. This experience was a retracing of their bodies, a reterritorialization, and like all such retracings, the grooves went deeper, and the pleasure/pain that followed grew more thickly and abundantly along the curves of its passing. Shosee's climax swelled and rolled her forward into a long series of shudders and aching whimpers, while Vanu's was more like the flow of the tide than the crash of a wave, a long, slow building of power into a crescendo that filled all hir awareness followed by a draining away as the ebb took hold.

<Have you had sex with people of other genders?> Vanu found hirself asking as they curled about each other in the long decline. Shosee's bren was now calming down, the embers fading back to smoky shades of grey, black, and brown. <I'm just wondering how that might be different. I don't know much about them, about other genders.>

<You know the children's contine?>

Vanu shook hir head. <Contine? I have no idea what you're talking about!>

Shosee shook hir head. <Children's rhyme? No? I can't believe how staid your culture is! Listen!

<First, dindiv, doer and poke;

Second, rindiv, king be-spoke;

Third, mindiv, middle man and maid;

Fourth, findiv, fire, fold and glade;

Fifth, sindiv, slide inside;

Sixth, lindiv, lamb innate;

Seventh, tindiv, triune pride

And all things dictate.>

Vanu was speechless, listening to these rhymes that Shosee recited in tones that retained echoes of her younger self and with a rhythm that had a ritual feel to it, her pseudo-voice emphasizing certain words. She also made gestures with her hands to accompany each line, and her face shone with glee at some of them. Such a combination of bawdry and subtlety! And there was so much here to understand!

<I don't know how to begin to respond,> zhe finally replied when Shosee had settled again. <That was wonderful!>

<Well, like most children's verse, it reveals more than one might think about what is going on.>

<So I'm "lamb innate"?>

<Most lindivs are gentle in their love-making,> Shosee acknowledged.

<And "triune pride"?>

Shosee nodded. <Tindivs often think they have all the cards, in the sense that they can take on any role. As I said, it may ostensibly be about genitalia, but in fact it's more akin to attitude than the mechanics of sex. There's another short set of verses about the latter, however. Do you not know this one either?

<Phallus, Malus, Apparatus;

Vagina, Regina, Ursa Minor;

Moelen, Gordian, Androgen;

Shoud, Unploughed, Endowed.>

Vanu shook hir head again. More subtlety. Did the children really know what it all meant? zhe wondered.

<It's very clever,> zhe found hirself saying. The shoud as unploughed, because nothing broke through the body's envelope, and yet, endowed nonetheless. Brilliant. Malus, zhe didn't know immediately what that represented. Obviously a reference to masculinity, but what else? And what about Ursa Minor?

<I think children like the rhymes and rhythms without always catching the full meaning of the phrases,> Shosee said. <But, in your case, you're not just a lamb, Vanu. I only meant to use that as a starting place. You're different. I don't know anyone else like you. You are so, I don't know, spiritual, in your lovemaking. Not spiritual in any kind of ethereal way, I mean. But still, every way you touch me is like a reverence. You make me feel like I'm some

endless gravity well, that you could keep going down and never touch bottom. It's not the way I normally understand myself, nor, I suspect, how others see me.>

<But you are deep, ama mine,> Vanu protested. <That is exactly how you feel to me. What does the rhyme say? "…fire, fold and glade"? That's a wonderful portrait of how it feels! I never expected, I had no idea. But of course, I had no basis for comparison. I've never had sex with anyone else. Although if the contine is accurate, then—>

<You've never had…?> Shosee exclaimed. She drew away from Vanu so that she could turn and look hir in the eyes. <Well, we'll have to do something about that. I'm sure I can find a few friends.>

<Now you're teasing me,> Vanu scolded her. <I have no interest in having sex with anyone else.>

<You don't?> She was mystified. <We come from very different worlds, then. In my world, people change partners all the time. It actually gets a bit tiring after a while. It's one of the reasons I like you so much. You are steady, not changeable like I am, or like my friends.>

<Why did you come to the Annex?> It was another of Vanu's saved up questions, one zhe had been waiting for the right moment to ask.

<Mmmm, my father is a senior member of the ECC here.> She flicked her eyes away from Vanu, then back again. <He wanted, he wants me to get experience with other types of *mycs* communities. Indeed, he is rather fascinated by your Kinship's idea of a Suffering God. In the ECC, we don't focus on God's suffering, or anybody else's, either. In fact, we don't even have any formal doctrine, in the way your Kinship has. The ECC is

more, I don't know, practical? The church tries to be inclusive. Not anything goes, I don't mean that, but, well, tolerant towards widely different beliefs. So sending me to the Annex was his way of training me in greater tolerance. And, look, it brought you to me, or me to you. Which is a blessing, any way you look at it!>

Vanu explained to her some of what Kinla Pater had said about the Suffering God. Shosee was interested. <I should get you to come round and talk to my father,> she told Vanu. <It would help satisfy his curiosity about the Kinship. Would you come, if I arranged it?>

<Does he know about us?>

<Not formally, no. He doesn't try to keep tabs on who I'm seeing. But if you come, he'll guess it. One look at you, and anyone would know! I gather it may be a problem for you if the Kinch find out?>

Vanu was horrified to discover that hir feelings could be read so easily, and said so.

<Mmmm, you are a bit transparent, sweetie. But no, he'd know because he can read me as well as you. We are becoming attuned to one another, and those with experience will recognize it. Our encounters have been anything but casual, haven't they? So why are the Kinch so ornery about sex? Is it any kind of sex, or just sex with partners from outside the Kinship that they object to?>

Vanu tried to explain, but hir own understanding was less than perfect, so it came out messy. <Let me get this straight,> Shosee summarized finally. <The Kinch believe that sex distances them from God. But you say this isn't part of the formal doctrine. So it's part of the informal doctrine. They tolerate sex between

lindivs, who are the only gender allowed within the Kinship. Now that's very odd—I've always found that odd. When I was there at the Annex, they sequestered me, isolated me from the Novices and even from most of the adult Kinch, as if I might actually be a source of contamination of some kind. It was very strange. The Kinch claim to be tolerant of others, but they are hardly tolerant of difference and variety within their own community. They should treasure difference, not berate it. Who decides these things, anyway, do you suppose? They don't use the Ido for such matters, do they?>

Vanu shook hir head. <Only about a third of the Kinch are Ido members, and so the Ido cannot be effective as a form of governance, as it can be elsewhere. No, there is a council that makes the decisions. They do consult the wider membership, but not on everything.>

<Mmmm, to me it's a great puzzle, although the pieces do seem to fit together. As your friend Kin... Kinla Pater,> she stumbled over the honorific, <as Kinla Pater notes, the doctrine of the Suffering God is not to worship suffering, but to be present for it. But if you got that mixed up, then you might think that suffering was good, and avoiding suffering was bad. So you would naturally treat sex as bad, because it gives pleasure, not pain. At least, some of the time. And you would seek to encourage solitude, and celibacy, as paired values. Solitude because it enhances pain, and celibacy likewise. And one way to increase solitude, is to promote a kind of social sameness, a communal homogeneity. Because social activities thrive in the presence of difference. So you would want to keep that out. How am I doing?>

<You're being very harsh and judgmental towards my community,> Vanu said, drily. <I thought you were in training for greater tolerance?>

Shosee stretched herself, and used a tether to pull herself free from the parflot. <You're right,> she said, sheepishly. <But I won't retract what I said, nonetheless. Perhaps I am being overly harsh. Well, it's time I got going. Will you come to the complex and meet my father? On your next free day?>

Vanu agreed, although zhe had reservations about the encounter. Zhe really didn't want to publicize their relationship, for that was indeed what it was becoming. Vanu wanted it kept private, and personal, and secret. But zhe understood that Shosee didn't have a secretive nature, that she was used to doing things in the open, and Vanu didn't want to change her in any way.

Vanu was on the way back to the Kinship House when zhe realized zhe had told Shosee nothing about Kinla Pater's remarks concerning hir vision.

XVIII

GREATBEAR

"The wordless teaching
The profit in not doing—
Not many understand it."

—Lao Tzu, *Tao Te Ching*, Accessed from the *All-Human Compendium*, *Theology*, Ido Era 1537

Vanu wasn't able to obtain another free day for three weeks. Kinla Pater assured Vanu that the busy season would settle down soon into something more sedate, but there always seemed to be endless chores—duties—zhe was required to complete. One of the Kinch, Kinla Hayden, had discovered that Vanu was a good organizer and motivator as well, and so Vanu found hirself organizing visits from various groups, and small Prayer meetings or open Ecumenical Gatherings involving representatives from the different churches and other *mycs* communities on the Rock. Zhe often worked eight, nine, even ten hours at a stretch, sometimes during the day and sometimes at other times. This left hir time for communal prayer, which zhe was expected to attend, an hour in the exercise gym, and then zhe needed to find refuge in hir nemo cocoon and sleep so as to be ready for the same kind of regime the next day.

Finally, although zhe had to make the request several times, zhe was granted a free day. Zhe contacted Shosee and arrangements were made. Shosee sent directions on how to find the ECC complex, and the next morning Vanu set out on this new adventure.

In order to discover more of the neighbouring environment, Vanu decided to set out along an unfamiliar route, rather than follow the same way towards the public court that zhe had followed several times before. The binup directions sent by Shosee should ensure that zhe didn't get lost, regardless of which route zhe took.

The way to the ceethree was straight up the Fold, but Shosee's family complex was westward, and so Vanu pushed off in that direction, skimming across the Rock at the edge of the Fold. Zhe had equipped hirself with a small jetpac—it stored both the oxygen zhe absorbed through hir vabren and the carbon dioxide hir body released. There was a small binach pressor that generated compressed carbon dioxide, and the jetpac could orient a miniature nozzle, giving hir the ability to dart forward without needing to use handrails, which were not plentiful on the Rock, unlike in the more artificial environment of the Fold.

Using the jetpac reminded Vanu that it had been a long time since she'd seen hir oggie friend. Jetsu would be wondering where zhe was, why zhe didn't come to see him. When zhe got back to the Annex, Vanu promised hirself that hir first order of business would be to go and see the oggie and apologize.

At first, the Rock was pretty barren in this sector, but after a while there were structures, some underground with the characteristic ochre-coloured metallo-fabric roofs, others soaring upwards at oblique angles. Zhe passed over a tube-like structure that zhe eventually realized was a threader corridor, stretching away on hir right across the Rock, but tunneling into the Fold on hir left.

Eventually, zhe realized zhe needed to abandon the more open spaces of the Rock, and found an entrance into the Fold. Inside, a maze of corridors crisscrossed the volume. There were also irregularly shaped enclaves, some of which appeared to be inaccessible private pards while others were open. Here, the route directions Shosee had sent were not so helpful. They told hir in which direction the complex lay, but whenever zhe took a corridor that seemed to run in the right direction, it would take a sudden turn and zhe would be moving away from hir goal. Hir binup gave hir actual paths to follow, but these were also useless. Zhe encountered dead ends where there weren't supposed to be any, and new openings where none were shown on the map. The three-dimensional nature of the maze made it hard to visualize where zhe was and where zhe was going. *A bit like life*, zhe reflected in frustration.

Finally, zhe came across another threader corridor. Using hir binup, zhe called for a threader. It was something zhe realized zhe probably should have done long before. Zhe had wasted a lot of time floundering about on hir own. Zhe was used to navigating the sparse, regular arrangements of the Annex, and this chaotic labyrinth had defeated hir. A threader turned up within minutes, its characteristic elongated shape known throughout the

Humanitat. Vanu boarded it, and within a short time arrived at the edge of the complex that was hir destination.

This turned out to be a huge cube buried in the heart of the Fold. Within the cube, wide, comfortable corridors followed a regular grid pattern. Vanu found comfort in moving through an environment with similarities to the rectangular spaces of the Annex. Once inside the cube, however, zhe was surprised to find that the whole structure was pressurized. There was an ambient atmosphere that transmitted sounds.

Shosee met hir at the main entrance, near the top of the cube. She was wearing another interesting bren, but more subdued than the ones she had worn when bent on romancing Vanu. This had slowly changing fractal patterns moving across her body, white and black. The Mandelbrot set, Vanu guessed. With her was a great bear of a man, not a mastodon, just large and well-muscled with the same dark skin as Shosee, bright blue eyes, a beaming smile, and even tufts of hair along the sides of his massive head.

<I'm so pleased to meet you, Kinla Vanu. My daughter thinks very highly of you. Come on in! We'll take hir down to the main lounge,> he added in an aside to his daughter. He was courteous enough to leave this on general broadcast so Vanu could hear too.

<I'm not actually a Kinla, Maestre,> Vanu hastened to explain. <I won't be until I achieve maturation status. Until then I am only a Novice. You should call me just plain Vanu.>

<And you shall call me Greatbear. I know, I know, I do look the part. How my parents knew what I would look like as an adult, nobody yet has been able to explain to me! Come on down and meet the rest!>

Vanu queried Shosee in private binup-to-binup mode. <What does he mean, the rest?>

She flashed a grin at hir. <You'll see.>

<I think I'm late,> Vanu said to Greatbear, as they pulled themselves along the corridor, using the occasional hold for leverage. <I'm not used to getting around in the Fold and I got lost, until I remembered I could call a threader...>

<We all use threaders in the Fold,> Greatbear told Vanu. <They are constantly modifying the innards, even the Crucium Institute can't keep up with the changes. You found the maps less than useless, I imagine? Never mind, you're here now.>

<Do you mind me asking? What is this complex we're in?>

<Shosee didn't tell you? I don't know where she puts her head sometimes! The centre of this cube is the main site for the Emergence Christian Church. I am, well, a sort of caretaker you might say, although sometimes I seem to also play a role as lay preacher and general counsellor for half the population of the Yard! Much of the ECC's ministry is done consensually, but we still do sermons from time to time. Grab hold of that bar, would you?>

Vanu grasped the bar indicated as the floor seemed to drop out beneath them. It was some kind of elevator, Vanu had heard of them but never actually seen one in operation. The elevator was one of the most ancient technologies still in use. The thing seemed to drop through several dozen levels before finally coming to a halt. Greatbear led them down another corridor, as long and as wide as the first one. In this one, however, there was a faint whispering sound. At first, Vanu didn't know what it might be, but finally realized it was the sound made by moving air, a sound so bizarre it drove home to hir the alien nature of this environment as nothing else could.

Finally, they entered a pard-like space, more luxurious than the starker corridors through which they had been moving. Here there was a patterned floor covering, albeit in dark, somber colours—browns and golds, blacks and purples in intricate geometric patterns. The walls were textured metallo-fabric, brighter in colouring than the floor. Vanu could discern no changing dynamics to them, as zhe had half-expected. Their decorative motifs seemed frozen in place. There were several parflots here, at different locations and heights, but they moved past these, through an opening in the back wall and into a second chamber.

As they skimmed on through, Vanu could hear voices, of all things, and a kind of braying sound that zhe realized must be laughter. A clutch of at least five people broke asunder as the three of them entered the pard—Greatbear had called it a "lounge," Vanu remembered—turning towards them with laughter still on their lips. But to Vanu's shock, they were all men, dindivs, and they were all exactly alike, junior versions of Greatbear himself.

‹These are my brothers,› Shosee told Vanu, in broadcast mode. ‹As you can see, the Kinch aren't the only ones to reproduce by cloning. We are the Greatbear clan. Only I am born exfolded, as you Kinch say.›

Outside the Kinship, despite what Shosee suggested, cloning was not a common practice. Vanu didn't judge it one way or the other. The trouble zhe had had with Dev did not mean that zhe condemned all clones. But among the Kinch, there was a mild rivalry between those born of a genetic pairing, the exfolded, and those born as clones, the infolded. From experience, Vanu found the dynamics among the clones from a common parent to be destabilizing, especially for exfolded individuals such as hirself. They seemed almost to communicate telepathically; if one smiled, then chances were they all did. In fact, in many ways Dev's behaviour had been exceptional—an infolded child with a mind of hir own.

<Don't listen to our little sister,> said one of her brothers, Vanu couldn't quite make out which, because his words were immediately echoed by several of the others. <She's jealous,> chimed in another chorus. <We're really a friendly lot,> added a third, as broad grins broke out among them.

<They are a rambunctious gang,> Greatbear commented ruefully. <Between my daughter and her brothers, I have to work to keep up! Now, let's all relax, and, if you feel up to it, tell us about yourself, Vanu. It's not often we get to chat with a Kinch insider. Your people tend to keep their distance.>

Vanu, who had been coached by Shosee concerning what elements of hir experience might be of greatest interest, told them as much as zhe could. There was no reason to hold anything back. Well, perhaps there were a few personal things Vanu didn't want to share. As zhe talked, Vanu thought about Shosee, about what this odd family taught hir about hir lover. Nothing obvious, perhaps, and yet a certain irreverence seemed to fit. Irreverence about what? Zhe didn't know. Vanu packed the thought away for another time.

Before leaving the Greatbears to go back to the Kinship House, Greatbear himself made a promise to Vanu. <If you ever decide to leave the Kinship, we could use your moral sensitivity here in our work with the ECC. I know you think of yourself

as very young, with questions perhaps about what life calls you to do, but I suspect you underestimate your talents and abilities. You have much to offer, especially to those who lack a moral compass. Even as recently as a few weeks ago, I would have said that about my daughter, but you see, Vanu, already you have changed her. You will always be welcome here. And if you need us for anything, please don't hesitate. Among my many roles, I am DeoFax representative for Plenum on the regional DeoFax Court, so I have some measure of influence, you see. Are you a member of the Ido, Vanu?>

Vanu shook hir head.

<Well, you might want to think about joining. It will give you more options, and we could certainly use your presence and participation in the local DeoFax community.>

As zhe left, Vanu sent Shosee a private communication. <I'll have a thing or two to say to you when next we meet,> zhe told her.

<Don't be too hard on me,> she replied. <You did enjoy yourself, after all!>

An unexpected wave of desire made hir tremble in anticipation of their next encounter.

XIX

THERE, BUT FOR THE GRACE OF GOD

"The world breaks everyone and afterward many
are strong at the broken places. But those that will
not break it kills. It kills the very good and the very gentle
and the very brave impartially."

—Ernest Hemingway, *A Farewell to Arms*, Accessed from the
All-Human Compendium, Literature, Ido Era 1537

After the meeting with Greatbear, Vanu and Shosee were able to meet a half a dozen more times. Vanu knew that time was running out. Zhe was destined to return to the Annex in another few weeks, and that would be the end of hir relationship with Shosee, unless Vanu returned to the Yard after attaining mat status. Although technically zhe would be free to do so, hir situation at the Kinship would not make it easy to arrange. Of course, Shosee was also supposed to return to the Annex for the rest of her training there, but finding places they could meet in private would be difficult.

As a consequence of these constraints and their dwindling time together, Vanu sought more and more opportunities to get away from the House. Fortunately, Kinla Pater had been right about the reduced workload, and Vanu was able to beg off from hir duties more often. They also changed the ceethree they used, to reduce the chance that they would become too familiar a sight to anyone.

Almost as an afterthought, Vanu followed through on Greatbear's suggestion to join the Ido. It wasn't anything zhe had given much thought to in the past. The Ido didn't seem to struggle with the kinds of issues that had been of concern to hir, but perhaps, zhe conceded, that was changing. Shosee also encouraged hir, so after a few more days reflection, zhe submitted a formal application via binup. Zhe was asked to stop in at a nearby argeet station, which zhe did on one of hir outings to see Shosee. Zhe spent a few minutes inside the device to have hir binup interface modified to support the Ido connection. However, after receiving the initial welcome message, zhe put the whole effort to one side. Zhe had neither the time nor the interest to explore the Ido linkup process at that moment.

Then, one afternoon when Vanu had been trying to connect with Shosee, to no avail, Kinla Pater came across to hir as zhe was exiting communal prayer. Since Kinla Pater rarely attended the prayer sessions, Vanu was surprised to see hir. <The head of Hospitality House has called for you, Vanu. I'm afraid I can guess what it's about.>

Vanu was met in the Hospitality Hall by not just the head, but the full council. There were three of them—Kinla Drude, the head, Kinla Sporeman, and Kinla Hayden, Vanu's erstwhile superior. Kinla Drude's sharp eyes, which belied hir warm mahogany skin, gazed coldly at Vanu, and hir mouth had a subtle twist to it that also boded ill. Kinla Sporeman was smaller and rounder but kindlier in hir pale facial features and expressions. Kinla Hayden was hir usual nervous self, warm brown hands constantly on the move. They were seated on real chairs, although these had tethers they could hold onto if they started to drift. Kinla Pater, stood next to the entrance, tethered placidly in place.

Kinla Drude addressed Vanu. <You can imagine my dismay when I was informed this morning that you have undertaken a relationship with the girl who was our guest at the Annex earlier this year. Whether or not this situation has been accepted by hir family, something I am still trying to discern, it is not acceptable to our community. In fact, it violates the rules that govern Novice conduct within the Kinship. Do you have anything to say in your defense, Novice Vanu Francoeur?>

Kinship names followed the lines of genetic descent within the community and hence preserved ancient family names from many cultural traditions, but Vanu rarely heard hir full name announced. Zhe thought of mentioning that Shosee had been fully participative, but decided this would not help hir case. So zhe elected to say nothing. Zhe wasn't overly worried. Zhe knew of many Kinch who had done equally reprehensible things, and not been severely punished. Ranee was a good example.

Kinla Pater chose that moment to move forward slightly. <I would like to bear witness that Novice Vanu has been an exceptional intern here. I'm sure Kinla Hayden will agree. We see many young Novices come and go, but Novice Vanu works hard and diligently, zhe makes almost no mistakes, zhe is careful

and thoughtful in hir relations with hir colleagues, and, I must add, zhe has been an exceptional friend. We should be cautious in how we judge hir, lest we damage a relationship which has been to our benefit.>

Kinla Drude looked severely across at Kinla Pater. <Thank you, Pater, your remarks have been noted. Is there anything else? Novice?>

<No? Well, as a Novice, your disciplining is, fortunately for us, not a direct part of our mandate. Therefore, I am sending you back to the Annex on the next transport, where you will stand before the Disciplinary Committee of the Novices. Your binup's ability to communicate outside this House has been shut off, and your movements will be restricted to the main House. You can go back to the pard you occupied when you first came here. Your duties have been terminated, likewise. The transport is due in three days' time. You will keep to your pard, and contemplate the severity of your disgrace!>

So that explained why zhe had been unable to reach Shosee. Vanu hadn't known they had the power to limit the functions of hir binup here at the Yard. Monitor it yes, but modify it? Wasn't that a violation of hir basic human rights?

Zhe was also unhappy hir sentencing had been deferred. Zhe would rather deal with the reality of hir punishment, whatever it was, than the expectation.

As zhe went to sleep that night, zhe wondered who had complained. Kinla Pater? That seemed unlikely. So who was responsible? Or had some chance event occurred, instead?

XX

CO-SCRIBE

"Historical chronology, human or geological, depends…
upon comparable impersonal principles. If one scribes
with a stylus on a plate of wet clay two marks, the second
crossing the first, another person on examining these
marks can tell unambiguously which was made first and
which second, because the latter event irreversibly disturbs
its predecessor. In virtue of the fact that most of the
rocks of the earth contain imprints of a succession of such
irreversible events, an unambiguous working out of the
chronological sequence of these events becomes possible."

—M. King Hubbert, *Critique of the Principle of Uniformity*,
Accessed from the *All-Human Compendium, Science,*
Ido Era 1539

*Additional commentary from the working notes of Doric,
Co-Scribe of the Sentiat, Ido Era 1539*

The story of Vanu Francoeur, up to this point, concerns primarily
hir personal growth and development, and only incidentally deals

with the larger community within which zhe grew to maturity. From this point onwards, however, hir story becomes enmeshed in the larger collective in ways that will have profound consequences, and, ultimately, affect the unfolding of the Crucium Crisis itself. This poses particular challenges for the Co-Scribe.

Let us begin with a quick reminder of how a Co-Scribe is constituted. Co-Scribes are collectives with a single, fused identity and persona. Our existence, of course, is directly dependent upon the technology of the Sentiat itself. In the era of the Crisis, and the period that led up to it, there was no Sentiat. The Ido served as the glue to hold civilization together. Sentience was shared within the Ido, but not, in general, fused. With the development of the Sentiat, the technologies of the Ido were recast to support collective fusion, albeit within the asynchronous tempo-modified pan-galactic environment that had become the norm for interspecies interactions. With the decision to consolidate existing cultures following the Crisis, work on the *All-Human Compendium* was begun, in parallel with similar efforts by the other extant galactic civilizations. The Co-Scribes were created to support those endeavours.

Participants within each Co-Scribe were drawn from many habitats across large expanses of space and generally also included representative members of other species. Our personas are emergent from these large collectives. Hence each Co-Scribe has a distinct personality, different strengths and also specific weaknesses. This persona's strengths, that is, those associated with Doric, include a particular susceptibility to understanding individual points of view. That is, despite the collective nature of our persona, we empathize with individuals and draw on individual experience to develop understanding of events as these unfold.

Oddly, however, this poses problems when we examine the relationship between individuals, such as Vanu Francoeur, and collectives, such as the Kinship. We sometimes encounter difficulties untangling the interactions, since these cross levels of aggregation. We either cleave to the individual experience, or to the collective, and can become confused when passing from one to the other.

We mention this merely as a word of caution. The modern reader, whether individual or collective, is generally more interested in individual perspectives than those of the collective, especially when examining these historical epochs. We therefore attempt to preserve our focus on Vanu's experience as an individual, and not get side-tracked into some of the collective issues that are nonetheless of interest to certain scholars. Occasionally, however, our focus may slip. We prefer that our readers be aware of these issues as they pursue their efforts to understand the origins of the Crucium Crisis in these documents. Let us now return to Vanu's story.

XXI

THE BOOK OF DOCTRINE

"Adoration's real name... is Research."

—Pierre Teilhard de Chardin, *Lettres à Jeanne Mortier,* Accessed
from the *All-Human Compendium, Theology,* Ido Era 1537

While confined to the tiny pard that had been hirs when zhe first
arrived, Vanu tried in vain to find a way around the blocks that
had been placed on hir binup. Zhe complained that zhe wanted
to access the matrix, but was told there would be time enough
for that later. It was a lonely three days zhe spent, trying to guess
at how Shosee would be feeling.

Eventually, zhe got to thinking about what Kinla Drude had
said, about Kinship doctrine. Zhe decided to check this out for
hirself. The Kinch had provided the room with a reading portal
on which was displayed the title page of the *Book of Doctrine.*
Vanu had tried to restructure the portal to get access outside the
Book of Doctrine, but this usually required a binup connection,
and even hir in-house link seemed to be shut down.

The *Kinship Book of Doctrine* was huge, something which Vanu had never before questioned. But Shosee's taunting questions and scepticism about many of the Kinship's values and practices led hir now to think about its weight. Must doctrine always be so voluminous? It was a kind of code of conduct, and, in Vanu's growing experience, the wellsprings of conduct were simple, not complex. Shouldn't the code be simple, too? It was the implementation of a code of conduct that was complex, not so much its roots. But the *Book of Doctrine* did not dwell on the ground of being, something that had long disappointed Vanu. Such fundamental issues were where Vanu's questions had tended to probe, but the *Book of Doctrine* gave little back for the effort it took to read it.

Kinla Val, and Kinla Pater, had taught hir more than any of hir lessons in doctrine over the years. And, curiously, Kinla Eugaine also had a kind of rough and ready understanding of their faith that, in retrospect, Vanu now realized was deeper than first appearances. The Kinch could do worse than place their children in hir care, zhe realized, unconscious that zhe viewed the Kinship almost as if zhe were an outsider now.

Zhe plunged into the reading of the weighty volume. Somewhere in these words and paragraphs, chapters and sections, there might be some insight into hir current plight. Kinla Drude spoke of hir disgrace. The *Book of Doctrine* should be able to cast some light onto what, exactly, zhe had done wrong.

The Book was divided into five main sections. The first was named *Faith*, but it was the smallest section. This was where the basic vision of the Suffering God was laid out, but little information was provided concerning how this understanding was to be used in everyday practice. Vanu had read this section many times in hir search for answers, so zhe now passed over it relatively quickly. The next part was titled *Prayer*, a much longer section already. Within this part of the book could be found the substance of the many hundreds of prayers recited during common prayer, as well as the formal prayers reserved for special occasions such as mat ceremonies, the vow of commitment to the Kinship, other swearing-in ceremonies such as when appointed to the Kinship Council or other committees, funeral rites, and so on.

The third section came under the heading *Community*. Vanu was not so familiar with this section, and had hopes that zhe might be able to find some answers here. Interestingly, a search revealed no mention of the work of the Core anywhere within the volume as a whole. Neither the section named *Community*, nor that which followed, named *Practice*, nor any of the *Appendices*, made any mention of the Annex, the Core or even the Plenum Nebula. Although the only extant Kinship community was here at Plenum, the *Book of Doctrine* had been written when there were hopes of a broader community, spread across many star systems, with perhaps many more forms of service to the Humanitat than those under the primary responsibility of the Core today.

The *Community* section, however, did lay out the diverse departments of the Kinch. This included, Vanu was interested to note, the Liaison Committee and the Hospitality Group. Perhaps the unfortunate naming of these groups was to be blamed on the *Book of Doctrine*. No wonder no one wanted to mess with it! It also laid out the organization of the Novices into cribs, the processes of education and training, and the apprenticing of Novices to different departments until each found their calling. Vanu was again interested to note that the *Book of Doctrine* presented the task of finding one's life work as the responsibility of the Novice, as assisted by the adult Kinch and the Committee of Oversight, and not as a unilateral decision determined on high and passed down as an assignment to the new member of the Kinship. The section made no mention at all of gender, sexuality, reproduction, cloning, exfolding versus infolding, or any other of the more litigious questions that preoccupied Vanu.

That left the *Practice* section, and the *Appendices*. Curious, Vanu jumped ahead into this last section, which contained hundreds of documents, apparently of a highly technical nature. Zhe realized they were amendments to the other parts of the *Book of Doctrine*, most of them procedural. There might be something in these texts, but it would take days to wade through them all, and a quick search for terms that interested Vanu yielded nothing at all. So, with the time that remained to hir, zhe went back to a more careful scan of Section Four.

At first, this appeared to be even more of a disappointment than the others. It was not an ordered layout of codes of conduct under different subject areas, as Vanu had naively imagined. Instead, it was a maze of procedures to be followed when practice became problematical. What exactly this *practice* was, and how one determined when it became a problem, was nowhere described.

But, as zhe began to read subsections of the text, the procedures started to make sense. There was an implicit sense of what constituted right practice here. You had to infer it, using the *Faith*, *Prayer* and *Community* sections as background guides, but it was there all right. Indeed, Vanu gleaned in these pages a description of the rich and layered way of keeping faith that zhe knew so well from the day to day encounters that made up life among the Kinch. And here, finally, in one of those subsections, innocuously entitled *Family Considerations*, Vanu found what zhe had been looking for.

The subsection nowhere mentioned specific gender issues, or even the word, "gender." It was no wonder that Vanu's searches had failed to find it. But the text offered procedures to follow if "communal homogeneity" was challenged. What did that mean, exactly, "communal homogeneity," and why was it considered to be important? Under a careful reading, Vanu realized that, historically, the Kinship must once have been a much more heterogeneous community than it was today. Although gender was not explicitly mentioned, the text did mention different "procreative potentials," which might be a backhanded reference to gender differences. Apparently, Kinch with different procreative potentials had been known to clash over issues "important to the future of the Kinship community." So, that might mean children. The need for communal homogeneity had emerged from these clashes, and the Kinch had apparently decided to adopt a social fabric that favoured communal oversight over "procreative practices"—in other words, sex.

Vanu wasn't certain zhe was making the right inferences, but the story seemed to hang together. It explained a lot. Sex between lindivs was tolerated because it was not procreative, and because it reinforced communal homogeneity. Sex with other genders, on the other hand, such as visitors to the community, was actively and firmly discouraged. The form of this discouragement followed the procedures laid out in the *Book of Doctrine* and, no doubt, its *Appendices*.

But something else was troubling Vanu about all this, although zhe couldn't put hir finger on it. Instead, zhe turned to the *Appendices*, trying to identify amendments relevant to communal homogeneity and procreative practices. But here, again, the Book stymied hir. A search for these terms brought hir to amendments of other sections and practices, but not to the particular amendments Vanu was certain were to be found in these pages. It was as if the Book had been designed to defeat hir.

And then zhe ran out of time. The transport ship had arrived.

XXII

RETURN TO THE ANNEX

"An idea is like a rare bird which cannot be seen. What one sees is the trembling of the branch it has just left."

—Lawrence Durrell, *Monsieur*, Accessed from the *All–Human Compendium, Literature*, Ido Era 1537

Despite the unpleasantness of the circumstances of Vanu's return to the Annex, both Ranee and Joh were present at the docking facility to greet hir. Whatever discomfort they might have felt over the events that preceded hir departure seemed to have vanished. They were delighted to see hir, and pulled hir along with them back to their pard, brooking no interference from the adult Kinch who had also been there to meet the ship's arrival. Faced with the determination of hir friends, the Kinch had merely told Vanu that zhe would be called to stand before the Disciplinary Committee in the next day or two, and let hir go.

<I thought I was the only one with a knack for getting into trouble,> Ranee chided hir, as they somersaulted into the pard, twisting and turning in their haste to get out of the common area.

Each grabbed hold of a piece of sleepnet to stop their movement. <I see it has rubbed off onto you, too!>

<You're going to have to tell us all about it!> added Joh, excitedly.

<Mmmmm,> Vanu replied, noncommittal. Didn't hir affair with Shosee reactivate the issue of hir refusal to be sexually intimate with Ranee and Joh? Zhe wanted to avoid recreating the same situation as that which had prevailed before zhe had left.

But Ranee seemed to know the broad details of the affair. Zhe claimed that the whole situation was the subject of debate within the Liaison Committee. <We didn't even realize she wasn't at the Annex any more, when we heard about the affair,> Ranee confessed. <However did you find her?>

<It wasn't actually like that,> Vanu said. <We ran into each other by accident. At least, I think it was by accident. And to be honest, really, she seduced me. I wasn't sure I wanted any kind of sexual relationship. I was still confused.>

<But you must have known the relationship was unacceptable to the Kinch!> said Joh.

<Ah, but did I? Unacceptable, why?>

They both stared at Vanu.

<Oh, I know what the argument is. But I've been reading the *Book of Doctrine*, and the real situation is much more subtle and complex than they would have us believe.>

<They?> Ranee focused on hir use of the pronoun.

<Well, the Disciplinary Committee, in this case.>

<You've been away longer than I realised,> Ranee replied. <Or your encounter with this... this findiv... has changed you.>

Zhe shook hir head. <I wouldn't have thought it possible. You've always been the most conscientious among us.>

<And I still am,> Vanu said.

Was Ranee right? Had zhe changed? Zhe felt the same tormented person as always. Or did zhe? Hadn't hir experiences with Shosee, and with the Greatbear family more generally, liberated hir from some of the torment? Yes, zhe thought, it was possible. Zhe felt more sure of hirself than when zhe had left for the Yard, that was certain. But wasn't hir recent, more critical perspective towards Kinship doctrine also based on hir innate tendency to ask questions?

Later, zhe went outside to look for Jetsu. Out here, the world was simpler. The oggies were clustered on the opposite side of the space platform from the docks. Here the dramatic colours of the nebula were largely hidden by the bulk of the platform. Vanu watched the oggies for a while. They were nestled into a small hollow in the edge of the aft wall of the Annex, rimmed by a wide raised lip upon which grew the ubiquitous greenbak that bedecked the hull. The presence of greenbak here suggested there might be a small leakage of gases from inside the Annex or of water vapour from the water reservoirs just inside the platform's skin. Such leaks couldn't be entirely avoided, and helped support the external ecosystems of the platform. The greenbak was a vacuum-adapted algae that stripped oxygen from gas or water vapour molecules, and stored the oxygen in small bladder-like fruits that clustered on its outer surfaces. The oggies harvested the oxygen from the bladders. In addition, they ate the barnaks that also clung to the outer surface of the space platform. The barnaks were carbon rich, and when the carbon combined with the oxygen intake, this generated the carbon dioxide the oggies used to jet about the station.

Like Vanu hirself, Jetsu was at the transition between being considered a child and an adult. He could be found, often enough, playing with the younger oggies, but more and more he held back with the adults. The adult oggies were still far more playful than adult humans, however. Right now the whole family was engaged in a game of "throw and catch," with the adults doing the throwing and catching, while the young were being flung around. It was a game, but a game with a purpose. The young oggies were learning to extend and contract their tentacles in mid-flight, and to use these to grasp hold of the tentacles of the adult oggies, without having to preoccupy themselves with issues of propulsion. Vanu enjoyed watching them immensely. It was so much more visceral a task than the kinds of things the Kinship tended to require of its members. And yet, "visceral" could be deeply spiritual, if you gave it the time and the presence it really demanded!

Jetsu, visible both because of his intermediate size and the distinct markings on his hide, didn't seem to know whether to stick with the throwing and the catching, or to allow himself to be hurled. The effort involved in throwing him was obviously more than for the smaller, younger oggies, but none of the adults baulked at doing so, or seemed to censure him in any way, and the sheer enjoyment he displayed at being thrown was equal to that of any of the younger oggies. Vanu envied him his dual status.

Eventually, the game wore itself out, and the younger oggies drifted away in small groups. Jetsu didn't join them. Now he obviously felt excluded. Vanu chose this moment to approach and hail him.

<Hey Jet, enjoying youself?>

<V'n'u!> the oggie responded, excitedly. <You stay 'way fr'm Jet? Lon'ly!>

The oggie's manner of communicating via binup was only partially rendered. Oggies tended to swallow the vowels, and syntax was very basic, but they were nonetheless able to communicate feelings quite well.

<Went starway awhile,> Vanu replied. 'Starway' meant to a distant habitat. <Am back now, to stay.>

<V'nu not go st'rway 'gain?>

Vanu shook hir head. The oggie anchored himself to a jutting set of bars. <Wan' show V'nu...>

<You have something to show me?>

Jetsu waved three of his tentacles in a circular motion that meant yes. He also held two tentacles towards Vanu, who grabbed hold. The oggie jetted away from the station and then along its length, towards one of the spinning sections. When they drew near, Jetsu used his tentacles to swing inwards to a location near the lowest edge of the platform. Because the Annex had a vertical structure, with lower floors more dedicated to maintenance, middle floors to residence pards and upper floors to management functions, the lowest floors projected many different structures through to the outer shell. This provided opportunities to the oggies that were much less present near the top of the habitat. Since oggies invested time and effort building up their dens, most oggies picked a location on or near the habitat underbelly for their efforts.

Jetsu introduced Vanu to a den that was extensive, even for oggies. Most dens were singly chambered. This one was composed of three distinct spaces separated by partial walls and offering numerous entrances and exits, also a feature of traditional oggie habitats. The dens were mostly anchored on clusters of barnak, another co-adapted species from ancient Earth. Barnaks fed on the interstellar medium, secreting particles into hard shells that accumulated on the exteriors of space platforms. Originally humans harvested the shell structures as building materials, but barnaks were never efficient enough to do the job properly, and later on other means had been developed, including the use of spiners. Eventually, like the oggies, they were left alone. In addition to the barnaks, which could form thick clusters, the oggies picked up strips of metallo-fabric, organic waste, the occasional stareye—an organism part plant, part animal—and a few metal struts to form their dens. That Jetsu had appropriated such a space for his uses was another sign that he was leaving his childhood behind. His den was both cosy and clever.

<This is super!> Vanu exclaimed. <Wherever did you find all these things?>

Although Vanu was impressed, zhe was also worried. Oggies weren't long lived, and their adult phase was often shortened by the demands of parenthood. The ecos who had adapted the species to space habitats had done their best both to lower their intake requirements—nutrients and oxygen, primarily—and also to lengthen their lifespans. Female oggies were more affected by the reproductive cycle than were male oggies, but life expectancies for male oggies were not long in the adult phase either.

It was another sign that Vanu needed to spend more time with hir friend, for time was precious, something zhe had already learned with Shosee.

<I also have an'th'r s'rprise f'r fr'nd V'nu,> Jetsu declared. <L'k st'rw'ys!>

Vanu didn't understand what the oggie was trying to tell hir for a moment. Then, as zhe turned hir gaze outwards, away from the Annex, zhe could see a moderately large shape looming quickly towards them.

<Wha...?>

The form slowed and turned, and a startled Vanu realized this was a jonah, another of the ancient deep sea creatures of Old Earth that had been adapted to function in the spaces between the stars. Just as the oggies were adapted from a cephalopod species, and the barnaks were said to be similarly derived from sea creatures, the jonahs were once a creature called a "whale." Like the oggies, but unlike barnaks, the jonahs' intelligence had been enhanced. Even more so than in the case of the oggies, it was reported.

Technically, these were all "co-adapted species," meaning that they were part of adapted eco-systems rather than individually adapted organisms. Even the jonahs were co-adapted, although they were the predominant members of their own ecosystem. They were a social species that tended to group together, and so their ecosystem consisted primarily of other jonahs. Jonahs digested organic compounds in the interstellar medium, and their bodies also included a "slow ramjet," allowing them to move large distances in interstellar space—hence their use as transports by humans. Under tempo reduction, the moderate speeds achieved by jonahs still made local interstellar trips viable.

Like their oggie cousins, the jonahs were equipped with a limited form of binup, allowing them to communicate with humans and to modify tempo. Even with reduced tempo, the magnificent creature drifted delicately up to the platform. Under tempo reduction, most movements seemed jerky and often extremely rapid, but the jonah's movements appeared graceful and slow.

<This my fr'nd Tee'hal,> Jetsu informed Vanu. <Tee'hal fam'ly n'r?>

An image appeared in Vanu's binup showing the relationship between the Annex and a nearby molecular cloud rich in organics. Although the jonah had a rudimentary binup, it didn't use language in the same, literal way as did the oggies. Instead, it communicated by images and feelings. Usually the binup was a poor communicator of feelings, but it seemed to work well for the jonahs.

<Tee'hal g'd fr'nd,> Jetsu commented. <Tee'hal, th's my fr'nd V'nu.>

A warm feeling of joy washed over Vanu. <I'm delighted to meet you, too, Tee'hal.>

Then a sensation of urgency and haste passed over Vanu, followed by a feeling of regret tinged with pleasure. This was further combined with the image of Jetsu and Vanu where they were currently located, against the backdrop of the Annex.

<C'nt stay?> Jetsu replied. <Unnerst'nd. Qu'ck vis't this t'me!>

The jonah sailed away, disappearing rapidly into the distance.

XXIII
DISCIPLINARY COMMITTEE

"Our care of the child should be governed, not by the desire
to make him learn things, but by the endeavour always
to keep burning within him that light which is called
intelligence."

—Maria Montessori, *Spontaneous Activity in Education*, Accessed
from the *All-Human Compendium, Science*, Ido Era 1537

A week after hir return to the Annex, Vanu was called before
the Novice Disciplinary Committee. There were five members
of the committee—the only one Vanu knew well was Kinla
Eugaine. This was hir first time before the committee, although
zhe had often coached Ranee for hir appearances. Now it was
Ranee who coached hir.

<The head of the committee is Kinla Truman these days.
Truman is a specialist in the *Book of Doctrine*—they say zhe
can recite it by heart! As you can imagine, zhe is a procedural-
ist, but not unkind, for all that. The two vice heads are Kinla
Eugaine and Kinla Bradach. Eugaine you know. Bradach is a bit

hardheaded. You'll need to be careful of hir. But Bradach doesn't know doctrine well, nowhere near as well as Truman. Bradach tries to wield the heavy hand of the law, but doesn't always succeed because of hir lack of knowledge of procedures. Eugaine will favor you, zhe always tries to act on behalf of the Novices. The two supplementary members for this committee are Kinla Safuki and Kinla Zyrgo. Safuki is not well known to me, but has a reputation for being fair-minded, provided you show that you are conscious of the needs of the community. Zyrgo is a specialist of the history of the Kinship. Remember the supplementaries are not permanent members of the committee. They are called in to address particular issues—that's why I don't know them as well as the other three. And I don't know why Kinla Zyrgo is there. It is unusual to call on a historian to be present!>

<Ah, but I think I know why,> Vanu replied. <Leave Kinla Zyrgo to me, I've done my best to be prepared for the historical argument.>

Ranee shook hir head. They had huddled together in the common area outside their pards, each nestled into a parflot. <I still can't get over how much you've changed. You used to be so tentative. Everything was a question. Now, you seem so sure of your answers. Of course, you are still my sib, and I'll do anything to help, but you need to be careful not to sound too sure of yourself. It will rub the committee the wrong way!>

<I haven't changed as much as you think,> Vanu said. <All the questions are still there. I'm just more insistent about getting answers when I believe they are just out of reach. Or when I think someone is withholding information I, or we, need.

No matter who they are, or think they are. But I promise to be careful.>

<And, it may sound strange to you, coming from me,> Ranee continued, <but I'm going to say it anyway. Don't forget to be sensitive to the presence of God. There's something a little, please don't take this the wrong way, you have a style of talking that is much less spiritual than it used to be. I'm not saying you're not spiritual. I'm just saying that you don't express as much humility as you used to. You've got to be humble before the committee, or they'll treat you as an example.>

Vanu was taken aback. This *was* a strange thing for hir friend to say. Not the bit about the need to be humble, that made sense for Ranee, who was never arrogant despite hir tendency to play around with the rules, but the need to be spiritual was uncharacteristic. Although, to be fair, Vanu knew that Ranee did have deeply rooted beliefs about the spirit, even if these rarely saw the light of day. And underneath the words, Vanu could feel that Ranee was right, zhe *had* changed. Before going away, Vanu's spiritual curiosity had found expression in questioning the fundamentals on which the Kinship was based—not, however, in the expectation of unearthing problems, but rather with a desire to understand, and understand deeply, the spiritual nature of the world.

Following hir encounter with Shosee, Vanu now felt that the Kinship did not hold all the answers zhe was seeking, that it embraced flaws which made its doctrine questionable some of the time, and that God, or the God of the Kinship, was in some way a slightly Crooked God as a result. How was that even possible? God didn't need to reflect the imperfections of the Kinship, wasn't that putting the 'scoop behind the starship,' instead of in front, where it belonged? God, even the Suffering God, perhaps especially the Suffering God, was Perfect. How could Zhe be Crooked? Wasn't it humans who were crooked?

Vanu needed to put these reflections aside, as hir hour was upon hir. The Disciplinary Committee was meeting in the Kinship Hall, the same space where Ranee's mat ceremony had been held. The Hall was far too large for this particular function. Vanu wondered if the choice of venue was meant to make her feel small. There was no one in attendance other than the five committee members and Vanu—the Disciplinary Committee sessions were always held *huis clos*, that is, without anyone else present. However, the Hall was not currently under spin. The committee members were hence held in place using parflots, although they were all five aligned in the same direction. Vanu was not given the support of a parflot, hence zhe was left to drift in front of the committee. There was one small tether, but its surface seemed moist and slippery, and Vanu felt averse to using it. Zhe had oriented hir body initially to line up with the judges, but if zhe did not hold onto the tether, zhe had a tendency to drift out of alignment. It was an awkward position to occupy, no doubt intentionally so. Vanu found hirself resentful towards the committee that it resorted to such tricks to bolster its position.

The senior Kinch, Kinla Truman, addressed hir words towards Vanu. Although the room was pressurized, they used the binup to communicate. Under tempo, spoken communications tended to be choppy and heavily distorted, so most people used pseudo-voice and the binup. <Novice Vanu, formal complaints have been submitted regarding your behaviour at the Hospitality House of the Yard. The substance of the charges are that you

have violated the Communal Practices Act, Section 94B, which stipulates that sexual congress outside of the Kinship community is incompatible with the long term goals of the community. Traditionally, there are severe penalties for this. This is a highly unusual and very serious charge to be brought against a Novice. We are perplexed, first of all, to understand how such a situation could arise at all, and secondly, how to proceed. In matters of Novice discipline, it is not our desire to punish Novices so much as it is to teach you, and we rarely apply the full force of the penalties formally available to us. But I must warn you, Novice Vanu, that this particular charge is rarely dealt with lightly. Now, would you please tell the committee, in your own words, how this situation came about?>

Vanu saw no reason not to explain, although zhe was annoyed they were citing a document to which zhe had not been given access. So zhe described as best zhe could, how events unfolded, beginning with hir attempts to obtain answers from older Kinch regarding questions of a spiritual nature which zhe believed were relevant to a preoccupation with sexual identity. Zhe described the chance encounter with Shosee at the Yard, and how things unfolded from there. Zhe did not mention the interaction with Ranee and Joh before leaving the Annex, relevant as the encounter was, as it involved the use of a forbidden technology, and zhe did not want to create trouble for hir sibs. Nor did zhe mention meeting the Greatbear family, although it was likely Kinla Drude would have told them about that encounter. Zhe also presented the relationship with Shosee in terms that were objective, even though zhe wanted to scream aloud hir anger at being kept apart from hir ama!

<While at the Hospitality House, you developed a friendship with Kinla Pater,> Kinla Safuki said. <Could you describe the exchanges you had with hir?>

Vanu looked thoughtfully at Kinla Safuki. Zhe had mentioned little about Kinla Pater, by instinct more than by design. Vanu didn't want to cause trouble for Kinla Pater, and, furthermore, zhe didn't believe hir exchanges with the older Kinch were relevant to the charges. <I spent months living in the same building as Kinla Pater and we had countless conversations. It is hard to remember any particular exchange and what was said. To my knowledge, none of them dealt with the specifics of my relationship with Shosee.>

<So you are saying that Kinla Pater had no knowledge of the relationship?>

Vanu hesitated, and then realized that the hesitation was noticed. <I think zhe suspected that something was going on. I don't know how much zhe knew.>

<Suspected or knew? Kinla Pater suspected something was going on, or zhe knew?> It was Kinla Bradach who interrupted this time.

<I think zhe suspected, until I was brought before the House Council. Then zhe knew.>

<Let me go back to something you said earlier,> Kinla Eugaine spoke kindly to hir. <You indicated that before you left the Annex, you were confused about your sexual feelings. Did you speak to anyone about this?>

<No. I went to see Kinla Val about another matter. I wanted to say something then, but I didn't. I felt ashamed of my feelings, and didn't know how to talk about them.>

<And were these feelings of shame concerned with simply having sexual feelings, or were these feelings already being directed towards someone of a different gender?> That was Kinla Bradach again.

<Both, I guess. No, I didn't realize I was confused about gender until the last few days before leaving for the Yard. I still find the issue of sexual feelings, in general, confusing.> Zhe paused a moment, then continued. <It seems largely a taboo subject within the Kinship. It wasn't until I encountered non Kinch, such as Shosee and her father, that I realized sex normally isn't considered problematic. Why isn't it dealt with more openly here? I should think all Kinch would benefit from a more open discussion about sex.>

A look was exchanged between several members of the committee, but nobody ventured to answer hir question.

<Also, based on what I read within the *Book of Doctrine*, it seems that the Kinship wasn't always so intolerant towards other sexual practices. That would also seem to suggest the need to at least discuss these issues.> Vanu had remembered Ranee's warning about hubris, and tried hir best to dilute the strength of what zhe was trying to say.

But the jury made no effort even to acknowledge hir argument. After a brief silence, Kinla Truman continued.

<Well, are there any other outstanding issues? Kinla Zyrgo, you have said little. What do your instincts tell you?>

Kinla Zyrgo said nothing for several moments, as if weighing what zhe was going to say. <You all know the seriousness of this issue. I recognize that the candidate has been struggling for some time, with very little guidance, on how to come to terms with

considerable inner turmoil. I also recognize that Novices seldom take the time to read the *Book of Doctrine* and to understand why we Kinch have the traditions we have. But none of that excuses hir behaviour, nor does it help us come to terms with the consequences, which may involve others and not just this Novice. In the service of the Suffering God, Novice Vanu must be led to confront hir inner demons and given the opportunity of guidance and counsel in order to do so.>

It seemed to Vanu that the statement lacked its conclusion. But the other committee members nodded, as if this confirmed some understanding they all shared.

<Indeed,> Kinla Truman said. <I think, then, that we are in agreement.>

Vanu was shocked. They hadn't made any effort to listen to or understand hir point of view! This wasn't the kind of oversight zhe expected from the Kinship authorities. They seemed more procedural, that is, following the letter of the law, and not truly spiritual. After all those lessons about the need to be present for the divine within any discussion! Instead, it seemed they had made up their mind ahead of time and the result was a foregone conclusion!

Zhe only half listened to what followed. Kinla Truman addressed Vanu more formally. <Novice Vanu, as I indicated in my opening remarks, it is not Kinship practice to discipline Novices in the same way we would require strict penance of an adult member. Therefore, this committee determines that you shall be confined to the Annex for a period of not less than three subjective years, that your attainment of mat status shall be postponed for that same period and that your continued education

and progress be subject to the oversight of Kinla Eugaine, as acting representative of this committee. You are also required to undergo a study of penitence as well as several guided exercises under the supervision of Kinla Eugaine. Please note that this committee's decisions are not subject to appeal.>

<And what if I formally protest?> zhe responded, despite hir own best efforts to rein hirself in. Hir arms flailed outwards, as zhe tried, but failed, to find the tether by feel, hence drifting at the precise moment zhe felt the need for an anchor. <You asked me to explain my actions! I assumed these would be heard, and not dismissed out of hand without further consideration.>

Kinla Truman's face tightened. <As I already indicated, there is no other body that can hear your arguments. There is the Council, but the Council supports this committee's decisions. And if you are not careful, we may find it necessary to impose additional sanctions. This session is adjourned!>

XXIV

MAT STATUS

"Every act of rebellion expresses a nostalgia for innocence
and an appeal to the essence of being."

—Albert Camus, *The Rebel*, Accessed from the *All-Human
Compendium, Philosophy*, Ido Era 1537

<...By what right do they revoke my access to mat status? They
claim not to be severe in their punishments, and then condemn
me to three more years without the autonomy and, well, the
dignity accorded to any adult Kinch! It is outrageous, an act of
cowardice! I thought them better than that. I thought such acts
beneath the moral integrity of the Kinship!>

Vanu was still furious, after ranting to hir two sibs for some
time. They were in hir pard, where zhe had confined hirself after
the verdict.

Ranee had been trying to calm hir down. <We need to think
their decision through, to at least try to understand their intent—>

<Oh, their intent is clear enough,> Vanu interrupted, waving
hir arms and losing hold of hir tether as a result. Zhe drifted

helplessly out of alignment, reminding hir of hir situation in front of the committee, but this didn't slow down hir stream of words. <They are intent on preserving the community against any perceived threat to its sacrosanct "homogeneity." I read the *Book of Doctrine*. I know what they are doing. They believe that if word gets around that I 'got away' with a relationship outside the bounds defined by the *Book of Doctrine*, then other Kinch may take advantage of the situation. Although where these others are to find non lindiv partners in order to carry out their satanic activities, no one will say!> Zhe grabbed hold of the tether and by sheer obstinacy realigned hirself with hir sibs.

<But why three years?> Ranee asked. <It does seem exaggerated. Some of my pranks had far worse consequences, and yet I never got any punishment worse than a few extra hours doing cleanup, or confined to my pard.>

<And why confine you to the Annex as well as put off your attainment of mat status?> asked Joh, hir ideas forming slowly, as they always did. <Don't they decide where we go, as Novices, anyway?>

<Good point,> added Ranee. <If they refuse you mat status, they also control your movements. So why stipulate confinement to the Annex? It should not be necessary to state it.>

Vanu stopped to consider both arguments, disconcerted. Zhe was still angry, but Ranee was right, there was more going on here than zhe had realized. <They can't restrict my movements off the Annex if I have mat status,> zhe said, thoughtfully.

<So maybe the goal is to prevent you from leaving?> Ranee wondered out loud.

Vanu shook hir head. <But why?>

<Maybe there's more than one idea about how things should be done? Within the Kinship, I mean,> Joh suggested.

<That's very clever, little sib,> commented Ranee. <Joh's right, that would explain why they stipulated you not leave the Annex as well as not be awarded mat status. Another group with different ideas might decide you could leave, unless it were forbidden. It would depend who had oversight over you. Eugaine may follow the ideas of the current Disciplinary Committee, but perhaps there's some sort of rebellion underway.>

<I always thought the Kinship Council was unified,> Vanu said, hir anger beginning to seep away. Zhe was like that, slow to anger but quick to let it go once it had been expressed.

<No, there's lots of argument,> Ranee said. <I've heard rumours of some of the disagreements, from my colleagues on the Liaison Committee.>

<So, maybe my leaving advantages another group somehow?>

<Is three years an important time interval for the Council?> Joh was making one of hir slow, thoughtful suggestions again.

Vanu scanned hir memories, but nothing surfaced. <Ranee?>

<Council members are appointed for three year intervals.> Joh had hir legs hooked around one of the horizontal bars near the entrance, while Ranee was tethered beside Vanu.

<Is it possible that my whole 'punishment' serves some political agenda within the Kinship? Was I being naive to trust in our leadership?> Vanu rolled hir shoulders in frustration, but kept hold of the tether this time.

<Possibly,> Ranee said. <My colleagues believe God works through such disputes, that God's will is not expressed only when

things are in agreement, but that disagreements are necessary to progress.>

Maybe, thought Vanu, thinking back to the vision zhe had had. It seemed to agree with Ranee's words. Dark roilings were as necessary to the future, hir future, as any paths of harmony. This wasn't the moment to dwell on that, however.

<Why not protest your mat status postponement, then?> asked Joh, again.

<I could protest to the Council,> said Vanu. <Kinla Truman even suggested that might be possible. However, zhe implied that the Council would support their decision.>

<Oh. You mean, even in the context of a divided Council?> Ranee asked.

<They must know that. We could try to register a protest, and see what happens, though,> Vanu replied.

<Too bad we're none of us Ido members,> Ranee said. <I'm not sure that mat status can be postponed for political reasons under Ido rules.>

Vanu raised hir arms again, then grabbed hold of the tether before zhe drifted away. <You're right, Ranee! I forgot to tell you. During my stay at the Yard, I signed on to the Ido. After I met Shosee's father, he encouraged me to join. I applied, was accepted, and had my linkup created, all while I was still at the Yard. I didn't think about its relevance in this context. At no time, neither when I was first brought before the Hospitality House Council, nor during this recent hearing, did I think to draw on those resources. I *am* a member of the Ido. With everything that has happened, I forgot about it!>

<Then that's the way to proceed,> Ranee said. <Being denied mat status is a violation of Ido rules! You could make a formal complaint!>

Vanu pulled hard on the tether, hir body surging upwards, this time unchecked. Instead of flailing, zhe was now moving like one of the oggies under jet propulsion, until zhe broke hir movement against the far wall. As zhe turned around to face them, zhe replied, <I need to figure out how to activate the link, but then, yes, by all means, I will submit a formal complaint!>

XXV

DEOFAX

"A society that is fearful of self-examination and exploration can't believably say that it trusts in God. Nor can it believably say that it values every living being. We must trust the totality of our nature, in terms of both its multiplicity and its oneness."

—Zenju Earthlyn Manuel, *The Way of Tenderness*, Accessed from the *All-Human Compendium*, *Theology*, Ido Era 1537

Vanu's complaint generated a lot of activity, far more than any of the three of them had anticipated. It wasn't just the formal proceedings. When Vanu logged hir activities via the Ido, documenting hir difficulties and the nature of hir challenge against the Kinship decision, the information entered the public domain. Zhe began to receive messages of support, both from within the Kinship community and from people farther afield.

Not only that, zhe had expected to interact with other members of DeoFax, but many of the messages of goodwill were from other Faxes. Zhe was familiar, of course, with the star sigil of

DeoFax, representing the vision of a universe opening outwards, the symbol of spiritual outreach via the stars, but now she began to see the other Fax sigils more and more frequently. The blue hand of UmaFax in its joyful pose, the green vines of EcoFax, framing the available space in a representation that was intentionally systemic, the red base of EngFax, that could be habitat or platform, and the embracing grey arms of IdoFax within its Taoist referents. Zhe had seen them all before, but now they took on a life of their own.

Each Fax, composed of a fraction of humanity spread out across the billions of worlds of the Humanitat, embraced a different vision of humanity's future. DeoFax members viewed spiritual matters as decisive, of course. EcoFax adherents believed that an ecosystemic perspective was paramount. EngFax were the technologists, and UmaFax the humanists and artists. IdoFax, although ostensibly proponents of paradox, were also often prominent leaders and visionaries. Besides the five main faxes, there were several smaller ones, the most prominent of which was NarFax, which grouped together those more interested in hedonism and drugs than actual human progress. And while Plenum was predominantly DeoFax, elsewhere in the Humanitat, DeoFax was in a minority. Only IdoFax were less numerous. Seeing the sigils affixed to or embedded within the messages reminded Vanu of the multitudes of points of view embraced by the Ido. Living within a dedicated *mycs* community, one lost sight of the broader perspective.

Most of these people were local, however. DeoFax was by far the most dominant faction within the Plenum Star Nursery and among its inhabitants. Comments from further afield would arrive, but they would take more time. Vanu kept hoping to see something from Shosee, but there was nothing. Following this spate of messages from well-wishers outside the Annex, other members of the Kinship started to comment. As Vanu moved about the Annex, strangers would accost hir with encouraging words, smiles, and gestures, particularly one involving grasping the elbow of the outstretched left arm with the bent right arm, clearly meant as a form of support.

Vanu also discovered the Plenum DeoFax forums—some of the messages zhe received referred to discussions within the forums, so zhe investigated. Zhe found evidence to support the conjectures zhe and her sibs had formulated, that there might be more than one political group vying to determine Kinship policy and activities. With Ranee and Joh, zhe had speculated on the existence of a rebel group, but the forums suggested there might be more than one dissident group, each with its own perspectives. Kinship policy per se was not debated within the forums, but references were made to policy perspectives, especially in the turmoil of comments about Vanu's 'crime' and hir punishment.

The DeoFax Court representatives in Plenum requested to meet with the Kinship Council at the Annex. Greatbear sent a private message to Vanu, letting hir know that he was coming, and that, in addition to meeting with the Council, the representatives wanted to meet independently with Vanu. The meeting was set for the end of the following week. The travel times involved precluded an earlier time. Greatbear needed three days travel to arrive, while the other representative came from the School, an additional five Ido Era days travel farther away. That Vanu's complaint resulted in preempting more than three person-weeks of travel was daunting, and underlined how seriously the matter was being treated. This didn't go unremarked within the forums either. There was speculation that Vanu's case provided a rare opportunity for other parts of the DeoFax community to delve into Kinship practices.

Two days before the expected visit, Joh shyly invited Ranee and Vanu to go with hir to the ball pit. As they passed the entrance, they were met by a broadcast cheer. <Va-nu. Va-nu. Va-nu. Va-nu.> There were at least a hundred people suspended within the large space of the ball pit, not quite the density of *sarde*, whereby people are packed in so they touch, but nearly so. In addition to broadcasting hir name, they were making that distinctive gesture Vanu had noticed earlier, the left arm stretched out in front, the right bent at the elbow so as the grasp the other elbow. Seen individually, the gesture was interesting if strange. Performed as a large group, in synch, the gesture became a powerful symbol in its own right. There were also several large flags with the DeoFax star sigil displayed prominently within them, rather than the more traditional Kinship emblem with its random field of ripples.

<What the...?> Vanu turned to Joh as the crowd of young people, many of whom, but by no means all, were Novices, quietened down to listen. Joh was clutching one of the flags that bore the DeoFax sigil.

<Your cause has generated not just interest and well wishing, but an actual movement,> Ranee explained. <It seems the Kinship leadership has been dictatorial not just with you, Vanu, but with others as well, and diverse forms of resentment were already felt. Your case has led some to organize, first to support your

complaint, but also to address other issues. Most of us feel that we would get a better hearing if the Ido were involved more fully.>

<Sorry if I seem singularly uninformed,> Vanu added in an aside to Joh, <but what is this gesture supposed to signify?>

<I can answer that,> intruded a once familiar pseudo-voice that Vanu had not heard in some time and had not expected to hear in this context. From out of the crowd, Dev moved towards them. <When we realized that the decision of the Disciplinary Committee was rooted in historical motivations, we started doing some research of our own. We found in the archives records of an earlier form of the Kinship community in which this gesture was used. The straightened arm signifies forward movement, while the bent arm that grasps the other signifies the constraining action of an intelligent and caring community. The Kinship was founded on both principles, which, when combined, were called the Caritas Principles. The Caritas gesture seemed an appropriate symbol for our contemporary concerns as well.>

<Dev has become one of the leaders of the movement that supports your cause,> Joh added.

<I found something more useful to do than making life miserable for younger Novices,> Dev joked. <I actually have you to thank for that, Vanu. Kinla Val Yatsen took me aside one day and had a very unofficial talk with me. I appreciate the fact that you hadn't set out to cause me trouble with an official complaint. Kinla Val helped me redirect my energies.>

The Caritas Movement, as they came to be called, were present outside the Kinship Hall where the meeting was being held between the DeoFax representatives and the Kinship Council. They made no rousing speeches, but exercised a quiet presence that was nonetheless keenly felt inside the room, as Greatbear reported afterwards in his private meeting with Vanu. The meeting lasted several hours, and involved the full Kinship Council of twenty-one members, as well as the members of the Novice Disciplinary Committee.

As the meeting drew to a close, Greatbear signaled to Vanu, who was outside the meeting room, and they met in Vanu's pard. Vanu wrapped one of the pard's sleepnets around hir so that zhe wouldn't have to constantly adjust hir position via a tether.

<I'd like to introduce Foresight Argo, our DeoFax rep from the New Pantheist Church, stationed at the School. As you know, Vanu, Maestre Argo has taken two weeks time from a busy schedule to come and meet with the Kinship over this matter.> Foresight Argo was an imposing, elderly findiv, not as large as Greatbear but with a regal bearing that drew the eye. She wore a brightly coloured bren, all yellows and oranges, over which were layered overbren garments in darker shades that contrasted with her light brown skin. She drifted over to where Vanu was resting in hir net-like arrangement, while Greatbear stayed near the entrance.

<Don't let Greatbear intimidate you, Vanu. He loves to take center stage and dramatize everything. Nonetheless, he is right to emphasize the gravity of the situation. There will be aspects of the case you probably don't grasp at this point. Although, you were in your rights to make a formal complaint. Indeed, this was the only viable course of protest open to you. You must realize, however, that the Ido has no jurisdiction over the Kinship in this matter.>

As Vanu tried to assimilate this shocking news, Greatbear took over from Foresight. <Now who's doing the dramatizing,> he chided. <What Foresight means is that the Kinship, as a community, functions independently of the Ido. Historically, this was a conscious choice on their part. Both of our churches, the Emergence Christian Church and the New Pantheist Church, chose to function within Ido oversight, but the Kinship chose differently. That being said, nearly half the adult Kinch are members of the Ido, and the Kinship Council cannot simply disregard the Ido's positions on issues of common interest. As your community has discovered, through the emergence of the Caritas Movement, the internal world of the Kinship and the external world of DeoFax are connected.>

<The purpose of our meeting with the Council,> Greatbear continued, <was to make clear the Ido's position on the matter of your rights as a member of the Ido, and to negotiate with the Kinship Council some form of acceptable compromise. And I have to say, to our disappointment, that although some progress has been made towards a solution, we are still at an impasse.>

Foresight continued after a brief pause, while Vanu shifted around in the netting in order to better view her. <The Council agrees that Ido members may have rights that are not always compatible with Kinship practices. They argue, however, that Kinship membership is a matter of choice. That Ido members who do not wish to conform to Kinship practices may freely leave the community and make their lives elsewhere. While this is true of adult Kinch, the matter of the rights of children who have not yet attained mat status is more complex. The decision against you, in its actual form, refuses to allow you to leave. Many on

the Council are sympathetic to your cause, but the Council as a whole defends the decision of its Disciplinary Committee.>

<But I don't want to leave the Kinship community!> Vanu exclaimed, rather perturbed at the thought. Zhe had never once thought that hir situation might lead to such a rupture. And then, as if to add to hir internal confusion, the thought, unbidden, came: *And what if zhe did leave, wouldn't that allow Shosee and hir to be together?*

<Understood,> replied Greatbear. <However, as long as the Kinship maintain their counter-argument that membership in the Kinship is a matter of choice, it is difficult for us to argue along other lines. Nonetheless, it is not yet the moment to give up. We are scheduled to meet with the Council again tomorrow, and perhaps we shall make more progress then. You should let your support group know that their actions, and presence, have an impact, even if the ultimate goal is still not in sight. The Council is nervous about its internal politics, and your Caritas group have played a role in increasing their nervousness. Okay? Any questions?>

Vanu twisted around in the netting again. Not for the first time, zhe wished the Kinship were more favourable towards the widespread use of parflots. <How is Shosee doing?> zhe finally asked. <I hoped she would have come with you.>

<She has gone to the School,> Greatbear replied. <It would have been awkward for her to have accompanied me. Given the charges, I mean.>

Vanu nodded. Of course. Zhe hadn't thought about that. Zhe quieted the roiling sensations that threatened to make hir lose hir sense of control, over hir own body at least. No point in stirring the beast from its harbour in the deeps. Although, it was hard to settle down with the memory of Shosee still lingering. And her critical mind, at the very least, would be so useful to Vanu right now!

XXVI

LESSONS IN PENITENCE

"...the highest function of ecology is the understanding of consequences."

—Frank Herbert, *Dune*, Accessed from the *All–Human Compendium, Literature*, Ido Era 1537

Despite Greatbear's encouraging words, the negotiations made no significant advances, even across several meetings between the DeoFax reps and the Council. Vanu wondered how much longer the outsiders could stay at the Annex. They were busy people with many other demands on their time.

Meanwhile, Vanu was required to meet with Kinla Eugaine to discuss hir penitence. Since hir discussions with Kinlas Val and Pater, Vanu had undergone a sea change in hir understanding of and sympathy towards Kinla Eugaine. Recent events, including hir presence on the Disciplinary Committee, hadn't changed that, although they had introduced nuances into hir appreciation of the older Kinch.

On the other hand, Vanu still didn't believe zhe hirself had done anything wrong. The notion of undergoing some sort of official penance and repentance posed difficulties for hir. However, Vanu decided that learning more about Kinship practices in this regard wouldn't hurt, and that neither would going through the motions of penance. It was the dissimulation that bothered hir. It wasn't hir usual practice to do anything zhe wasn't wholly committed to, nor did zhe like the idea of hiding hir true thoughts from someone zhe respected.

Vanu met Kinla Eugaine in the tiny chamber the latter used as an office, located on the periphery of the large, multi-chambered, zero-gravity space they called the Crib Nursery. The Nursery was inside an enormous bubble that jutted out onto the Machine Platform near the centre of the Annex. It consisted of a honeycomb of small chambers organized in concentric spheres around the centrally located exuterus devices and their associated regrowth units, or argeets. The younger cohorts of crib sibs lived, studied, exercised and prayed in their group pards in the surrounding shells under the guidance of roving teachers and guardians. The latter were artificial beings sometimes channeling human guardians and sometimes not. Watching over the young was a task that rotated among certain groups of adult Kinch.

As a near adult, Vanu found it strange to be back in the once familiar environment of the Nursery, even if Kinla Eugaine's office was on its edge. In the year or two following the move of Vanu and hir siblings to their pard cluster, Vanu had visited younger friends among the other cohorts, but these visits had ceased. It had been years since Vanu had last entered the Nursery.

<Ah, there you are!> Kinla Eugaine greeted hir as Vanu pulled hirself in through the open entrance. <Use the parflot, I prefer the tether.> Vanu followed instructions, but the parflot's particles seemed to follow an unusual trajectory, sliding around instead of just vibrating as if they were somehow fluid. But that was impossible, of course—it must be hir imagination. <Now,> Kinla Eugaine went on, <I realize you are here under protest. I won't be requiring anything of you that you are not ready and willing to commit to. I know you are a dedicated and principled Novice. Don't misunderstand me, I do take issue with what you've done. I hope to bring you to understand the nature of the wrongs you have committed, and the boundaries you have crossed, but we shall proceed one step at a time. All right?>

At Vanu's nod, Kinla Eugaine continued. <Now, let us talk about the Kinship as a community. Remind me what our motto is?>

<'From fulfillment into grace, from the inner heart to divine transformation, we surrender ourselves to God's path of suffering, sacrifice and awakening.'>

<That is so, yes. And I'm sure you think you understand those words. You've asked many a question about them over the years! Let me tell you this, however: as an oldtimer I speak from experience. Every time you think you understand those words, they turn around and bite you from behind! They are far more enigmatic than they are explanatory.

<For example, what do you think is meant by fulfillment? If you think about it, it is an odd place to start. You would expect fulfillment to be an end, not a beginning, wouldn't you?>

<I always felt our lives of dedication to God were a kind of fulfillment,> Vanu replied. Zhe hesitated, intrigued by the direction of the discussion. <The motto starts there because our lives start there.>

<Harrumph. Yes, that is a very thoughtful answer, and does you credit. But fulfillment can also be a trap, an illusion. As you get older, you'll realize how easy it is to feel fulfilled, but how hard it is to be fulfilled. Even within the community, within the Kinship, we suffer from this truth!>

Suddenly, Vanu understood something about what the old Kinch was trying to tell hir. When zhe thought back over the state of fulfillment zhe had experienced in Shosee's company, real as it had felt, zhe had been conscious that the sense of fulfillment was precarious, and sometimes, that all was not as it seemed. And over the past few days, despite the triumphs of engaging the DeoFax reps in the discussion over basic rights, there had also been an emptiness there that disturbed Vanu. Was the feeling of fulfillment always accompanied by a sense of emptiness? And was that why fulfillment was a beginning, and not an end?

<I see that,> Vanu finally answered. <Fulfillment carries its own emptiness. Is that what you mean?>

<I have never heard it stated better,> Kinla Eugaine answered, a note of respect in hir affirmation. <Now, skipping over grace, we shall come back to that very important concept later, what do you make of the second clause, the bit about the inner heart and transformation?>

<I've always found that obscure,> Vanu admitted. <Or maybe too obvious? My ability to transform myself, or our ability as a

community to achieve transformation, requires delving inwards. It seems obvious, somehow.>

<Those words have troubled some of our greatest scholars, Vanu, so you are right to view them with some trepidation. And your reflection on the communal element is particularly interesting. But why is transformation a goal? Either for yourself, or for the community?>

<I always assumed that... I don't know... getting close to God, required a transformation. Zhe seems so, unattainable, how could I possibly approach God without a divine transformation, like the one Siddhartha describes?> Although the Kinship was rooted in Christian ideas, it drew some of its ideas from Buddhism as well.

Kinla Eugaine was silent for a long minute. <I begin to doubt my understanding of events,> zhe finally replied. <As usual, I might add. Your answer bears witness to more wisdom than I have heard in many a year from the Kinship Council, which rarely talks about these matters with the depth you've given them. I'm going to have to think more about what I've been asked to do here. So, let us try once more to review your actions in the light of our communal motto. I accept your interpretation of the need for transformation at the individual level. What about as a community? And are you sure of your understanding of the words 'divine transformation'?>

Confused by the sudden shift, Vanu thought through the expression again. What did Kinla Eugaine mean? What other interpretation was possible? 'From the inner heart to divine transformation'... And suddenly, the answer jumped out at hir. Why, Kinla Eugaine was right, there was another way to view the text. Not as a transformation of the human towards the divine, but as

God transforming Hirself! In which case, the 'inner heart' might refer to God's inner heart... and we, community or individual, were called upon to be present for this 'divine transformation'! Vanu wondered how zhe could ever have seen anything different in those words, now zhe saw it!

<I see it, now!> Vanu said, excitedly. <It is our function, as a community, to be an instrument for God's transformation, for God's emergence. That is why we follow, why we must follow, the path of 'suffering, sacrifice and awakening'.>

<That is why we must surrender ourselves to that path, yes, that is our task. We shall come back to that term, too, the word 'surrender'.> Zhe was silent again, thinking. <Do you think the path is easy, Vanu?>

Vanu shrugged, but again, zhe realized Kinla Eugaine wanted more. <The obvious answer is 'no,'> Vanu finally echoed hir inner argument. <But you want me to go deeper than that. So, I guess you are saying the path is hard in ways that aren't obvious?>

<Indeed. What might those 'hard to see' ways be, do you think?>

Vanu stirred in the parflot. It was so much more comfortable than the nets in which they slept inside their pards! And as hir mind lingered momentarily on that idea, zhe realized it pertained to Kinla Eugaine's question. <I think...> Vanu started, but then stopped in confusion.

<Go on. What do you think?>

<I don't know how to say it. I was thinking about how much a parflot provides comfort and support compared to the sleepnets we use in our pards, or the flat benches we use in other parts of the Annex. But the Kinship... eschews, is that the word?...

eschews the use of such simple comforts for the most part. We are provided with less comfortable seating surfaces and sleeping arrangements. I used to think that was because we serve the Suffering God, but I have come to realize that is not the way things work. Instead, I think that we are being encouraged to be present for the path of 'suffering, sacrifice and awakening' in our seating and sleeping arrangements, in simply not taking the comfortable path, but rather one that involves more hardship. So that is an example of the hidden ways in which our path is not easy?> Which would mean, Vanu realized with a start, that even if zhe were right about Shosee and the reaction of the Kinship Council, there was another sense in which zhe was wrong. She had exhibited a form of hubris, of pride, that was not commensurate with the teachings zhe aspired to follow. And this was what Kinla Eugaine wanted hir to think about.

<Yes, that is one way of looking at it. I might also point out that the path may appear straight to you from here, but that it is anything but straight. It doubles back on itself, frequently stalls, and sets off in totally unexpected directions. Furthermore, down each segment of the path, things risk becoming difficult in ways we can't even begin to imagine from our position here, at this moment in time. I don't mean to sound ominous, but my experience of life is that there are many unexpected turns on the way.>

<What about the part about grace?> Vanu mused, thinking more about Eugaine's words on the complexity of the path. <I understand the general idea of grace, but I think I may be missing some of what is meant by that term.>

<Yes, grace. Grace is both simple and complex, it is all a matter of perspective. What does it mean to you?>

<As I understand grace, it is God's way of forgiving us when we go astray?>

<You might think that, yes, but there is more to it than that. Remember what we said about divine transformation?>

<You want me to take God's perspective again? Then grace is, hmmm, an opening to... God's process of... accepting the world? I'm not sure.>

<Don't worry about it. We should stop there today. I want you to think more about this, and we shall meet again soon. You have given me at least as much to think about as I believe I have given you. I may want to consult someone before we see each other again. And Vanu, thank you, I shall not let this pass without some follow-up, I promise!>

Vanu didn't make much sense out of these final comments. In any case, zhe was preoccupied by the chain of thought Kinla Eugaine had led hir into. For, although zhe wasn't ready to give up hir struggle for the recognition of hir mat status, zhe had gained a deeper understanding regarding the nature of the Kinship as a community, as well as hir own spiritual journey. Zhe needed time to think it all through.

XXVII

GENDER TROUBLE

"I hold it that a little rebellion now and then is a good thing, and as necessary in the political world as storms in the physical... It is a medicine necessary for the sound health of government."

—Thomas Jefferson, *Letters*, Accessed from the *All-Human Compendium, Literature*, Ido Era 1537

As things turned out, the meeting never took place, since events overtook both Vanu and Kinla Eugaine.

The morning following hir interview, the final meeting between Greatbear, Foresight and the Kinship Council was scheduled to take place. Greatbear had informed Vanu that the negotiations were stalled. The Kinch refused to make any concessions regarding the rights accorded to their young. This, despite the pressure from both the Caritas Movement and turbulence among the adult Kinch, the latter expressed in intense discussions going on throughout the Annex.

The Caritas Movement had requested a public meeting with the Council on the occasion of the final meeting with the DeoFax representatives. Although the Council had been trying to downplay the importance of the movement, they did agree to meet with a small delegation outside the Kinship Hall at the close of the discussions.

Vanu had seen neither Joh nor Ranee for several days. That morning, zhe crossed paths with Joh in their common pard. <Have you seen Ranee?> Vanu asked. <I've been hoping to ask hir about the reactions of hir colleagues on the Liaison Committee to all these events, but zhe is not responding via binup and I haven't seen hir in several days.>

Joh looked guilty. <You should come to the meeting with the Kinship Council. It's scheduled for some time after 14:00. Ranee will be there.>

<All right,> Vanu replied. <I have been staying away from those encounters. I didn't want people to feel confused by my presence there. However, since it is the last day of the discussions with Greatbear and Foresight, it may be all right this time.>

The Council meeting didn't break up until past 15:30. Greatbear sent a private message to Vanu saying there had been some unexpected progress at the last minute. The Kinship Council had agreed that children within the Kinship community did have rights, including the right to an appeal of decisions viewed as unfair, but that it was an internal Kinship matter how such an appeal was handled. As a result, the DeoFax representatives were not leaving empty handed, but rather with a formal promise that some procedural mechanism for appeals would be set up in the near future.

When the Council members finally emerged, there were tired smiles on several faces. Greatbear and Foresight were to be guided back to their ship following the meeting with the Caritas Movement. The waiting Caritas group, as well as a number of well-wishers and supporters, among them Vanu, were tethered at various locations in the atrium outside the Kinship Hall. The head of the Council, Kinla Chou-Foc, finally came out, flanked by Greatbear and Foresight. The Caritas group, led, Vanu noted, by Dev, and including Ranee, met them face to face, and with bodies aligned.

It was Dev who broadcast the message on behalf of the Caritas group. <Although we understand the Council has agreed to institute an appeals process for the decisions of the Disciplinary Committee, we believe this concession to be too little, and too late. The Kinship youth should have the right to participate in all Council decisions. In particular, the Caritas Movement that we represent disagrees with current Kinship doctrine which stipulates that all members must be of the same gender and sexual orientation. In light of these disagreements, and in solidarity with Vanu Francoeur, four among us have undergone the procedure of changing gender from a lindiv to a tindiv.>

In the subsequent furor, Vanu almost lost sight of Ranee, who zhe realized, with considerable shock, was one of the four. Dev, it seemed, was not, nor was Joh. The four of them had temped up and entered a regrowth tank for the operation, which had taken four months of realtime, although less than a day at standard Kinship tempo.

The transformation from lindiv to tindiv was a major procedure. The lindiv, or la-gendered, the norm within the Kinship, were equipped with the shoud, the second skin whose sensitivity could be consciously modified in a variable way across the body. The tindiv, or ti-gendered, involved modifying the shoud to introduce the moelen, the fleshy extension in the pelvic region that could fold either to take on a phallic or a vaginal form. Both the la-gendered and the ti-gendered were widely treated within the Humanitat as neutral genders, but the ti-gendered, like the mi-gendered, were bi-gendered rather than strictly neutral.

The Caritas Four, as they were quickly named, had succeeded in raising the bar on the pressure tactics being applied, and by the same token, dramatically increased the turmoil already present among the adult Kinch. But it wasn't until much later that Vanu was able to engage Ranee in a private conversation about hir actions. They met in the common lounge area outside their individual pards.

<So, little sib, you're not the only one who can cause trouble in the Kinship!>

<Trust you, Ranee, to make a joke out of it! The Council is not likely to treat this as a joke, however. I wish you'd come to me before deciding to do this.>

<So you could talk me out of it? For once, little sib, I've found a prank that has some bite to it! And you made me curious, Vanu, regarding other forms of sexuality, and gender, than the one the Kinship would enforce upon us. I much prefer the versatility of the moelen to the staid virginity of the shoud. In fact, I think this gender is much more me than the old one. There are so many more possibilities for getting into trouble! It's time the Kinship evolved to accept a more heterogeneous community!>

<You haven't read your history, Ranee. The Kinship was a more heterogeneous community in the past, and gave that up. There is a need to understand why that happened—otherwise, we will never be able to reverse the trend. And just because I have been unable to fit myself within those constraints, doesn't mean that others must break the mold!>

<You're wrong, despite your good intentions. The mold as you call it, was stifling us! Don't you realize that the pranks I have engaged in all my life were my own form of protest? You've done us all a favour! And if what you say is true, things are even worse than we thought. We've devolved! That's crazy! Why would God require us to be all the same in order to worship Hir!>

XXVIII

CROSS CURRENTS

"...the best way out is always through."

—Robert Frost, *North of Boston*, Accessed from the *All-Human Compendium, Literature*, Ido Era 1537

Vanu had been right to be worried. The Kinship Council took the new events very seriously. And although the DeoFax representatives, Greatbear and Foresight, wanted to stay, they were in no position to demand this. None of the four protesters were Ido members. Vanu had asked Ranee about that, about applying, but Ranee had hir own ideas on the matter.

<Don't you see, Vanu, your move to involve the Ido was brilliant, but it wasn't for everyone. Despite my firm conviction that the Kinship needs to change, I consider this to be an internal matter. We Kinch have to work it out between ourselves. If our community is not strong enough to accommodate these changes, then what is it for?>

Ranee had a point, Vanu conceded. And the Council wasn't united on the issue. There were deep divisions. Rumours were rampant about putative decisions that the Council was reaching. But even in the presence of those divisions, the Council reached its verdict, and, as Vanu had foreseen, the result was not encouraging for Ranee and hir three co-conspirators.

The published decision was several pages long, but it came down to a judgement of exile. Ranee and hir colleagues were to be banished from the community. Convenient, thought Vanu. Send them away where the Council no longer has to think about them. Furthermore, in Vanu's opinion, by expelling the Caritas Four, the Council was reneging on its internal responsibility to its own members! Especially with regard to the other three, excluding Ranee, who were all children. The fine print of the decision presented the act as a 'breach of faith' and a 'violation of the sanctity of the body.' The latter, if upheld, represented a condemnation of a common act carried out throughout the Humanitat. And as to any breach of faith, Vanu's conversations with Ranee had confirmed quite the opposite—it was an act of confirmation of faith!

As an adult Kinch, Ranee had a right to appeal, and used this right. None of the other three had attained mat status, but they submitted a document calling on the right to appeal as recognized by the Council in its deliberations with the DeoFax Court members. Vanu also submitted a request for an appeal for hir case, on a similar basis, a way for hir to act in support of hir sibling.

Vanu tried hard to convince Ranee to revert the process, especially in the light of hir own changed understanding of the situation. <As an adult Kinch, you are in a very different position than the other three,> Vanu argued. <Also, you've made your

point. By reversing the process, you'd be declaring your wish to stay within the community, an act of contrition. I agree we want to change the way the Kinship operates, but you can't do that from the outside. We need you here, where you can do the most good. I'm sure if you presented yourself to the Council, after reversing the procedure, that you'd get a hearing. We know there are several dissident voices on the Council. Please consider it!>

And finally, Vanu made progress. Ranee talked things over with the Caritas leadership, and with the other three, and all agreed that Ranee wasn't in the same situation as the others. They saw that there could be advantages to hir staying within the Kinship, rather than allowing hirself to be expelled under protest.

So Ranee entered the argeet and emerged several hours later, returned to hir lindiv status. Zhe then presented hirself to the Council head, Kinla Chou-Foc, who took hir changed status under advisement. To the dismay of both Ranee and Vanu, however, the Council determined that, although Ranee would no longer be expelled from the Kinship, zhe would be sent to the Kinship community at the Station for the foreseeable future, ostensibly still a part of the community but de facto excluded from the Annex. The remaining three of the Caritas Four were being kept on at the Annex until the appeals procedures could be worked out. By reversing the gender change, Ranee had ironically worsened hir situation. Zhe had been effectively exiled, and, apparently, immediately.

Vanu was also awaiting a response to hir request for an appeal. In the meantime, zhe was expected to continue hir meetings with Kinla Eugaine.

Zhe was disappointed not to have received any word from Shosee yet. Perhaps zhe should take the initiative and send her a message?

XXIX
DISSIDENT MOVEMENT

"Rebellion cannot exist without a strange form of love."

—Albert Camus, *The Rebel*, Accessed from the *All-Human Compendium, Literature*, Ido Era 1537

Kinla Eugaine had confirmed Vanu's next meeting with hir, but had suggested they meet at a different location than hir office. Surprised, Vanu had to look up the indicated location via binup. It was an observation port on the other side of the Machine Platform from the Nursery Block, jutting out from the main office section. Unlike the Nursery, the walls here were transparent, but the bubble was barely larger than the central core of the Nursery. Vanu used a passenger elevator to get there. Zhe arrived late. Finding the location and the most appropriate form of transport took more time than zhe had expected. Why the devil did Kinla Eugaine want to meet hir out here?

The answer revealed itself when Vanu entered the observation space. In microgravity, perspective is always a matter of orientation. As Vanu entered the space head first, zhe had the impression zhe was rising into the observation bubble. The floor of the Machine Platform was a colossal wall that cut off the view in that direction. As zhe moved towards the small group tethered near the centre of the space, zhe reoriented hir body to their alignment, and the Machine Platform became the more familiar floor.

The group included Kinla Eugaine, Kinla Val, Kinla Pater, whom Vanu was surprised to see, and two other, rather aged figures zhe didn't know.

<Sorry to spring this on you, Vanu, but there was no way to warn you without revealing our hand to the Council. Let me introduce you to my co-conspirators, two of whom you know and two you do not. Kinla Murakino is one of our best historians, and Kinla Tarech was a former head of the Kinship Council. Both Kinla Val and Kinla Pater, you already know. I use the term co-conspirator with trepidation. We are not plotting anything as dramatic as overthrowing the current Kinship Council, but we are the main part of the dissident movement, and we need to work out a strategy to go forward from where we are. We were hoping you could help us.>

<I'll be glad to do anything to help, if you think I have something useful to contribute.>

Kinla Pater took up the thread. <As a dissident movement, I'm afraid we are rather unorganized. As you may have guessed, not all the adult Kinch are in agreement with the recent decisions the Kinship Council has adopted. That said, finding a way to challenge them is... awkward. It is not only their treatment of you or even of the Caritas Four that we object to, but rather there are long-standing differences over the interpretation of

the principles upon which the Kinship is founded. However, your own... defiance of Kinship customs seems to have acted as a whirlpool around which these debates have gained new energy.

<The Council,> Kinla Pater went on, <although still dominated by a group one might call the Purists, is more and more split. The Purists believe that the Kinship is diminished by allowing change to enter our practices. They use a kind of pseudo-historical perspective to advocate a "return to traditional values." The problem, of course, is that the Kinship has never been a static community. In fact, the whole vision of an Emergent God is predicated on a community with the courage to change, to allow new understandings to emerge within our midst.>

There was a half attempt to interrupt on the part of Kinla Val, but Pater overrode hir and went on. <The growing presence of the Ido within the Kinship membership has long been an irritant to the Purists. The arrival of the DeoFax delegation brought this particular struggle to the surface.> Zhe paused a moment, looking at Kinla Val, as if daring hir to comment. <Even with the current composition of the Council, there was a lot more sympathy for their arguments than the Purists would have preferred. The leadership tried to close off the discussions quickly, but as you know, concessions were finally adopted...>

<Are you a member of the Council, Kinla Pater?> Vanu asked. <I hadn't realized...>

<No, I have long been viewed as a troublemaker by the Purists. My position at the Kinship House at the Yard is partially an attempt to keep me away from the larger group. You see, as a former head of the Core, I have influence among the older Kinch. Kinla Val is, however, a recent appointee to the Council.>

<I had drawn the conclusion that you were not a fan of the Ido,> Vanu ventured to suggest to Kinla Val.

<And you would be right. My appointment to the Council appears to be in part the result of that perception. But my objections with regard to the Ido are not the same as those of the Purists. They dislike the Ido because its edicts result in a decrease of their authority. My disagreement with the Ido is that it enhances the reliance of people on making decisions based on certainty. The Ido acts as a substitute authority, which is why the Purists would like to see it disappear. I would like people to make their own decisions.>

<We all agree on that, even if we have different ideas about how to change things,> added Kinla Pater. <The stalwarts among us are Kinlas Eugaine, Tarech and Murakino, although there are others, not yet willing to declare themselves openly.>

<And until very recently, I was among the undecided,> Kinla Eugaine confessed. <I bear witness to the growing dissatisfaction with the current leadership of the Kinship.>

<But what exactly do you expect of me?> Vanu asked. <I have no voice on the Council, in fact, very little power at all. I'm not happy about my situation, nor that of my sib, Ranee, but I'm really not the rabble rouser others take me for. My... defiance... as you call it, was a very personal affair. Although I am sympathetic to the cause of the other three members of the Caritas Four, it is the plight of Ranee that concerns me the most.>

<And it is precisely there where we think you can make a... a contribution,> responded Kinla Val. <Ranee is in a situation that is different from you or the others, in that zhe is a recognized adult. Hir sentence of exile to the Station is unprecedented. We

believe that you could make a formal protest to the Council in
this regard. And to say that you have no power is to shortchange
yourself, as you must realize by now. Your actions are watched
by many, and may still influence those who are as yet undecided.
And there is a certain caution in the way the Purists have been
reacting to your actions. It is easier for them to discipline your sib
than yourself. It gives you an edge, a certain level of freedom. We
further believe there is far more sympathy in support of Ranee
than of the other members of the Caritas Four, precisely because
zhe is an adult. A formal protest will have an impact...>

<But I am not a recognized adult! Wouldn't it be better
coming from one?>

<It might,> Kinla Pater conceded. <Vanu is right. As the only
person not on the Council, I propose to support hir protest. Let
us co-submit such a plaint, if you consent to do this. Because as
Ranee's sib, your voice still counts.>

Vanu nodded. <All right, if you think it will make a difference.
None of my earlier protests seem to have made much of a dent,
but I'm willing to try once more.> Although, hir own concerns
seemed to have receded as the political situation developed. All
Vanu had wanted was to have the ability to leave the Annex and
return to the Yard to spend time with Shosee. Regardless of what
else happened, that seemed an increasingly unlikely outcome,
not the least because Shosee was no longer present. Of course,
Ranee's situation took precedence, but it did not displace Vanu's
personal concerns. And then there were Kinla Eugaine's earlier
remarks, about Vanu's lack of humility. How should that issue
come to bear on events? Should Vanu abandon Shosee, despite
hir inclination? It was all still very confusing!

Vanu was dismayed, however, on hir return from meeting with the dissidents, to find a despondent Joh telling her that Ranee had already been sent away. Zhe had been allowed no opportunity to bid farewell to hir sibs, hir friends or hir colleagues. Access to hir binup was also blocked. Events were proceeding far too quickly for Vanu to even grasp, let alone find a place in hir heart to develop a response.

XXX

JOH

"If they don't like you for being yourself, be yourself even more."

—Taylor Swift, *Interview*, Accessed from the *All-Human Compendium, Popular Culture*, Ido Era 1537

Vanu quickly formulated a protest with regard to the disappearance of Ranee. Zhe notified Kinla Pater, who co-signed it, and submitted this to the Council. The protest was couched in neutral terms, but, in reality, Vanu was deeply concerned. Despite hir doubts concerning aspects of hir own behaviour, the Council appeared to have lost its hold on reality. The dissidents confirmed this. It was an unconscionable move on the part of the Council leadership to have Ranee removed without even the possibility of communicating with hir family. Furthermore, despite hir sympathy for the dissidents' position, Vanu had started to feel that both zhe and Ranee had become pieces in a power struggle. Vanu needed to find a way to break free of the situation into which zhe had been immersed, to take matters into hir own control. But how?

In the meantime, Vanu tried hir best to cheer up Joh. Zhe explained about the formal protest as zhe got it organized and sent. <See, there is hope. Ranee may have been sent away, but with time we will be able to contest those actions. Life is long, and there will be lots of opportunities for other alternatives, I assure you!> Vanu almost convinced hirself with hir own arguments.

<You think so?> Joh asked. <It's my fault, you know. Ranee's exile, and everything!>

<That's not at all true, Joh, and you know it! It's the fault of the Council! Furthermore, their heavy-handed tactics may backfire on them, yet! How could it possibly be your fault?>

<You don't understand.> Joh looked miserable. <I was the one who put the idea into their heads! About the gender change, I mean. It was my idea!>

<What?>

<It was at a Caritas meeting. We were discussing how to help you, and I said what somebody needed to do was to undergo a gender change operation in solidarity, since we couldn't simply go off and find non-lindiv sexual partners. The others thought it was a great idea, especially Ranee. Originally, I was going to do the change too. But Ranee convinced me otherwise. I allowed Ranee to convince me that it was the kind of thing zhe could get away with, one more prank. I feel terrible about the way things turned out. The Council didn't treat it as a prank at all!> zhe wailed.

<Ranee never expected them to treat it as a prank, Joh,> Vanu told hir. <Zhe knew it would be different this time. Zhe said that to mollify you. And you can't take responsibility for

Ranee's actions. Zhe's free to make hir own decisions. To deny that is to fail to respect Ranee. I know you mean well, Joh, but Ranee knew what zhe was doing, knew zhe risked punishment.>

To Vanu's surprise and discomfort, the younger sib slid into Vanu's arms. Joh sobbed for several minutes, while Vanu tried to stem the tide. <I don't care! It was still my idea! If I hadn't got involved in that stupid Caritas movement, Ranee never would have gotten involved either. Zhe only got involved to keep an eye on me. We both felt so helpless!>

The talking brought on thicker and denser bouts of tears and for some time Vanu could make out nothing coherent from the jumble of words.

Since hir sojourn at the Yard, zhe had been distant from Joh, who spent much of hir time away from their pard cluster in any case. Vanu had often been left to hirself. Indeed, the other sibs had moved out during the time Vanu had been away. Zhe had been surprised by Joh's active involvement in the Caritas Movement, especially with Dev there. Ranee's involvement had also surprised hir, but for different reasons. Ranee had gained in maturity since Vanu had left. Although Vanu had worked hard to convince Ranee to reverse the gender operation, zhe was none-theless proud of hir sib's actions on hir behalf. Joh's involvement seemed different. Vanu had assumed Joh had followed Ranee into the movement, not the other way around. Zhe now needed to reassess hir younger sib, who also showed signs, despite hir acute sensitivity, of growing up.

Then, as the sobbing ebbed, Vanu realized that Joh was caressing hir in more intimate ways. Not wanting to hurt hir sib at this vulnerable moment, Vanu allowed the caressing to continue, and, with reluctance, began to respond.

There was no taboo in the Kinship against sex between siblings, beyond the taboo against sex in general. Vanu knew that there were cultures where such practices were proscribed, but usually, as zhe understood such things, these taboos were partly to reduce the kind of genetic limitations that might result from pregnancy. Here no such preoccupation could be relevant, since reproduction was carried out only by artificial means.

However, although there was no taboo, Vanu hirself was not comfortable with sexual intimacy with hir sibs, for reasons zhe didn't understand. It crossed a line, somewhere, one zhe hadn't even known was there. But now, faced with Joh's desperate need, Vanu gave in and gave hirself over to the act of making love with Joh.

The experience was very different than hir encounters with Shosee. Not so much because of the different gender mix, but rather because Joh's love-making came out of a neediness for the comfort and assurance that intimacy provided, rather than from a feeling of mutual attraction and shared adventure. Vanu was conscious throughout the encounter of the other's shaken core, of the instability present in hir partner's every caress, the trembling supplication of every kiss. And yet, despite hir resistance to the act of surrender, there came a moment when Vanu felt the connection catch hold. Not the connection between hir and Joh, but rather the one inside hirself, like a circuit closing. Zhe shuddered as zhe entered one of hir long, slow, quivering climaxes. It didn't feel right, and yet it happened just the same!

As Vanu sank from the intense states of orgasm into calmer waters, hir thoughts turned again to Shosee. Zhe remembered the tremulous passions they had passed through together. Would Vanu ever see her again? Greatbear had mentioned she had gone to the School. Was that true? Vanu wondered. If so, what was she doing there?

And finally, inevitably, Vanu began to question the relationship between sexual intimacy and God. What about that vision zhe had had following hir first sexual experience? At the time, the vision had seemed compelling. Now? It was but a distant memory. Why did Vanu feel there was a connection between sex and God? Perhaps sex was simply another part of everyday human experience, another way of "walking with God," as Kinla Pater had explained to hir. Must there be more?

Vanu felt certain there was, although it was hard to say exactly why. Was it related to what Kinla Eugaine had suggested to hir? That is, that the passage to a greater connection with God was fraught with difficulty? Could sex play a role in making that connection possible? And the fact that sex itself was complicated—as Vanu had found out—was that a reflection of the difficult paths involved in walking with God? But it wasn't only a question of connection, nor the act of surrender implicit in sex. There was a humility there, a sense of extreme vulnerability, of being open—but to what? To one's partner, yes, but also to something else....

Joh stirred from where zhe had been curled against Vanu's body. This slight movement broke into Vanu's drifting thoughts, and the insight that trembled just outside hir grasp, withdrew and dropped away from hir conscious mind.

XXXI

ORACLE

"All spiritual truths are contingent."

—Ionian Nazari, *Third Testament*, Accessed from the *All–Human Compendium, Theology*, Ido Era 1537

Following Vanu's encounter with Joh, and the news about Ranee, zhe felt at an impasse. The way forward had become restricted to a narrow channel, and in the turbid waters it was unclear towards which of a limited number of directions zhe should turn. Furthermore, whom could zhe ask for advice? Ranee was gone. Joh was out of the question. Kinla Val and the others were engulfed in their power struggle. Shosee had not responded to any of Vanu's efforts to reach hir. Maybe zhe should try one last time? Zhe sent a new query, then set thoughts of Shosee aside.

The thought of Shosee and her father, however, reminded Vanu of something zhe had nearly forgotten. In the turmoil and fast-paced action of the hearings, Vanu had viewed Greatbear as an ally, and the recent interactions had all but overwhelmed the memories of their initial encounter. But in addition to his role as Shosee's father, Vanu was reminded that Greatbear had persuaded hir to join the Ido. And the Ido was more than just its Court system. Zhe had forgotten about its larger role. The Ido could serve as the confidante zhe sought! Zhe queried hir interface, and in place of the normal neutral information environment presented to hir in overlay on hir visual field, zhe found hirself swimming in a thick, emotionally layered sea of flickering sensations. Moments after the initial shock, a presence manifested itself in hir vicinity.

<Can I be of help?>

Again, although the query was presented in pseudo-voice via the internal channels of the binup, it was accompanied by a warm sense of concern and Vanu found hirself responding in a manner not unlike the one zhe adopted towards Kinla Eugaine.

<How do I, uh, consult the Ido?>

<First time?> It could have been amusement, but it wasn't; it was too gentle for that.

Vanu non-verbally acknowledged that truth, and zhe registered the fact that hir reaction had been picked up without any need on hir part to subvocalize.

<You need to formalize a *question*,> the pseudo-voice replied, but the word wasn't 'question'. Or rather, it was, but it was nuanced and modulated by a complex series of changing emotional states and meanings that suggested something much more global than a question. More a state of mind, a kind of personal history that ended in an open query.

Vanu was fascinated by this unusual interface, unlike anything zhe had previously encountered. Indeed, zhe was charmed. Zhe quickly moved from hir awkward first response of formulating phrases to a much more complex and flexible exchange about states of mind, intentions, and fleeting memories, a constellation of feelings and ideas that encapsulated hir current state of turmoil and the problems zhe faced. Without coming to a definitive resolution in a 'question,' hir query was rather an open-ended plea for guidance, for some form of feedback to the knotty matters that concerned her. Zhe didn't know if the Ido could deal with such a messy query, but the presence seemed to accept it without resistance.

Vanu turned hir thoughts towards timing. Could zhe expect a reply anytime soon was the gist of her uncertainty. Zhe sensed a momentary hesitation, as if the presence had withdrawn itself to consult elsewhere, then the return to full attention.

<The Ido agrees with your assessment that these are weighty issues, and requests time to determine an appropriate response. If you wish an immediate answer, however, a provisional one can be provided. You may consult the following documentation for more information about the limits of the Ido's decisions.>

So the query environment had its limitations, Vanu noted. Straightforward statements still had to be made using pseudo-voice, especially, zhe suspected, if there were legal ramifications. Zhe struggled to recall what zhe knew about the Ido. It might be considered unwelcome among the Kinch, but there was nonetheless some discussion about its strengths and weaknesses, albeit probably laced with more than a few mistaken perceptions.

Although its primary mode of operation was as a source of personal advice and counsel about life's difficulties, Ido decisions were in many contexts legally binding. Or if not binding, at least they served as a legal reference. You could ignore the suggested actions, but if you did, and someone challenged your right to act in that way, you would need to explain why you didn't follow the Ido's counsel, and you'd better have a good argument.

For trivial matters, about which the Ido was often consulted, these considerations were rarely invoked, but not infrequently what looked like a trivial decision might have important implications for other people, and the Ido tracked such things. It was assumed that if you consulted the Ido, you were aware of these consequences. But if you were a member of the Ido, and you didn't consult it for important decisions, you weren't scot free either. If someone lodged a formal complaint, and their arguments were Ido-sanctioned, they were likely to win their case. Only if you weren't officially a member might you have an equal say, but in that case the plaint would be handled by the OutFax Court.

So there were real consequences of becoming a member. From a distance, it might look restrictive. Why would anyone sign on to such a system? In fact, and in practice, the Ido had a reputation of pronouncing wise counsels, and it was a hard system to corrupt. There were rumours that some exercised undue influence over the Courts, but that route wasn't easy. There were lots of checks and balances.

Of course, early on in its development, people realized that the Ido also offered a solution to the problem of government. According to the binup, in the tumultuous early days of the Humanitat, following the arrival of universal access to binach, governments had collapsed along with much of the economy. The emergence of the Ido, with its focus on collective wisdom, offered an alternative to traditional governance structures that quickly became viable, and then the de facto standard. The Faxes had emerged later, as new alliances formed within the post-binach social fabric.

That was what Vanu knew about the Ido, but zhe had never realized how engaging the Ido consultation process could be. Because the Kinship tried to discourage its members from joining the Ido, zhe had simply never thought much about what the process might be like.

Right now, zhe had a decision to make. Allow the Ido to make a tentative suggestion concerning hir future plans, or wait for it to provide a more complete reply, however long that might take. On impulse, Vanu would have opted for the immediate answer, but zhe had no real confidence in the quality of the Ido's choices and zhe was hesitant to be bound, in hir future activities, by such a process. Moreover, during these reflections, an idea had entered hir mind, and zhe had hir doubts it would correspond to the Ido's idea of a wise course of action. So, better wait for its more complete pronouncement, whatever that might be... and get busy.

XXXII

ACTION!

"You cannot avoid the interplay of politics within an orthodox religion. The power struggle permeates the training, education and disciplining of the orthodox community. Because of this pressure, the leaders of such a community inevitably must face that ultimate internal question: to succumb to complete opportunism as the price of maintaining their rule, or risk sacrificing themselves for the sake of the orthodox ethic."

—Frank Herbert, *Dune*, Accessed from the *All-Human Compendium, Literature*, Ido Era 1537

In the wake of hir encounter with Joh, and then with the Ido, Vanu felt compelled to move away from the roles and expectations that had been laid down for hir, and do something unexpected. Zhe would take matters into hir own hands. Zhe even had a bold idea how to do this.

Since the leadership had decided that Ranee's presence at the Annex was exacerbating the divisions among the Kinch, and that a swift and de facto removal of the source of the frictions might lead to calmer spirits, Vanu concluded that if Ranee could be brought back, this might provoke the changes that needed to occur. There were no guarantees, but passively accepting the situation ran against hir growing sense of anger over their treatment at the hands of the Council. Not just hirself, but more especially of hir sib. Indeed, Kinla Val had confirmed that the decision to send Ranee away had been taken without the approval of the Council as a whole.

How could that be organized? Was it something Vanu could do? Go after Ranee and bring hir back? Maybe. Although, there would be no possibility of stealing one of the arships, even if zhe knew how to pilot one.

But there was an alternative—a desperate one, true—but one that might offer a chance of success.

Vanu had remembered hir encounter with the jonah, Tee'hal, Jetsu's friend. The Kinch, in general, refused to use jonahs as regular transport ships, as was done elsewhere throughout the Humanitat. They believed that jonahs were intelligent creatures worthy of dignity and respect, and had a right to service-free lives. But Vanu felt that, if zhe asked Tee'hal and the latter consented to help in this way, as an act between friends, then it shouldn't violate the Kinship precepts in this regard. And the jonah couldn't be controlled from a distance by someone trying to prevent her departure, the way an arship could. Nor did Tee'hal need a pilot. The more Vanu thought about the jonah, the more zhe became convinced that the ploy might work. Zhe would have to go through Jetsu, but was sure the oggie would collaborate.

What about Joh? Vanu hesitated to share hir plans with hir younger sib, but knew that Joh would be devastated to be left out of any attempt to go after Ranee. And, indeed, Joh was adamant about coming, when Vanu explained. Vanu hadn't the heart to say no, even though it was dangerous, almost certainly foolhardy, and risked getting them both into far more serious trouble with the Council leadership. Vanu was already in trouble, but Joh was not. Joh, however, could not be dissuaded.

Nevertheless, Vanu was determined to see Jetsu alone. Having Joh along would complicate the explanations, and Vanu was already preoccupied with how zhe was going to explain things to the creature. So they arranged for Vanu to pick Joh up later if zhe could secure the cooperation of the jonah. They would stay clear of the docking area, but Vanu suggested that Joh wait for them out on the Machine Platform, near the observation port where zhe had met with the dissidents. The location was far from the main thoroughfares of the Annex, and there was a good chance the pickup would go unobserved out there. Vanu assigned the job of organizing supplies to Joh, a way of keeping hir busy and distracted. They did need to ensure they had enough opacs and elpacs to last the trip, there and back again, and some extra bren kits so they could stay clean and healthy. Joh readily accepted the task.

Vanu found Jetsu at hir new habitat. Interestingly, the oggie appeared to be sleeping. His skin kept changing colour. Vanu had no idea that was even possible. The colours cycled through a deep purple and warmer oranges. Was it a side effect of dreaming? Vanu was sorry to disturb hir friend, but time was important. The oggie awoke quickly when Vanu touched him, and was as happy as usual to see hir friend. But the creature was not stupid. <Someth'ng wr'ng, V'nu? Jetsu h'lp?>

<Yes, something is wrong, Jetsu. I need to go starway, to find my sib, Ranee. You remember Ranee?>

The oggie twirled his tentacles, a sign of assent. <R'nee old'r sib? Came t'see's when you st'rway.>

Now that was news! Jetsu hadn't mentioned it the last time zhe had seen him, and neither had Ranee. Vanu felt grateful to Ranee, who had taken the time to go and visit hir oggie friend.

<Ranee's in trouble. I need to go starway to find hir. Do you think Tee'hal could help?>

The oggie rotated his tentacles again.

<G'd'ea! You w'n me t'ke you Tee'hal? I l't h'm know we c'm'ng!>

Jetsu wrapped two of his tentacles around Vanu, then gave a powerful push away from the platform. A few moments later, Vanu realized the oggie was using his jets to propel them even faster.

Vanu didn't know where the jonahs were located. They weren't tethered to the station the way the oggies were. They were a nomad species that moved from one locale to another, looking for new food sources—molecular clouds within the interstellar medium rich in organic compounds, often called shoals. Inside the Plenum nebula there were many such regions, including several not far from the Annex.

<You know where Tee'hal is located?> zhe inquired of the oggie.

<N't f'r,> confirmed Jetsu. After thinking about it, Vanu remembered the jonah herd had been nearby when Vanu had

first met Tee'hal. Even if the jonahs had drifted further out since then, it was unlikely they would be far away.

After about 30 minutes the view of the nebula, in its reds, golds, blues and greens, became hazier. They were entering a moderately thick shoal, albeit a small one. There was a flash of movement and then the oggie slowed his movement by reverse-jetting to reach the near stationary jonahs.

When jonahs were adapted to function in the hard vacuum of space, a longitudinal cavity was created in their bellies, large enough to contain three chambers that could accommodate two or three vacuum-adapted human passengers. These included a small chamber for resting, a larger chamber for working and a chamber for carrying equipment. The internal organs of the jonah were shifted and substantially modified using binach and advanced bioengineering techniques.

Tee'hal now opened his access port, allowing Vanu and Jetsu to pass inside. However, Jetsu balked and refused to enter. <J'tsu stay 'tside,> the oggie confirmed. <Not l'ke 'nsides!>

<You're sure?> Vanu asked. <What did you say to Tee'hal? I need to make certain he's willing to help.>

<W'n't go 'n'wh're if he n't 'gree!>

Jetsu was right. A jonah couldn't be forced into doing anything it didn't want to.

<Tee'hal? I need to get back to the Annex to pick up my sib.>

Vanu received an image of the Machine Platform, of the location where zhe had agreed to collect Joh. The jonah had picked the exact destination from the confused images zhe had sent. <That's it, yes!>

The jonah left the shoal and headed towards the Annex. <Are you still with us, Jetsu?>

<I st'y st'rw'y,> came the enigmatic reply. Tee'hal sent an image of Jetsu clinging to the upper sail plane, once one of the creature's fins, now one element of the creature's collector for the cosmic particles that fueled its movement. They were on their way!

XXXIII

MACHINE PLATFORM

"Be broken to be whole,
Twist to be straight.
Be empty to be full.
Wear out to be renewed.
Have little and gain much.
Have much and get confused."

—Lao Tzu, *Tao Te Ching*, Accessed from the *All-Human*
Compendium, *Theology*, Ido Era 1537

Vanu was elated. The jonah had agreed to help, and they were headed back to the Annex for the supplies they needed and to pick up Joh, then they'd be on their way to the Station and Ranee. Finally, zhe felt that things were going better, after weeks of frustration. It was encouraging!

There were still many dangers, however. Vanu was hoping that they would get away from the Annex before their efforts would be discovered. Even if their binups were still being monitored, as seemed likely, the realisation that things were amiss should take time, and the will to act on that perception, even longer. But even if their efforts were detected, they should still be able to reach Ranee at the Station without being stopped, simply as a result of the limitations of the physics of interstellar travel. Interceptions in space, while possible, were complex to achieve and required preparation and time. It would be far simpler for them to be intercepted once they arrived at the Station. Vanu was hoping, however, that if they were fast enough they might arrive before the Kinch, who were slow moving even at the best of times, could react. Indeed, the physics of space travel should work in their favour, since there would be little spare time for a message to reach the Station before they themselves did.

Vanu reached out binup-to-binup to contact Joh. At first, there was no answering signal. Then, just as zhe was preparing to try again, Joh's binup-mediated voice came through in a confusion of words: <No, they're coming! Stay clear! Do not—> Then the communication was cut off.

Trouble, Vanu realized. It had all been too good to be true.

Tee'hal sent an image to Vanu of the Annex looming before them—the jonah was coming up on the target location. But as Vanu studied the image, zhe realized something altogether unexpected was happening. One of the giant machines anchored to the Machine Platform had moved—indeed, was still moving. Throughout hir entire life, those machines had remained dormant and unused. Now one of them was being operated.

The machine crawling across the Machine Platform towards the waiting figure of Joh, tiny by comparison, was some kind of construction beamer. These behemoths were used to create massive beams and wall segments from the raw particles provided by harvesters that trawled the interstellar medium. The machine could not have much in the way of materials right now, as there were no harvesters in operation. It might contain a limited supply in an internal store, left over from the days when the Annex was constructed. From the distance at which Vanu was viewing it, the beamer appeared to lumber along slowly, but zhe guessed it was moving fast enough to outmaneuver a solitary human. It sidled laterally across the Machine Platform, its movement resembling that of a large crab—indeed, it had pincer-like appendages like those of the ancient crustacean.

The beamer was a large cube, more than two hundred meters in each dimension, upon which were attached half a dozen large, articulated arms. Two of these, near the base of the machine, were hauling it along by grabbing hold of bars that jutted out from the Platform. The machine must be floating several meters from the Platform surface. The role of the articulated arms was to keep that massive mass on its course. Who was operating the machine? Vanu wondered. It was an act of near insanity

<Joh! What's going on? Are you all right? We're almost there!>

The jonah swooped towards the tiny figure as the monstrous beamer drew near.

With a start, Vanu realized what they had to do. <Joh, temp up! Temp up! Set your tempo to five!>

Vanu coordinated with Tee'hal and Jetsu to reset their tempo. At a tempo of five, instead of the usual 800, they might have a chance at forestalling whatever that operator had planned. They also stood a better chance of dealing with the physics of the various moving bodies out there. Five was uncomfortably close to realtime for hir vacuum-adapted bren, however. Vanu could feel the sudden, deep chill as hir bren tried to supply heat at a rate faster than it leaked away.

Vanu wasn't sure Joh had heard hir instruction, but it might not matter. <Tee'hal, I need you to swing in as close to Joh as you can get. Jetsu, do you think you could catch Joh *and* the supplies as we move by them? Before that beamer… before that machine gets there?>

Both creatures assented. Vanu didn't have time to test their resolve further. At the change in tempo, the forward motion of the beamer had slowed dramatically, but so, of course, had their own. Nonetheless, Tee'hal put on a burst of speed, twisting his body so that the Machine Platform became their ceiling. As they swept past, the oggie grabbed Joh. A few moments later, Joh clambered through the access portal, holding hir slight body away from the soft walls to counter the sharp movements of the jonah's maneuvering efforts, still wrapped in the yellow splattered flag of DeoFax, now both dirty and rumpled. Zhe held a crumpled bag between hir hands.

<Need t' go 'gain f'r s'plies,> Jetsu confessed. Obediently, Tee'hal jetted around for another pass.

<I've got a few!> Joh asserted, holding out the bag, but Vanu could see these weren't enough.

They would have made it, but at that moment the operator of the beamer showed hir hand.

<Watch out!> Vanu called to Tee'hal as a huge, horizontal shape shot forward from the beamer towards them. Tee'hal twisted and lurched, causing both Vanu and Joh to crash into the sides of the chamber. Suddenly their binups were filled with a keen wailing, a cry of pain, that almost caused Vanu to lose

consciousness. <Tee'hal? Are you all right?> zhe finally managed to call out.

In answer, the jonah sent Vanu an image of mangled flesh still clinging to the sailfin. Jetsu was gone, leaving only a few flickering pieces of tentacle behind. And the Annex was dropping away behind them as the keening wail of the jonah accompanied them into the void.

XXXIV

TRANSIT

"We all come from darkness, you have to remember that. And we sleep during the night to escape that fact... We'll all return to darkness one day, when the sun burns out."

—Ian Rankin, *Set in Darkness*, Accessed from the *All-Human Compendium, Literature*, Ido Era 1537

Vanu didn't know which of them felt worse. The jonah was still emitting its keening, flooding their binup communications channels, albeit at a low volume now. Joh was curled into a ball and barely acknowledged Vanu's half-hearted attempts to get hir to talk. And Vanu hirself would have preferred to join the other two in their pain, but knew that was not an option. They had set their tempo back to 800. The physics of interstellar travel meant that they gained nothing by operating at faster tempo on the long leg between origin and destination. In fact, Vanu believed they would have to temp down further still if they were to survive the journey with the few supplies they had managed to recover.

Jetsu was gone. Dead. The hollow in Vanu's belly was unprecedented. The operator of that foul machine had launched one of its stored beams at them, intending to hit the jonah, but the massive projectile had hit Jetsu instead. The oggie hadn't had a chance. Vanu wished zhe could allow hirself to wail like Tee'hal, but zhe had to hold things together. And zhe was appalled that one of the Kinch had done this. It was unthinkable. The Kinship valued life above all else. Vanu had thought the Kinch incapable of such acts of barbarism. Would zhe ever be able to forgive them for this? That they could let this happen!

And how had their little escapade been discovered? There was one likely answer that Vanu didn't want to accept at all. Time to get Joh talking, zhe decided.

<Joh, I need you to tell me what happened. We must figure out what our next steps are, and what is likely to be our reception when we arrive at the Station. For that, I need information. Listen to me, Joh! I'm the one who just lost a friend. You've got to give me some answers!>

<They found out.> It was said in a pseudo-whisper, but at least zhe was talking.

<Who found out? And how?>

<When I went to the stores. We didn't have enough opacs in our pard cluster, so I had to go to the stores. And while I was there, loading them into a carryall, zhe surprised me. Maybe zhe had a trace on my binup? Do you think?>

<Who, for fitchu's sake, Joh. Who followed you?>

<It was Dev.>

<Dev? But zhe's in our camp!>

<I don't know.> Vanu could see that Joh was confused. <I thought so too. When Dev realized I was packing away stores, zhe demanded to know what I was doing. I told hir. Like you, I thought zhe was with us. But then zhe went crazy, telling me that we were spoiling everything, that the movement was in sight of its goal, that we mustn't interfere, that we must stop what we were doing. Zhe was furious. I didn't know what to do.> Joh stopped and gazed at Vanu, stalled.

<Go on, then. What happened?> Vanu urged, impatiently.

<I took what I had and fled to the rendezvous point. Dev said zhe would come after me, that we had to be stopped, but I paid no attention. Then, as I was moving though the access port to the Machine Platform, Kinla Chou-Foc ordered me to stop, and to come back inside. I don't know how they found out. I didn't stop, though.

<But then that machine started coming at me. There was nowhere I could go to escape.> Great shudders passed through hir frail body.

Dev! What the fitchu was going on? It was apparent that Dev was acting independently of the Council leadership. Why did we need to be stopped? Vanu wondered.

Zhe must have had something to do with Ranee's forcible removal from the Annex. The Caritas Movement, or maybe just Dev, were trying to escalate the tensions. And judging from Vanu's encounter with the dissidents, zhe might be succeeding! But to use violence to try to stop them? That was beyond any kind of reasonable action.

Still, that meant the violence probably wasn't the action of the Council leadership, which meant they should be all right when they arrived at the Station. Vanu had feared they might be physically seized upon arrival. Zhe was breaking the terms of hir confinement, and that might have consequences.

<We need to temp down, Joh. We don't have enough opacs to make the trip at this tempo. Or elpacs, for that matter. The Station is five days away at humorn tempo, in an arship. In a jonah, I don't think we can travel that fast. We need to temp down in order to fit the trip into a day's subjective time. Have you ever done slow time before?>

Joh shook hir head. Vanu continued. <Well, they say we won't notice the difference. Tee'hal will have to maintain a faster tempo, to navigate effectively, but he will be used to that.> They made the changes and settled down for the trip.

They spoke little on the remainder of the journey. Joh was in a bubble of misery. Vanu made several attempts to break through, but was rebuffed. Vanu was uncertain about the causes of this distress. Zhe didn't believe Joh had been particularly close to Jetsu. It was more likely Ranee's absence that was at its root

Tee'hal was still audibly sad, but didn't seem to blame Vanu for hir friend's death. Instead, the jonah sent hir an image of the Station, insisting they continue their journey. Vanu appreciated the dedication of hir friends, but no matter how zhe thought about it, Jetsu's death seemed so unnecessary. Something had gone seriously wrong in the Kinship to allow such an event to occur. However, zhe needed to keep hirself together, and not give in to the emotion the way hir companions had done.

Later, Joh recovered enough to talk more. <I'm really sorry about the oggie's death,> zhe said softly. <I know he was your friend. I feel responsible for what happened. I just never dreamed

Dev could act so irrationally. I thought zhe had gotten over that kind of behaviour.>

<There was little you could have done, cara,> Vanu finally replied. <It was more an accident, I think, that the beam hit Jetsu. Although if it hadn't been the oggie that was hit, it would likely have been Tee'hal, and we might not have survived either. Jetsu died saving us. And, truth be told, he might not have had that much longer to live, anyways. He was entering his mating cycle, and oggies often don't survive that stage. But I will miss him terribly.>

<I miss Ranee,> Joh complained, as if that were the subject of their conversation.

To Vanu's dismay, hir younger sib slipped into hir arms, seeking comfort. Vanu pushed Joh away forcefully. <I need to be left alone for a while,> Vanu said, by way of explanation. Joh looked stunned, then turned away and curled up into a tight ball again, that damnable flag with the yellow stars wrapped around hir. *Fitchu!* Vanu thought. But zhe couldn't always prevent Joh from feeling hurt! Right now, zhe felt incapable of offering consolation. And why was Joh still wearing that flag?

XXXV

STATION ENCOUNTER

"Thinking begins when conflicting perceptions arise."

—Plato, *The Republic*, Accessed from the *All–Human Compendium, Philosophy*, Ido Era 1537

The Station was the main docking facility for the different habitats within the Plenum Nebula. Every star system within the Humanitat had a docking hub to support the traffic of long distance transports, mostly arships but also jonahs. Although the Plenum Nebula was much larger than any one stellar system, it actually contained only a fraction of the human population usual for such a volume, and so was provided with only the one docking facility.

Vanu was impressed with its compact shape and size. Zhe remembered hir first view of the moonlet that was the Yard, with its untidy extrusions and mottled surface. This habitat, in contrast, was spheroid, some thirty kilometers in diameter, although it had a large gap in its side which served to berth ships. Indeed, you could see the onion-layered structure of the habitat where the docks sliced down into its skin. The bright O star that served as anchor for its orbit sailed past at regular intervals in the distance, the result of tempo slowing

A small shuttle was sent to take passengers from them, since jonahs couldn't be accommodated inside the berthing area. The jonah was then referred to an artificially maintained grazing cloud where he could join others of his kind until needed again.

<We probably won't be here long, Tee'hal,> Vanu told hir friend. <Then we'll get you back home.>

The Station was really a small city. Despite having attempted to contact the Kinship Hospitality House by binup ahead of time, no one was at the docks to greet them. *Just as well*, thought Vanu. They looked up the location of the House—it was halfway across the Station. Vanu requested a threader.

The area near the docks was busy. Although the Station was a microgravity environment, it was pressurized, and movement within it was chaotic. Lots of people in brightly coloured brens were swimming past, some dragging freight boxes and others not, either streaming towards the ships or moving away from them. Vanu remembered that the Station residents were predominantly members of the New Pantheist Church. Zhe wondered if the brightly coloured brens were a fashion choice that resulted from the church's precepts. Zhe remembered that Foresight Argo had been NPC, and also wore bright garments, so that seemed likely.

While most of the Plenum habitats were quiet, the Station appeared to be more commercial in the sense that it supported a greater variety of enterprises offering many different products to both visitors and residents. Here, outside the closed environment of the Kinship, things functioned as they did everywhere within

244

the Humanitat, as a highly sophisticated gift economy. Vanu had learned during hir time at the Yard that the system functioned well. In the context of the abundance created by ubiquitous use of binach, there were few misadventures. When conflicts did arise, these were handled via the Ido and the Fax Courts.

The spindle-shaped threader arrived promptly. Vanu set the vehicle's walls to a high degree of transparency and raised hir tempo closer to realtime so that the world through which they moved, operating as it did at humorn tempo near to 800, appeared to function in slow motion. Although the vehicle tended to stay largely within special conduits dedicated to the threaders, it also passed across open areas. Vanu wanted to get a sense of the activity going on, so zhe watched closely as they crossed these. As they moved further from the docking facilities, the environment became less busy. It also presented itself differently than did either the Annex or the Yard. Vanu caught sight of quite a few people wearing elaborate head pieces. There was also, unexpectedly, more park space, indeed, more areas where vegetation grew. Although there were gardens within the Annex, these were in general walled off from the main passages. Here, the vegetation spaces seemed both more haphazardly located, and less constrained by walls and barriers.

Vanu had hirself and Joh dropped directly at the House. There was no point in being subtle. Hir attempts to reach someone by binup had continued to prove futile.

The House turned out to be a small pard cluster located in a quiet residential area on the seventh level inward from the outer skin. It looked like some sunken city in an underwater kingdom. They pushed themselves free of the threader, using tethers conveniently located, and passed into a small atrium. There, they were finally able to accost someone. A tall figure, presenting hirself as Kinla Lorca, greeted them.

<You're too late,> zhe said when zhe learned their identity. <Your sib has already left. You need to turn around and go back to the Annex. We have no interest in dealing with you, here.>

<What do you mean Ranee has left? Left to go where? Back to the Annex?>

<I thought you knew. Kinla Ranee has joined the Core Service. Zhe left the day before yesterday for the Core.>

<No!> Joh blurted out. <Zhe wouldn't have joined the Core without consulting us. You've forced hir somehow, pressured hir into doing this.>

Kinla Lorca, a frail, pale-skinned indiv almost certainly past hir second century, looked nonplussed. <Not true. I can't imagine anyone trying such a thing. You can't work in the Core under force, the work is far too challenging for that. No, Kinla Ranee proposed this hirself. It seems zhe had been thinking about it for some time. Indeed, zhe underwent some of hir initial training under tempo acceleration before hir departure. We didn't ask for hir motivations. That will be done by the Core Assessment Team, along with hir evaluation assessment, once zhe arrives at the Wellhead. Zhe should be arriving there about now.>

This information passed down Vanu's spine like a shock wave. What the…? What was Ranee up to? Would zhe really take such a momentous decision without consulting hir sibs? Things were happening too fast. Although, given the way tempo worked, and space travel, Ranee might have spent weeks at the Station on accelerated tempo while Vanu and Joh were en route.

In the commotion that followed, a new figure made an appearance. To Vanu's surprise, it was Shosee. Hir heart rhythm became staccato for a few cycles. <You promised you would call me when they arrived,> she said, addressing Kinla Lorca.

The Kinch shrugged. <You're here now. I told you we wanted as little to do with them as possible. Take them with you when you go!>

<I got your message,> Shosee told Vanu as they stood outside the House, waiting for a new threader to come.

<Which one? I sent several!>

<I only received the one,> she said. <Are you going to introduce me to your friend?>

Joh was still withdrawn, but hir eyes flicked upwards as Shosee spoke. Zhe said nothing, however, turning inwards again.

<Joh is my sib,> Vanu explained. <Our other sib, Ranee, was forcibly removed from the Annex and we are trying to catch up to hir. However, Kinla Lorca claims zhe has gone to the Core, apparently voluntarily, although that is very unexpected. Do you know anything about it? How long have you been here?>

<Not long. I scrambled to get here from the School. Originally, this was going to be a stopover on my way to the Annex, but when I contacted the Hospitality House, Kinla Lorca informed me your sib Ranee was being brought here, so I changed my plans. But by the time I got here your sib had left again, and I was going to continue my original journey when I got word you had arrived. You've had quite a tumultuous time of it since I last saw you! I had news from father about it all.>

<Shosee is the, uh, friend I spent time with at the Yard,> Vanu explained to Joh, who remained despondent. Vanu had a

momentary glimpse of what Joh must be feeling. This was the person who had replaced hir and Ranee in Vanu's intimate world. Zhe wished zhe could make it up to Joh, but was again stymied by the fact that zhe couldn't take the responsibility of Joh's own growth away from hir. Sure, it hurt, but getting over such things was what growing up meant, wasn't it? Although, right now, the source of Joh's turmoil was not so much Vanu or Shosee, as it was Ranee. Vanu needed to find a way to let Joh know that zhe, at least, still cared.

The threader whispered up to where they were standing, and Vanu gestured Shosee to join them inside. Shosee hesitated. <I'd rather we found somewhere we could talk privately,> she said.

<I understand, and I wish we could, but we really need to go after Ranee. The sooner we catch up to hir, the better. But perhaps you'd like to come with us? I'm not, um, making any assumptions, but I value your ideas. Three heads are better than two! Joh, you won't mind?>

Joh said nothing. Vanu adjusted hir pseudo-voice to communicate privately with Shosee. <I'm hoping you will have some thoughts about how to reach Joh. Zhe had taken the news about Ranee hard, even before this latest news.> Where Vanu alone had failed to connect with hir sib, maybe zhe and Shosee together would succeed. It changed the dynamics of their interaction.

<All right, I'll come,> Shosee agreed, in broadcast, not private mode. They enmeshed themselves into the vehicle's parflots and the threader started to move. The House dropped away behind them as the vehicle looped around and found one of its dedicated transport tubes. This time, Vanu barely glanced out as they travelled. Hir gaze was held captive by Shosee. <I wanted to explain,

Vanu. After you were sequestered, father convinced me there was little I could do by staying at the Yard. He suggested I return to the School until there was more news, or until an opportunity arose to do something more.>

<I thought you had abandoned me,> Vanu said. <I sent a whole slew of messages, but you didn't answer any of them.>

She shook her head and shrugged. <As I said, I heard nothing. I didn't think it would help for me to go to the Annex. I would be a stranger there, an outsider, and I rather doubted I would have been welcomed this time around.>

Vanu could see her point. Zhe had assumed Shosee would have come anyway, but from a practical point of view, what she said made sense. And the moment one of Vanu's messages had connected, it appeared she had left the School immediately.

The rush of relief that welled up from within at this realization almost overwhelmed the equanimity zhe had been struggling to regain since she had re-entered Shosee's presence. Although, the tidal surges that swept through hir were not as overpowering as they had been at the Yard. If zhe worked at it, maybe zhe could maintain an even keel?

<Any thoughts about Joh?> zhe said privately.

<Well, I can understand hir reaction, I think. Maybe just give hir time?>

Vanu nodded. <I thought the same, but I am aware that sometimes when I opt for that, what I am actually doing is avoiding my own feelings, since I have to be conscious of those to be able to talk to Joh.>

<Well, if zhe is anything like me, zhe may be in need of signs of physical affection. People process emotional stress via their bodies generally.>

The threader chose that moment to make a sharp turn, and then its flank opened. They were back at the docks. Vanu pushed down hir diverse reactions and organized the shuttle they needed to regain access to their jonah. Zhe did take a moment, however, to place a gentle hand on Joh's back, who, despite initially shrugging it off, allowed it to stay after zhe persisted. There would be time to deal with the questions that had arisen after they were on their way, Vanu reflected.

XXXVI

THE CORE

"If all time is eternally present
All time is unredeemable."

—T.S. Eliot, *The Four Quartets*, Accessed from the *All-Human Compendium, Literature*, Ido Era 1538

Additional commentary from the working notes of Doric, Co-Scribe of the Sentiat, Ido Era 1539

The Crucium Matrix technology was the linchpin around which the events we historically call the Crucium Crisis developed. And given Vanu Francoeur's ultimate role in the Crisis, it behooves us to untangle hir relationship with this technology from the early years of hir development as a person, since this coloured hir later actions. The Kinch played an active part in the extension of the matrix technology during the heyday of the Third Exodus, and the key to understanding the Kinship project is to be found in the location they called the Core.

The work undertaken within the Core was of a delicate nature. Essentially, the Core was a sensitive tuning fork. The Crucium Matrix was the set of star-spanning q-fields that provided the carrier waves serving as the substrate for the Ido calculations, that is, that supported the oracular functions of the Ido. Q-fields had been discovered once humans were able to investigate high gradient gravitational fields. Q-fields were generated from changing gravitational fields, in a way that partially paralleled the generation of magnetic fields from changing electrical currents. Q-fields were hence a second order phenomenon. Once discovered, human ingenuity led to the ability to measure low intensity, low energy q-fields, and, eventually, to manipulate and harness them. Q-fields, compared to gravitational fields, decayed more slowly as a function of distance. This made them ideal candidates for supporting a star-spanning computational environment.

Setting up such extensive q-fields, however, required adjusting the gravity gradients inside stars in such a way that resonance effects were created, through constructive interference. If done correctly, this resulted in a coherent, sustained field. The Crucium Matrix was maintained by fine-tuning the gravity gradients inside a sufficient number of anchor stars. Furthermore, this substrate could be extended to larger regions of space by anchoring new stars outside the currently active region or, better still, by anchoring star clusters. The main, central part of the matrix was anchored on two stars, Ascent, a few light years from Old Sol, and a neutron star near the Crucium Institute, some five thousand light years from Sol.

The Plenum Nebula initiative was an attempt to create a much stronger anchor for the Crucium Matrix at a location further afield from its main anchors. Other large anchoring projects were also underway with similar goals. The Messioph project, completed, was one of these which had focused on the development of an anchoring cluster in the galactic halo, and hence well outside the region spanned by the Humanitat. The new Messicaven project was its logical sequel. Also a halo project, it sought to extend the matrix in the opposite direction from Messioph. But these projects relied on the Plenum initiative for their effectiveness. Without the Plenum anchor, the matrix would be too thin and too weak to take advantage of the new extensions.

A star's gravity gradient was adjusted by using devices to modify the gravitational and magnetic fields, and hence to regulate the q-field phases. Magnetic fields in stars affect the gravity by providing buoyancy to the ambient gases. Devices were installed either in orbit around stars, or, sometimes, deep inside them. Resonance was measured using a "tuning" star, that is, a star tuned to the resonances created by other neighbouring stars. Small changes in the gravity of neighbouring stars affect the resonances measured in the tuning star. Furthermore, variable stars were used as clocks—they caused the matrix fields to fluctuate in precisely timed ways. Both tuning stars and variables contributed to creating the matrix substrate.

The work at the Core, therefore, consisted of measuring the impinging q-fields and providing feedback to the engineers involved in installing the tuning devices around other stars, so that the entire initiative would produce the desired anchoring effect. Because the Plenum stars existed inside a cluster roughly sixty light years in diameter, each time the cluster was tuned the process took, typically, several hundred realtime years. This was because the fields needed to propagate out and back again sufficiently often to settle into their new state. In realtime, and with propagation speeds below that of light, this took many times the light diameter of the cluster.

Since the Plenum Nebula was a stellar nursery, another part of the work consisted of seeding the nebula so as to increase the number of stars it produced. This meant that new stars were constantly being added, and a subset of these stars had to be integrated into the matrix anchor as well. At tempo ratings in the Core of 20000, a typical adjustment of the q-fields in the nebula would stretch across two or three days subjective time, while more than a hundred realtime years would pass, and months at humorn tempo. This high time differential meant that the tuning could be handled in one multi-day Core visit, hence facilitating the coordination efforts in addition to the softening of the harsh effects of the stellar interior on the human visitors as a result of the high tempo setting.

Tuning stars were generally selected among G-type main sequence stars. This was because hotter, more massive stars had convective cores. The gases were under constant motion, and particle radiation was much higher. Also, the thick convective envelopes of cooler stars were less advantageous. G-type stars were characterized by radiative transfer regimes, meaning the gases were not very mobile. Only the electromagnetic radiation moved up through the star. Not only that, the nuclear fusion characteristic of these smaller stars was slower and less energetic than in their more massive cousins. These were therefore the safest stars for humans to work in.

Access to the Core was a multistage effort. At the so-called Wellhead, the main residence pards were maintained for Core workers and the entire platform was heavily protected by degenerate matter shielding. From this, qubes could be lowered to several positions inside the star: just above the photosphere or stellar "surface," inside the convective envelope, and at several depths inside the radiative core. Typically, a person would spend no more than a month's continuous subjective time inside the star. People were rotated through shifts while inside the Core so that no one person was exposed for too long a time to the residual particulate radiation whose effects on the body couldn't be entirely eliminated. A month's time in the Core, however, was nonetheless four humorn tempo years, and hence nearly three and a half millennia in realtime.

XXXVII

FROM STATION TO CORE

"There is a darkness in terrestrial things / That will not suffer long too glad a note."

—William Blake, *The Marriage of Heaven and Hell*, Accessed from the *All-Human Compendium, Literature*, Ido Era 1537

The Core was a mere five light years from the Station. At humorn tempo, that was only two and a half days away. If they shipped out for the Core now, they might still be able to talk with their sib before zhe was sent down into the star's photosphere. Once Ranee began the descent, zhe would be incommunicado, and the high tempo meant zhe would be lost to them.

It took longer to set out than Vanu had expected. Joh had come out of hir shell long enough to insist that they should acquire a small two-person flyer, so that they weren't dependent on others to leave and enter the jonah. It seemed a good idea, although Vanu was impatient with the delay. They also had replenished their supplies of elpacs and opacs. This was doubly important now that they had a new passenger to accommodate as well.

They got no interference from either the Hospitality House or the Station authorities, who had no formal relationship with the Kinch, nor was there any sign of pursuit. There were a few raised eyebrows about their youth, but no serious opposition. Perhaps the Kinch had less authority outside of their community than Vanu had always supposed. Vanu also wondered about hir own status with the Kinch. Was zhe considered to be more mature, or less? Ranee seemed to have been given the benefit of the doubt.

Vanu noticed that Joh was behaving more normally. Zhe was not quite so withdrawn as earlier. Zhe had even started to banter with Shosee, treating her like an older sib. When they finally did get underway, the atmosphere was a lot more relaxed than Vanu had anticipated.

They were now floating in the main chamber within the jonah, where they had reset tempo to humorn for the final leg of their journey. Vanu had switched out hir depleted elpac for one with a spicy cranberry mix similar to the ones zhe had favoured at the Yard, when zhe and Shosee had been intimate. Zhe sipped on the mixture now. Zhe had also taken care of replacing Joh's elpac. Instead of using opacs, they were now connected to ports in their parflots that drew on their stored oxygen supplies.

<Now tell me about everything that happened after our tryst was discovered by the Kinch,> Shosee said. The explanations were long and detailed, full of asides and probing questions. Joh, who withdrew again to begin with, actually listened to some of it, and chimed in a few times.

<So if you were to summarize the issues that concern you still, what would they be?> Vanu realized zhe had missed Shosee's frank questions about hir life. Back at the Annex, nobody spoke

so directly. It was lovely to be back with this person who called things by their true names.

<I suppose I grew up with the idea that the adult Kinch had some kind of deep knowledge about the things that matter. And some of them do. But as a community, with the exception of a few indivs, they really don't seem to have much more of an idea than we Novices did. They know how to get by, they have experience with their own ways of practice, but they are equally fraught with doubt and uncertainty.>

<And how is that a problem? A disappointment, I could see. But a problem?> Shosee focused her gaze more directly on Vanu.

<No, you're right. It's not their doubt or uncertainty that distresses me, it's their arrogance to presume to know what is right for us, Novices and younger Kinch, without really listening to our voices.>

<Are you sure that's what bothers you?> Shosee shook her head impatiently, squirming around in her parflot. <I mean, what about this chase after your sib, Ranee? You assumed to begin with that zhe had been taken by the adult Kinch, but later you found out that your own allies had played a role in having hir taken away. And now, you've been told that Ranee has moved on under hir own volition? So it seems to me that the situation is more complex than you imply.> She paused, then added, <I'm only judging based on the things you yourself have told me. In some sense, your own people were complicit in the initial departure, and your sib is complicit in the second stage of the affair. So what is really bothering you?>

Vanu was distracted by Shosee's movements. Zhe forced hirself to focus on the question. <We don't know for certain that

Ranee isn't being forced in some way,> zhe said. <But never mind that, let's assume you're right. I still think the senior Kinch have been rather too casual about their assumptions. They defend a set of rules that have never been clearly defined or justified. I guess, ultimately, what bothers me is they don't seem to have a place for someone like me in their system. Only if I conform to their ways of doing and being.>

Shosee nodded. <Now we're getting to the heart of the problem, I think. What do you mean by their system? Their understanding of the world? Or of God?>

<It's not about understanding,> Vanu said. Zhe rolled hir shoulders. <I think most Kinch accept that how each person understands God is different. No, it's about how we care for each other, despite our different understandings. The Kinship community only seems capable of caring if one conforms to acceptable behaviours.>

<And what about your actions is so different, Vanu, from theirs? What is it about your way of believing that is unacceptable, do you think?>

To Vanu's surprise, it was Joh who answered from hir parflot just behind Shosee's.

<Your body's responses. And your sexual inclinations. You don't conform.>

Was that what hir experiences amounted to? Vanu wondered. Was it all about sex, and not about hir engagement with the world? But no, it wasn't sex that was the problem. It was hir interest in the other. The Other. The Kinship didn't seem to want its members to be outwardly focused, to be attracted towards someone outside the Kinship, as Vanu was. Although the situation with Ranee had shown hir that perhaps hir sib was more of a stranger than zhe had assumed. And Joh also was becoming someone unexpected. So maybe the Other was closer to home than zhe had understood—or even than the broader community realized—as zhe reviewed the events that led up to this moment.

Still, the Kinship persistently rejected opening itself to the Other. They had closed themselves away from the Humanitat, and from the Ido. For them, acceptable practice meant being turned inwards, to their own kind. It was a community organized as a family. They treated God as an intimate partner, a known companion. They were infolded.

Vanu made a gesture of negation. <I understand why you think that, Joh, but I think that is not, ultimately, the issue. I mean the Caritas Movement isn't only about me and my problems with the Kinch. It came into existence because my problems are emblematic of deeper issues, and those issues have to do with being more accepting of different ideas about behaviour, and community, and, yes, faith.> Zhe pulled hirself free of hir parflot and drifted over to the dresser, the unit that allowed them to change their protective brens. <Where my practice is different is that I want to embrace other ideas. It's why I became so interested by you, Shosee. You can see that, right? The Kinch have shut themselves away too long from the wider human community.>

But while that argument had its strengths, Vanu was uneasily aware that Joh's comment had also been truer than zhe was willing to admit.

<Although the fact they were willing to allow me to function as a guest at the Annex suggests they are not completely closed to the outside world,> Shosee pointed out.

<I guess,> Vanu said. <Maybe it depends on how much effort one has to put into recognizing difference within the community. Your arrival at the Annex was a way of encouraging an outsider presence, but not really an opening up of the inner heart to change.>

<Again, I think you are being overly simplistic,> Shosee said. <There are different groups with different ideas within the Kinship, right? Your allies, Kinla Pater and even Kinla Eugaine are hardly in agreement with the actions of the core leadership, by your own admission.>

<But they are a minority. I think we're going to have to agree to disagree on this issue. Now it's time for you to tell me about your adventures since we parted ways.> Vanu thought for a moment that Shosee would resist the change of subject, but she allowed Vanu to steer her towards calmer waters.

<Well, although I have been worried about you, I must admit I have started to enjoy my time at the School. I've been learning about some of the other religious communities, not just here, at Plenum, but more broadly speaking within the Humanitat. There are so many!> Joh moved back to the parflot in the corner of the chamber, while Vanu and Shosee continued their exchange.

Later, after Vanu requested a break to rest and process, each withdrew into their personal bubbles, Vanu to the sleeping chamber while Shosee and Joh stayed in the main area. Vanu checked with Tee'hal about their location and transit route.

The Core wasn't far from the Station. The Station was in orbit around a star that was itself a member of a small open cluster. These were mostly hot O and B stars that had formed from the nebula, but there were one or two somewhat older stars, F and

G dwarfs. The Core was located at a G dwarf. Well, not "at" it, but "in" it! That was why it was called the Core. It was from the Core that the stellar engineering which constituted the primary work of the Kinship within the Plenum Nebula was coordinated.

Upon their arrival at the Wellhead, Vanu didn't actually intend to dissuade Ranee from hir new adventure. On the contrary, zhe admired hir sib, although the move surprised hir. Never would zhe have thought of Ranee as Core material. But zhe did need to talk to Ranee about what had happened, about how Ranee had come to be spirited away, and why zhe had made this important decision without at least checking in with hir sibs. And Vanu was also convinced that Joh needed the closure involved in talking to Ranee. It had become obvious to Vanu that Joh's emotional stability was bound up in hir sexual intimacy with Ranee. Vanu couldn't play that role with Joh, much as zhe loved hir sib.

Vanu adjusted hir tempo to match that of the jonah, still functioning near realtime. ‹Tee'hal, how are you doing?› Vanu hardly needed to remind hirself of the grief the jonah had expressed over the loss of Jetsu. Vanu hirself still experienced the event as a travesty of what the Kinship community supposedly represented, although zhe had begun to view the oggie's disappearance as a part of hir own growing up. Was it not, in a way, an example of how the universe had a tendency to surprise hir at every turn? That Vanu would never again hear the joy and excitement when hir friend greeted hir constituted an absence that throbbed as a physical pain in hir belly and heart, but zhe was also aware of how lucky zhe had been in hir unusual relationship with the oggie.

<Starway's calming solitude,> was what Tee'hal gave hir by way of reply. As usual, although the expression made overall sense, there were things about it that escaped Vanu's understanding. <New frien' solace?>

Shosee *was* a form of solace, Vanu realized, surprised the jonah even knew the word, or the nuance of emotion the word evoked. <Yes, Tee'hal. What can I do to help you?>

<Swim two swales. Harmonize. Will sing to little one.> Did the jonah mean Joh? And what about the two swales? Vanu and Shosee? Another subtle concept the jonah seemed to know and understand.

Some time after Vanu re-adjusted hir tempo to that of hir friends, Shosee signalled a request to see hir. Vanu assented and Shosee entered the sleep chamber.

<I'm worried about your sib, Vanu. You need to talk to hir.>

<Yeah,> Vanu acknowledged. <Zhe's shut hirself away from me. I thought zhe had changed when you came on board, but I guess not. Zhe's clammed up again.>

<And so your response is to ignore hir?>

<No. That's not my intention. I assume when zhe's ready to talk to me zhe will.>

<Because zhe always talks to you about everything? Zhe always shares hir inner states with you? I don't think that approach is going to work. If it ever did.>

How to explain to Shosee about the complexity of Vanu's intimacy issues with hir sibs? And the confusions that may have arisen as a result of Ranee's relationship with Joh? It had all become so complicated! But maybe she was right. Vanu had been waiting for Joh to indicate some kind of willingness to talk, but every time Vanu had attempted to make contact the other had turned away. Maybe zhe needed to try again, and with a different approach.

XXXVIII

THE IDO RESPONDS

"The eye sees only what the mind is prepared to comprehend."

—Robertson Davies, *Tempest-Tost*, Accessed from the *All-Human Compendium, Literature*, Ido Era 1537

As if the universe were also conspiring for hir to face the issue of hir relationship with Joh, the Ido finally responded to Vanu's earlier request for guidance. In the rush of events since they had left the Annex, Vanu had almost forgotten the fullness of the interaction environment that was the Ido, that sense of being surrounded and uplifted. Zhe was just preparing to go back into the common room when the contact descended as from above, like a shroud that dropped down across hir shoulders and upper torso, an almost physical sensation that thrummed with energy. It was an odd experience, paradoxical, combining a feeling of lightness with a sense of weight.

There was also a tentativeness to the initial contact. Presumably, if Vanu had been in a situation where accepting the interaction might be dangerous or difficult, zhe could have postponed it. But Vanu accepted the connection, albeit with some trepidation. Should zhe inform it of recent events? Zhe wasn't sure, so zhe left the question to one side for the moment.

<First, we will present you with a summary of the query, as understood by the Ido, accompanied by a few explanations of the context within which a solution is offered,> the gentle pseudo-voice declaimed. So, it was back in its legal mode, Vanu realized, reassured, although there was still a sense of warmth, meaning the emotional interface wasn't dormant. <The young adherent is DeoFax and resides in the Plenum Star Nursery, within the bounds of the *mycs* community known as the Kinship of the Suffering God. This is hir first official consultation of the Ido services. As a result the Ido response is only partially guaranteed. No penalty will be applicable in case of failure to comply.> Vanu relaxed. Hir actions were not going to be judged one way or the other. Now zhe was curious what the system's response was going to be. Was there a chance it could actually offer help?

<There are several components to the querent's question, and these are based on the complex historical antecedents of hir situation. Zhe has been involved in a relationship which is acceptable within Ido statutes but which is proscribed by the community of which zhe is a member. Hir involvement has led to disciplinary action and sanctions on the part of the latter. Second, hir right to attain mat status has been revoked as part of these sanctions. Zhe has lodged a formal complaint with the DeoFax Court in this regard. Normally, the Court would have upheld hir rights, but it is bound by the extant contract between the Crucium Institute, representing the interests of the Ido, and the Kinship

Council, representing the Kinship. The contract grants certain aspects of decisional autonomy to the Kinship in return for its work to support the expansion of the Crucium Matrix. This has interfered with the Court's ability to defend the querent's rights in this matter.

<Furthermore, the querent's sibling, Ranee Francoeur, following an action undertaken in support of the querent, has likewise been sanctioned, and removed to a distant location. However, it appears that this situation has been adjusted and no outstanding issue remains. Finally, the querent is preoccupied with the well-being of another sibling, Joh Francoeur, for reasons that may be viewed as personal. The formal query concerns the latter two contexts, and may be summarized as a concern for the emotional stability of the younger sibling given the numerous perturbations experienced by all three siblings over the course of recent events. Does the querent accept this summary as a valid representation of the query?>

Vanu was astonished. How had the Ido managed to extract all that information from hir fleeting emotional states expressed during hir last interaction with the system? Obviously, it also had access to the neuws and forums, wherein many of these events had been discussed. That bit about the contractual arrangements between the Kinship and the Crucium was interesting, but not, perhaps, the main thrust of hir current query. The system had, indeed, honed in on the issue that preoccupied Vanu. Although zhe disagreed with the assessment concerning Ranee, that 'no outstanding issue' remained, zhe wasn't sure hir disagreement would make a difference. Zhe also wanted feedback about the situation with Dev, and the attack which had killed Jetsu, although zhe recognized that this had not figured into hir original query. Still, perhaps zhe could raise the issue?

<I agree up to a point. There has been a change in the situation concerning our interaction with the Kinch.> Zhe focused hir emotional attention onto the attack and the loss of Jetsu. Remembering the oracle's remarks about hir first query, zhe attempted to frame the problem more clearly.

<The new situation is noted,> the persona continued. <Our remarks about the earlier situation should be taken under advisement, as a result. Do you wish a quick assessment for this new point? It will be integrated into the answer for your earlier query.>

Vanu nodded hir assent. Zhe didn't want to wait any more for a new answer. At this point, zhe wanted to hear what the Ido had concluded. So zhe assented.

<The Ido recommends that the querent's sibling Joh be provided with emotional counselling from a sufficiently qualified and informed adult. The Ido notes that the querent is no longer at hir primary habitat, but is en route to a facility called the Wellhead. There are several individuals there who could serve as counsellor, people who would have the sensitivity to delve into the emotional nuances of hir state of mind. If the querent wishes, some suggestions could be offered. Note that this decision is provided within the standard format. In future interactions, if the querent wishes to select an alternative format, the change will be noted. Alternative formats include engrams, verse, and structured rites. If explanations of these terms are required, please refer to the appropriate documentation.

<As for the second issue raised by the querent, our quick response is that the Kinship appears to have acted irresponsibly

in this regard, and legal action may be pursued, regardless of the contractual relationship between the Kinship and the Crucium. If the querent does not wish to pursue legal action, the Ido will undertake negotiations with the Kinship or support the querent in such actions as zhe chooses to conduct. Does the querent have additional questions concerning either issue, or something else to ask?>

The disappointment was substantial. Counselling? Okay, involving someone other than Vanu might make sense, but zhe had hoped to obtain guidance in hir own dealings with Joh. Zhe had actually begun to hope that the Ido would be able to provide a viable solution to hir problem. Something that would engage with Joh at the level zhe needed, that would fill in the gaps in Vanu's own ability to respond. An adult Kinch of the right kind could, indeed, provide such assistance, but such an intervention under their current circumstances would not be easily arranged. Even back at the Annex, Vanu doubted Joh could be persuaded to attend such a session, not right away. Furthermore, it was a solution zhe could have organized herself, without the Ido suggesting it. Zhe simply hadn't had much of an opportunity to do anything of the kind, with everything that had happened!

On the other matter, the second point concerning the events just before their flight from the Annex, zhe was more satisfied with the answer. Or was zhe? The oracle seemed to be preoccupied with the legal ramifications of their actions, whereas the legal issues were the least of hir preoccupations. Zhe wanted, first of all, a clear procedure on how to move forward, and some idea of the goals towards which zhe should be moving. The Ido's response was less oriented to longer term goals than it was to more direct gains.

All that build-up, that sophisticated assessment ability, and it came, in the end, to this. Vanu had hoped that the supportive emotional environment provided by the Ido connection could have been used to help Joh. This response was not that. Unless…?

Vanu formulated hir dissatisfaction with the answers into a query state, and added the following more direct question: <Our ability to seek counselling right now is limited, despite the value of the suggestion, and I am worried for my sib's mental well-being. Would it be possible to organize some kind of provisional arrangement?>

There was a momentary pause, then a request for more information. <We sense in your query the presence of another issue that you have not explicitly raised. Another person is present?>

Vanu had forgotten to update the persona concerning the presence of Shosee. Something in hir query had alerted the Ido, however. <I should have mentioned that earlier, you are right. Another person has joined us on this part of the trip, my ama Shosee Greatbear. She is from—>

<The Ido is familiar with this person. We will need a few minutes to integrate the new information. Are there any other updates we should know about?>

Vanu shook hir head, and formulated a negative. Then zhe noticed a withdrawal of the presence, as if it were a person who had turned their attention away. As far as zhe knew, the presence could not be a person. Rather, they were said to be some kind of teach, a machine intelligence, a set of algorithms. Indeed, they tended to use first-person plural as a pronoun. There were literally trillions of such interactions occurring in each second across the Humanitat. Perhaps zhe was holding the Ido to too high a standard—how could it possibly provide effective answers to everyone with whom it interacted? But then zhe remembered how hir initial expectations had been low. It was the quality of the interaction that had raised hir hopes.

The persona was back. <Two different kinds of intermediate support could be offered. The first is a form of personalized coaching, using a systems response. That is, we could coach you directly. But Maestre Greatbear is also known to us. Although young, she has had some experience as a counsellor, within her functions as pastoral assistant to her father. You could work with her, and we will observe only, and make additional suggestions if this is judged necessary. Would that be acceptable to you?>

Vanu was relieved. Zhe hadn't realized that Shosee had experience as a counsellor, although it made sense. And working with Shosee, rather than with the disembodied persona of the Ido, was much more comfortable. <All right,> zhe said. <How should we proceed?>

<For us to be able to observe, you will need to consent to provide access to your visual field, and auditory and tactile inputs. That will allow us to form a more complete understanding of the interaction.> A consent field was input into hir visual field and Vanu assented to the proposed consultation.

Vanu contacted Shosee and explained the arrangement zhe had set up with the Ido persona. <It seems like a useful approach,> she commented. <And it is true that I was involved with helping someone with severe depression before.>

Vanu passed into the main chamber where Joh was curled up in the corner parflot zhe had staked out since they had left the Station. Shosee also came to join hir. <You need to do the main talking, though, Vanu. I doubt Joh trusts me the way zhe does you.> Vanu nodded.

<Joh?> Vanu ventured. No reaction. Zhe drifted closer and the other stirred, turning hir face towards Vanu.

<Leave me alone!> Joh said, and turned hir back to Vanu.

<Can't you at least tell me what I have done to hurt you so? I almost feel it might have been better if I had left you behind as I had originally thought. Was I wrong to bring you? I thought you had wanted to come.>

Joh rolled hir shoulders, but kept hir back towards Vanu and hir body folded inwards.

<You need to approach hir physically, touch hir,> Shosee told hir in private mode via binup. <It's through physical contact that people can be reached, usually, provided there is trust and safety. Zhe will want you to get closer,> Vanu overruled hir own reluctance and obeyed. <You need hir to give you permission, however.> Vanu reached out hir arm, and caressed the back that Joh presented to hir, with the utmost delicacy. The back quivered, but remained a curved shield.

<Zhe doesn't want me to come close!> Vanu said. <Zhe just doesn't. Zhe wants to shut hirself away.>

<Nobody wants to shut themselves away. Remember, zhe is doing hir best to reach you. Never doubt that. But you have to make the effort to overcome the obstacles that prevent hir from doing so.>

<How?>

<You have to help Joh break free from the state zhe's in. It's not easily done, however.>

<How, then?> Vanu asked.

Shosee addressed Vanu's sib. <Joh, nobody is going to abandon you. On the contrary, you have more friends who love you than before. Not just me, but you made other friends through the Caritas Movement, I'm sure you did.>

<…nee…> The pseudo-voice was garbled, but at least Joh had reacted to Shosee's affirmation. Vanu was both impressed and stricken. Of course that was the issue! Joh felt zhe had been abandoned, first by Vanu and then by Ranee! Shosee had understood immediately what Vanu had failed to understand for many days, weeks even. Mainly because Vanu had been preoccupied by hir own distress and discomfort over their physical contact!

<We will catch up with Ranee, I promise you!> Vanu told Joh. <We will catch up with hir and find out what's going on. And Shosee is right about me, too. You are my sib, Joh! How could you imagine I would abandon you, no matter what else is going on in my life?>

Joh's back unbent slightly. Vanu slid hir hands up along hir sib's flanks and around to the front of hir torso. Joh's body lost some of its rigidity. Zhe allowed Vanu's arms to reach around hir. Zhe remained curled forward, however.

<Listen, Joh. It's true that I have developed some new relationships since I went to the Yard. If you're honest with yourself, you will recognize that I was unhappy before I left, and happier afterwards, despite the circumstances of my return. Aren't you pleased that I have found a way forward in my own life? I'm not

going to leave you for my new friends, though. That is never going to happen. I promise you.>

<…nee left.> The words were better formed now, and Vanu understood them. Zhe was making the same promises Ranee must have made to Joh at an earlier time, or at least, that Joh assumed Ranee had made, and Ranee seemed to have reneged on hir promises. Working at the Core meant that effective contact would be more or less impossible. So if Joh believed Ranee had betrayed hir, then what guarantee did Joh have that Vanu wouldn't also do so?

<Maybe Ranee left of hir own free will. We don't actually know that for certain, yet. But if zhe did, then maybe zhe had hir reasons. We all have to find our own path, you know that. I don't think zhe will have left because zhe is rejecting us, even if zhe has gone to work in the Core. Ranee has to follow hir own inner calling. We need to have the greatness of spirit inside ourselves to wish that for hir. Just as we wish the same for you, when you figure out what it is you must do.>

<Leave me alone! I need to think,> Joh said, while the tension in hir back started to relax. Zhe was still curled away from Vanu and Shosee, but it seemed less a configuration of rejection than one of gestation. Vanu took it as a hopeful sign.

<All right, we will leave you to work things out on your own for the moment,> Vanu said. <But we will not be far, and if you want to come and talk about things, we will be thrilled.>

<What do you think?> zhe asked Shosee in private mode. <You think I should stay with hir, physically?>

<Not necessarily. But you should be ready to do so, if zhe makes the slightest effort to open hirself to you. I think you did connect with hir, which is a beginning.>

Vanu queried the Ido persona one final time. <It went as well as you could expect,> was its comment. <Although like your friend Shosee, we believe you should be more physically present for your sib than you have been.>

Vanu acknowledged the advice to hirself. Ultimately, what the Ido persona had given hir was the confidence to accept Shosee's counsel without questioning it. They might have gotten there without help, however, left on their own. So was the Ido really useful? For Vanu, it remained an open question.

XXXIX

PROGRESS!

"All actual life is encounter,"

—Martin Buber, *I and Thou*, Accessed from the *All-Human Compendium, Philosophy*, Ido Era 1537

Three hours later, Joh drifted into the sleep chamber where Vanu was resting. Vanu welcomed hir into hir parflot, passing hir arms around hir sib and holding hir close. Shosee, in a separate parflot, was sleeping. Vanu had been watching her; everything about her still held hir in thrall. Her father might be bear-like, but in sleep, she was like a doe, both graceful and awkward.

<I'm sorry to be such a source of trouble to you,> Joh said.

Vanu squeezed, and protested. <You're never a burden, little one,> Vanu replied. <I just wish I knew what to say to reassure you.>

<You did fine,> Joh said. <Although, I guess I'm still scared about Ranee.>

<Scared? That's a strange thing to say. Scared of what?>

<I'm worried zhe has run away to the Core to get away from me.> There was a quiver in Joh's pseudo-voice. Sometimes Vanu wished they could speak with their real, biological voices, rather than this binup-mediated simulacrum. Zhe was certain that nuances of expression were lost as a result. The overgames zhe had played hinted at such a difference.

<No. Ranee wouldn't do that. Put the thought out of your mind, Joh. Zhe loves you, just as I do. We only want what is best for you. You can see that, can't you?>

<I guess. I wish I could be as relaxed about it as you are.>

<Relaxed about what, Joh? About what Ranee is doing? There is nothing relaxing about the mix of information we have been receiving about that. I may look relaxed to you, but I am not.>

<You're not? Oh.> Zhe sounded confused. <You seem so calm, though.>

<You know my temperament makes me calm a lot of the time. But you have your own strengths, Joh. You internalize the world around you. I struggle to do that. It's a great way to process things.> And it was a useful practice, zhe realized, to recast what hir sib said and did into more positive terms.

Joh shook hir head. <No, it's like living inside a constant storm. I yearn to be steady and stable the way you are!>

Vanu was about to reassure Joh that zhe was more stable than zhe knew, but interrupted hir own process. It was insidious, this tendency zhe had to discredit Joh's internal ways of processing the world by affirming hir own. <Well, maybe if we were all more chaotic, we would be more tolerant towards different ways of doing things. Stability has a tendency simply to reaffirm the status quo. I have been struggling to find a way out of that!>

<Maybe,> Joh said, but there was more energy in hir torso now than there had been, despite the doubt zhe expressed. <What must it be like, do you think, to go down inside a sun?> The sudden change of subject left Vanu at a loss for how to respond.

<You mean, at the Core? I don't know,> Vanu said. <Hot and uncomfortable, I've always assumed. It's not like you can see much, right?>

<No, I guess not. But I've always thought it must be like being inside God. Filled by the power of creation. I can understand the allure.> Did that mean that Joh was becoming reconciled to Ranee's choice? It seemed to be a good sign. <How long do you think someone could survive down there, without the protection of the shielding?>

<Are you worried about Ranee in case of an accident? Although there's always some danger, procedures have been in place a long time, you know. At the Yard, I met an older Kinch who had spent most of hir life working in the Core. I think it's safe enough.>

<But just supposing?> Joh insisted.

Vanu shrugged. <I don't know. They say the alpha particles will cause permanent damage to the body's cells, but how long that takes I don't know. And if one set tempo to a high value, maybe one could survive for a long time, objectively speaking. Although in subjective time, it would all go by in a flash.>

Joh seemed satisfied with the response. Zhe snuggled down against Vanu's body in the parflot. <Are you feeling better, cara?> Vanu found hirself asking, despite hir best intentions. Zhe wanted reassurance, but didn't want to put pressure on hir sib to respond to anyone else's needs instead of hir own.

But Joh said nothing. Vanu tried again. <Tell me, cara, what can I do to help you feel more connected, more grounded?> Zhe remembered what Shosee had said. <More in control?>

Joh shrugged, hir shoulders moving against Vanu's chest where zhe held hir sib. <Maybe just let me know more what your plans are? You often assume I will just follow along, without actually asking what I think about it all.>

Vanu nodded. It was true. Zhe had simply assumed that Joh didn't want to be bothered with the decision-making. Another insidious habit.

Zhe noticed, however, that hir own body thrummed with the energy their exchange had generated. Vanu had not been looking forward to the heart-to-heart with Joh, and had been agreeably surprised by the sense of wonder that had emanated from hir sib. Zhe seemed to have become more reconciled to Ranee's new situation. Vanu needed to be careful, however. Joh might be in a better state of mind than zhe had been, but that didn't mean that relapses weren't possible or even likely. Zhe needed to watch the situation, and do what zhe could to interrupt any tendency for things to drop back into despondency.

Zhe would mention this to Shosee when she awoke. Between the two of them, maybe there was a way through.

XL

THE WELLHEAD

"We are all, every one, condemned to believe that if we could ever make another human understand everything that went into every act, we could be forgiven."

—John D. Macdonald, *Dress Her in Indigo*, Accessed from the *All-Human Compendium, Literature*, Ido Era 1537

As Tee'hal approached the Wellhead, Vanu hailed the occupants via binup. Zhe identified themselves and indicated their desire to talk with Ranee.

<Hello, I'm Kinla Soffo. Let me check if Kinla Ranee is still at the Wellhead. Zhe was scheduled to descend today.>

<Why the rush?> a sober sounding Joh asked, although zhe didn't broadcast hir question beyond Vanu and Shosee.

Vanu agreed. It was as if Ranee was actually running from something. From them, perhaps? Why? Such haste did not make it any easier to manage Joh's fluctuating states of mind.

Kinla Soffo was back. <I'm sorry, you've just missed hir. Zhe started hir descent only about an hour ago, humorn tempo. Once

they're on their way down, we can't reach them while they are in motion. When they get to one of the stations, it is possible to reach them on an emergency basis, but not during descent. That means zhe cannot be reached for three months at humorn tempo. I'm really sorry.>

<And is there no way to, say, join hir? Could we descend and meet hir down there?> Vanu asked.

<No, our protocols forbid it. The qubes are cramped spaces already, and they are entirely sealed. Even if you went down in another qube, you couldn't communicate with hir. Also, binup communications don't work well down there. There is too much interference from the star's electromagnetic fields. The only way we can communicate with hir is through the q-fields themselves! That's why it is limited to emergency contact only. Using the q-fields to communicate interferes with the basic operations. I can let you into the Wellhead, and you can go through hir personal effects, if you like. Maybe zhe left a message. But that is as far as I can go.>

<We'd like to come over,> Vanu stated, speaking for all of them. <If only to better understand what you do!>

Then zhe had a thought. Zhe spoke to Shosee and Joh in private broadcast mode. <We only have a two person flyer. Do you think we could all squeeze in?>

<I'll stay here with Tee'hal, if you like,> Shosee offered. <While I am curious to see how things are done at the Wellhead, there will be other occasions for me to do that. Do you mind if I keep you company, Tee'hal?>

The jonah assented. They received a feeling of discomfort, however. The Wellhead was located close to the star, within its extended corona, and conditions weren't ideal for the jonah. For short periods of time he could maneuver there, but he expressed the intention to move away from the star for a time, until Vanu, Joh and Shosee were ready to leave.

Vanu and Joh snapped opacs onto their brens for the trip across to the Wellhead, to ensure they would have an adequate supply of oxygen. Joh loaded several opacs into a separate pouch on hir bren.

<You're going to be all right, Joh?> Vanu found hirself asking, reaching out hir hand and stopping Joh from climbing onto the flyer. Zhe was still worried. Joh had been doing better, but seemed to have withdrawn again, perhaps in anticipation of what they were about to learn about Ranee.

Joh nodded, but pulled away from Vanu's touch and boarded the flyer. Vanu wanted to shake hir sib, to wake hir up, but knew that was not the right move to make. If only zhe could work it out! Zhe thought of asking the Ido counsellor, but shook hirself free of the idea. Now wasn't the right moment to address the issue. As soon as they had worked out what had happened to Ranee, what zhe was doing, Vanu would have a heart-to-heart with Joh. That was clear. And then there might be time to arrange for a counsellor from among the Kinch present.

Vanu boarded the flyer, and piloted it across the short distance to the access port for the Wellhead. This was an egg-like structure which looked to be tethered to the star by a gossamer thread that dropped away beneath it. The construction looked ungainly, a beached whale thrown up by the seas it served, although Vanu had to dampen the brightness of hir visual field to even perceive it properly. Vanu also had a momentary thought about what the

Wellhead represented. It was like a guardian, or a gatekeeper, a Saint Peter at the pearly gates, not just to support those who went down into the Core, but also to screen out the unworthy.

Onboard the structure, they were met by Kinla Soffo, who turned out to be a charming and sympathetic individual, much younger than Kinla Lorca had been, and quite tolerant of their checkered history. The Kinship Council leadership had forwarded a warning about Vanu and Joh, along with the information that someone would come to collect them, but Kinla Soffo waved that away. <Here at the Core, we are far from the internal squabbles of the Kinship Council,> zhe said, <and try to keep clear of getting involved. This work requires a dedicated mind and a clear conscience, and politics does not mix well with those requirements!>

This position about Kinship politics corresponded to Vanu's memory of some of the things that Kinla Pater had talked about in relation to work in the Core. They had a different attitude towards what went on in the Kinship. Certainly Kinla Pater had, but it seemed that others here shared that point of view.

<I am really sorry you missed your sib,> Kinla Soffo continued. <Kinla Ranee is newly arrived, as you know, but was very keen to undertake the initial training session down the well, and we had no reason to question hir motives. And as I say, once they are on their way down, there's very little we can do. Even if we were to try to pull them back, it would still take weeks to achieve success! The high tempo ratings of Core work lead inevitably to slow reaction times. But we understand about family. Although we may choose to separate ourselves from our sibs, we try to give as much support to the latter as we can. So I'm at ease letting you sift through hir pard here at the Wellhead.

This is common practice, leaving messages or mementos behind when going down the well. Here we are. I'll leave you here. Let me know if there's anything else I can do for you.>

Vanu had hir doubts that they would find much in Ranee's Wellhead pard. They were used to sharing things directly, binup-to-binup, and their pards, although not empty of personality, were more places to sleep than to live. However, in this particular case, Vanu was quite wrong. Ranee had left them an image recording, triggered by their idotags.

<Hey sibs!> The three-dimensional figure of Ranee, larger than life, filled the central space of the pard. <I know you've been trying to catch up with me. I'm sorry I have to break the news via a recording, but I expect to be out of touch by the time you finally get here. Listen, I know it looks like I'm running from something, but it's not so much you two as myself. It wasn't the Kinship Council who got me shipped to the Station, no matter what you were told. It was Dev, or the Caritas Movement, I'm not sure how to separate the one from the other. Dev convinced me that there was a mutiny on the Council in preparation, and that if they thought I'd been forcibly removed, it might help swing things, so I allowed myself to be persuaded. But then, while en route to the Station, I got to thinking about what I really wanted to do with my life. I know you all think of me as the joker in the group, but I haven't been happy working in the Liaison Committee. I feel anybody could do that stuff, and I want to be of real service, not just to the community but also to my understanding of God. And I think working in the Core could give me the kind of satisfaction I truly crave. I know it

sounds sudden, but I've thought about this long and hard, and I think you two, of all people, will understand, more than most.

<I also feel I've taken advantage of you, Joh, over the past several months. I know I initiated things between us, initially almost as a lark, but later more seriously. When Vanu left us to go to the Yard, I was hurt at first, but we both know Vanu better than anyone, Joh, and there isn't a soul more true to who zhe is. Vanu is a model to us all. In fact, my engagement at the Core has more to do with Vanu's example than anyone else I know. If Vanu can't engage with us intimately, it's because of who zhe is, not because zhe doesn't love us or care deeply for us. We each have to find what works for us, and you'll find your road, Joh, I'm sure of it. So I'm letting you go, too.

<This is what I want to do. It is me... perhaps not the old me, but the me I aspire to be, the me I like, for the first time in my life, I think. The gender experiment helped me understand that the old me needed to change. This is the me I need to be, without standing on anyone else's shoulders. So, please, don't try to come after me. You'll hurt yourselves, first of all, and you'll finish by hurting me, too. I want you two to celebrate knowing me, to be proud of what I'm doing, to support my right to be myself. And I want each of you to do that for yourselves, too.

<So I'll say goodbye, now, not because we won't see each other again. We almost certainly will, but we shall be very different people when we do. I wouldn't have it any other way!>

Vanu's heart did several somersaults while zhe listened to this. Zhe was, indeed, proud of the person Ranee had become, although zhe did feel that Ranee had avoided them rather than face them directly. Wondering what Joh's reaction was, Vanu turned, but Joh had gone. And now Vanu could sense hir absence in hir binup. At first only mildly concerned, zhe searched for Joh via binup, but to hir dismay, Joh had cut off hir link. What now?

Vanu contacted Kinla Soffo and explained. Joh must have accelerated tempo to slip out unobserved, zhe realized. Kinla Soffo checked the station logs. <It seems your sib took your flyer and left by the access port a few minutes ago. I assumed you had called back your jonah.> A few minutes at humorn tempo would be almost two days realtime. Plenty of time to do something precipitous, if that was what zhe wanted, even if zhe set tempo to a more comfortable range.

Vanu demurred. <No, the jonah's moved away for the time being. Can we access your sensor field and see where zhe is headed?>

Using hir zoomer, connected to the Wellhead sensor field, Vanu followed the path of the flyer, panic beginning to take hold. <Joh is dropping down through the corona, into the sun! How long will zhe be able to survive down there?> Vanu asked, remembering hir earlier conversation with Joh, about surviving within the sun. Zhe had assumed at the time that Joh had been worried about Ranee, but it now appeared Joh had had this in mind all along.

<Not long,> Kinla Soffo replied, soberly. <The corona has a high particle density and energy, and the photosphere is convective. Both environments are toxic to an unprotected human, even under tempo reduction. And if zhe has engaged tempo reduction, hir reaction times will be too slow to pull up before zhe kills hirself. It's suicide to go down there unprotected!>

<Well, do you have a vehicle that offers some kind of protection? Something that would keep me alive while I go after hir?>

<We do have an automated maintenance vehicle we use to undertake repairs of the tuning devices placed throughout the envelope. It can be operated remotely, via the q-fields. It doesn't have a lot of power, though. It won't be able to boost hir back out, and it is too small to carry a person. But you may be able to communicate with hir... maybe the binup will work up close, or... I really don't know. It's not much, I know. We've never had anyone do this before!>

XLI

DOWN THE WELL

"Love is the unfamiliar Name
Behind the hands that wove
The intolerable shirt of flame
Which human power cannot remove.
We only live, only suspire
Consumed by either fire or fire."

—T.S. Eliot, *The Four Quartets*, Accessed from the *All-Human Compendium, Literature*, Ido Era 1537

Vanu reached Tee'hal and Shosee via binup.

\<We're headed back,\> Shosee told hir. \<But it will take time. Tee'hal needed sustenance. If the Kinch people can send across a flyer to pick me up I can join you, but in the meantime you should get to work looking for hir.\>

\<Tee'hal, I am sorry I didn't think about your needs for nourishment,\> Vanu broadcast.

\<S'allri'...\> the jonah replied. \<T'k care yo'r frien'. S'f'r me, I s'ng starway.\>

<Sorry Tee'hal. You're going to sing?>

<S'ng starway f'r yo'r frien'.>

Vanu had no idea what this meant, but didn't have the time or the attention to ask more. <Kinla Soffo will send someone across, Shosee, as soon as you let them know.>

Kinla Soffo had installed Vanu inside the main observation deck in the Wellhead. The observation deck provided an immersive experience of the environment through which the remote maintenance vehicle, or RMV, was moving, including separate visualizations of the luminosity, magnetics, temperature, gravimetrics, neutrinos, particle density and energy spectrum. Kinla Soffo also offered to control the vehicle. <It's not that complicated to operate, but you don't have any experience with it. And making sense of the readouts requires considerable training. Let me do this for you. You can still watch everything and be right beside me, right here.>

The remote had been at work within the photosphere, not far down from where Joh was still dropping under controlled descent. It was fortunate that Joh was using hir braking rockets to slow hir descent. If zhe had let hirself drop like a stone, zhe would be long gone. While Joh's actions might be suicidal, zhe wasn't stupid.

Kinla Soffo was trying to get the RMV to climb back into the corona, but the vehicle was resisting hir attempts to do so. Although the older Kinch was directing it remotely, the RMV had certain levels of built-in intelligence that couldn't be overridden. Furthermore, the device was operating under slowtime. Just as humans were protected inside the stellar atmosphere by higher tempo ratings, so were machines. The RMV was temped down less than the human workers were. The rate was a mere 2000, but this still made the machine react sluggishly to the commands it received, sent via q-fields. Vanu and Kinla Soffo were operating at a tempo of 200, hence significantly faster than humorn and faster than the RMV.

Furthermore, the vehicle was designed to work in dense environments rather than near vacuum. It was not designed to operate within the corona. They would have to wait until Joh descended far enough to be able to manipulate the vehicle to reach hir. Fortunately, it had been working in the vicinity of the elevator shaft, and hence was close enough to be able to reach Joh provided hir location could be clearly identified.

How long did they have? Certainly not hours! Minutes, perhaps? Seconds? Or was it already too late to reach Joh?

Rescue was, as had been pointed out by Kinla Soffo, likely impossible, although Vanu had had the glimmer of an idea that might help. Zhe wanted to talk with Joh to at least suggest it. And if zhe was wrong, and Joh had no thought of returning, then at least Vanu would try to gain some form of closure, some sense of what Joh was trying to do, or why zhe was doing it.

The surroundings through which the RMV swam was a thick soup. At visible wavelengths, you could see nothing at all. The sensors were dampened so as not to be overwhelmed by the intensity of the radiation. The magnetics showed the oriented field lines, but these were roiling and sliding around. There were pockets where the lines thinned out and the ambient environment became less turbid. At microwave frequencies, you could see a little farther, but it was still a turbulent and murky soup.

The neutrino sensor, on the other hand, showed a faint mist in every direction. Not much help. Within the maelstrom of energies that constituted the stellar photosphere, they needed a radiation signature unique to the flyer that Joh was using, so as to be able to pick it out from the noise on the sensors. In principle, the flyer would look darker, because the light was redshifted by the high tempo value, but they would never see it in this thick soup. And, of course, the flyer was tiny, while the star was immense. Was it a completely useless exercise?

<Is it all right if I ask you questions while you are working?> Vanu queried Kinla Soffo.

<Yes, of course. It will be necessary, in fact. I have to say, I'm not at all certain we will be able to find hir down there. Remember, hir flyer is no more than a speck!>

<Could we find a frequency range where the flyer might be more visible?> Vanu asked.

Kinla Soffo said nothing for a few heart beats. Then: <The peak solar radiation will be redshifted by the flyer's tempo field towards the upper edge of the radar bands,> zhe said, softly, making the adjustments to the sensor to bring up the relevant visuals. <The sun is dark enough in that range that we may be able to pick out the vehicle. But there will be a lot of noise. There is no guarantee.>

<Still, we do know roughly where to look, right? Based on the descent parameters you determined earlier.>

Kinla Soffo nodded, and Vanu observed a box appear on the radar visuals. <If zhe is to be found, hir vehicle trace should be within that box,> Kinla Soffo said. <I'll keep shifting the frequency. Maybe it will show up in one of the bands more than

the others. And in the meantime, I will be moving the RMV towards that sector, so resolution should get better, too.>

Vanu stared at the image for a long time. Zhe could see nothing, no bright spots, although there was a constant movement, a kind of boiling effect, as regions emerged and then faded in succession. Still nothing. *Keep looking*, zhe told hirself. Joh was out there, and not so far away as to be undetectable. Zhe willed the flyer to show itself, then realized what was needed was more a prayer than force of will. It was a practice zhe had resisted of late, but now was not a time for protest. Zhe silently recited the Prayer of Acceptance, from the Third Testament, not because it seemed particularly appropriate, but because it was one zhe loved and remembered, although it was not popular among the Kinch: 'Let all that flows in the wild world pass through me without judgment or sorrow. Allow me to accept all acts within which I am complicit, whether or not I am in agreement. All that is Other is part of me, and all that is me is Other.' Zhe repeated the recitation, over and over, hoping, praying for a sign.

And then, as if in answer to hir silent prayer, Vanu saw something. Not even a point, more like a fleck, there for a moment and then gone. <I saw something,> zhe said, hir pseudo-voice almost a whisper. <Just for a moment. Keep cycling through the radar bands, maybe?> Just more flicker and turbulence, no sharp point. Then, the background went darker. They were near the edge of a sunspot. Could that be…? And, suddenly, Vanu found the fleck again. <There it is again. Do you see it?>

Kinla Soffo glanced at the image, and nodded. <Yes, I've got a fix on it. It's still hard to work out distance, but if we can see

it, it can't be far. It still seems to be above us, though, dropping steadily.>

<So it should be coming towards us.> As zhe watched, the point seemed to gain an aura, and then a ghostly shape. The image processing now had had a chance to work on the scene and the contrast between the bright point and the background became stronger.

<Now that we have located it, I'm going to try to get a fix from the orbital sensors as well. We should then be able to determine its true location relative to the RMV.> Kinla Soffa's pseudovoice rambled on as the flyer came closer. Vanu began to make out its general form in the RMV's field of view, a glowing figure against the darker background. The background fluctuations were now barely discernible in contrast as the image processing suppressed them.

Would Joh see the RMV as the tiny craft moved in towards it? Unlikely, Vanu thought. The RMV was also under its own tempo field, but at a lot slower rating than that of Joh. In order to survive inside the sun, Joh would have had to set tempo to a value close to the 20000 used by the Core workers, whereas the RMV was operating under a tempo field of about 2000, a factor of ten lower. Joh's reaction times would also be at the slower rate.

<We need to catch hir attention somehow,> Vanu said. <Could we try via binup? Using the RMV to boost our signal? At close range, it might be possible.>

<Maybe,> Kinla Soffo said, after a moment. <The binup uses radio waves among others to communicate. Even red-shifted, it should pick up the signal. Try it.>

<Joh? Are you there? Can you hear us?> Vanu set hir binup to general broadcast mode and repeated the phrase several times, but to no avail. Zhe also tried setting it to the private channel zhe often used with Joh, and used the call signal to alert hir. <No response,> zhe finally said to Kinla Soffo. <Is there something else we could do? Could we use the RMV to physically nudge hir? That might be enough to catch hir attention.>

But Kinla Soffo shook hir head. <That seems not only difficult but also dangerous. Both the RMV and the flyer are being buffeted randomly by the turbulence in the photosphere. Although indications are that we are close, to physically connect would be like, let me see if I can find an example you would understand…>

<Two netterball players connecting in a ball pit that is constantly changing spin. Yeah, I get it. But we should at least try. We've come this far. And as for the danger, isn't the RMV smaller than the flyer? We only want to nudge it, not to give it a front-on collision. Although even that shouldn't be fatal.> Vanu thought it strange to be discussing danger in such a wild context. Wasn't the danger already excessive, without any action on their part at all?

<All right, I'll do my best. You're right, we've come this far.> Kinla Soffo focused hir attention back on the maneuvers. <If I can get close enough, I'm going to try to match velocities so that we can sidle up and 'nudge' it, as you suggested.>

It was going to be a near thing. The flyer was accelerating as it dropped, an indication that it was no longer under powered flight, or only weakly so. Gravity had taken control of its dynamics. This made for an added problem. If it came down too fast, matching velocities would become difficult.

But then the flyer began to slow its descent. Joh must have realized zhe was nearing the photosphere and started to apply the braking rockets more strongly. At a high tempo rating, the response of the flyer would be sluggish. Its ion drive was designed to work in the near vacuum of space. It was highly doubtful it could function inside the dense burning gas of the star the way the RMV was designed to do. Once the flyer hit the photosphere, its braking rockets would fail. It would have some limited buoyancy inside the photosphere, but left on its own, it would sink.

<I am adjusting the tempo rating of the RMV closer to realtime,> Kinla Soffo said. <It will make it more responsive to my efforts at control. We may lose the RMV if we leave it too long like that, but that is okay, as long as it does the job it needs to do here and now.>

A brief pause, and then Kinla Soffo continued. <Now I'm giving it a small descending velocity.> Vanu appreciated the running commentary. It was hard to tell what the older Kinch was doing without it, since most of the control happened via binup. The next set of maneuvers seemed to take an endless time. As if sensing Vanu's impatience, Kinla Soffo started to maintain an ongoing patter. <The slight delay between our location here at the Wellhead and the RMV is making the speed adjustments more difficult. It's like, trying to catch the netterball when you can only use jerky hand motions. Wait a moment! Here it comes! Nope, we missed it. It's still there, though. Here it comes again! I think we hit it this time. A glancing blow, but it should have affected its movement in a tangible way.>

<I can see it!> Vanu exclaimed. The image loomed closer again. Vanu wished the controls of the RMV were in hir hands.

Zhe felt sure zhe could do something more substantive to get Joh's attention.

The flyer had a cylindrical fuselage, and two cone-like open cockpits, each with a heatshield that flared outwards, one for each occupant. Joh would be inside the rearmost cockpit—this was the normal mode of flight when used by a single person. The image suddenly lunged forward, and the RMV seemed to have lodged itself against the forward edge of the cockpit in front. <Can you hold it there? Maybe give it a forward velocity? If you could lodge it there, inside the cone of the forward cockpit, we could give it a series of speed bursts.>

Vanu had an idea. They could use the speed bursts to communicate using Morse code. As children, like young people everywhere, and across the centuries, zhe, Ranee, and Joh had played with communicating via Morse codes. Zhe hoped Joh still remembered how to interpret Morse. It was a terribly slow way to communicate, and you couldn't say much, but in the absence of binup-based communications it might still be effective. Provided Kinla Soffo could keep the RMV lodged in place.

Kinla Soffo nodded, struck by surprise. <I didn't expect to land in there. Your idea is a good one, though. A bit more and...> After several tries, zhe succeeded in lodging the RMV into position. <I'm resetting tempo to 2000. As far as I can tell, the two vehicles are now falling together. I'm really quite amazed.>

Now, how to get Joh to pay attention? Vanu's sib may have realized something was going on, as the RMV had given several shoves to the flyer that might have been felt. Given the turbulent medium, however, Joh could have assumed the star's turbulence was the cause of the sudden movements.

The only thing Vanu could think of, was using the RMV to push the flyer forward in sudden bursts. At the tempo of 20000 that Joh would have used to survive inside the star's envelope, zhe would feel it as a jerking motion. And if they were bursts forward, there was less danger of dislodging the RMV. <Do you think I could take over the controls at this point?> Vanu asked Kinla Soffo. <All I want to do is give it bursts of speed. If you show me how to do that, I should be okay.>

Kinla Soffo looked at Vanu and nodded. <I have transferred the controls to your binup. You will see an overlay field showing the main controls in your secondary visual field. The control for burst acceleration is clearly marked.>

Vanu toggled between hir two visual fields and identified immediately the control activator the elder Kinch had indicated. Zhe tapped it once to test it, and the image shook. So zhe got down to business. <I am resetting tempo to 20000,> zhe told Kinla Soffo.

Then, using Morse code on the bursts, zhe created first an S-O-S to get Joh's attention by maintaining the burst for several seconds for the dashes and just tapping the control for the dots.

Vanu wondered how Joh could answer, but hir sib used a similar device to send answers back. Instead of boosting the flyer's engine, however, zhe braked. Which was clever, Vanu realized, since it ensured the RMV wouldn't be dislodged.

V A N U?

Y E S, Vanu answered.

At tempo of 20000, each exchange of messages was taking more than a day realtime. While the flyer was sinking into the sun, its speed of descent meant it would stay within communications range for weeks or months realtime. The real problem for maintaining the exchange would be the loss of power when the flyer's engine gave out.

Now Vanu got down to details. R E S C U E ?

M A Y B E, came the answer, not the one zhe had feared. N O T — S U R E — H O W ! Vanu didn't know either.

W H Y — T H I S ?

W A N T E D — T O — S E E — W H E R E — R A N E E — L I V E S

B U T — W H Y — T H I S — W A Y ?

T O — L O O K — I N S I D E — G O D ? — A M — S O — S O R R Y — V A N U — — R E M E M B E R — O U R — T A L K — — A M — N O T — L I K E — Y O U — — N O T — A — G O O D — K I N C H — — P L A N N E D — T H I S — S I N C E — T H E — S T A T I O N — — Y O U — A L M O S T — C O N V I N C E D — M E — N O T — T O — — Y O U — A N D — S H O S E E — M A K E — A — G O O D — P A I R !

J O H ! — — I N C R E A S E — T E M P O — — Y O U — M A Y — S T I L L — S U R V I V E — — W I L L — F I N D — A — W A Y — T O — C O L L E C T — Y O U

? — — I — G U E S S — — W I L L — T R Y — — S T I L L — H A P P Y — I — C A M E ! — — I S — B E A U T I F U L ! — — M O T O R — W I L L — B U R N — O U T — S O O N — T H O U G H

D O N T — F O R G E T — T O — R E S E T — T E M P O !

Would zhe follow through on the suggestion? Even now Joh seemed uncertain whether zhe wanted to let go of her life, or find a way forward. Vanu cursed hirself for hir failure to respond adequately to Joh's calls for help. If Joh did reset hir tempo to an arbitrarily high number, Vanu would still need to work out the means to go pick hir up. And that wasn't going to be easy!

Once the flyer lost its motive power, it would sink within the star until its tempo-adjusted mass buoyed it up. So maybe it wouldn't drop all the way, but stop short of the centre. They might be able to drop another elevator into the star, and pick hir up that way. At some immense cost, of course, but possible. If the Kinch were willing. It would take decades, however, perhaps centuries, even by humorn tempo reckoning.

V A N U ? Trying to catch hir attention? As if zhe was doing anything else right now!

T H E R E — I S — A — K I N D — O F — M U S I C

Tee'hal, Vanu realized.

Y E S — — T E E H A L — S A I D — H E — W O U L D — S I N G — T O — Y O U

I T — I S — G O R G E O U S ! — — W I S H — Y O U — C O U L D — H E A R — I T — W I T H — M E !

Vanu agreed, even knowing where that would place hir. But if zhe adjusted hir binup, zhe should be able to catch the edge of the… A strange music welled up around hir. Like panpipes, with their quality of the breath inside the hollow sound of wood. Although, it wasn't only sound, but rather sounds mixed with images, and tastes, surges of movement, all undulating within strands of space-time, booming and surging, spilling out across the intervening distances. Was that how the jonahs perceived space? Vanu wondered, awestruck. And how was the jonah able to do it? Not via binup alone; as Kinla Soffo had explained, the electromagnetic fields were heavily saturated.

I — C A N — H E A R — S O M E — O F — I T, Vanu messaged back.

T I M E — T O — F O L L O W — T H E — S T A R — S O N G — B E Y O N D — T H E — E D G E — — S E E — Y O U — T H E R E ?

There was a last, major burst of the engines, and in the jerky motion, Vanu realized that the RMV had been dislodged. Zhe had no means, now, to query that final message, to try to determine what Joh meant. What did zhe mean, 'see you there?' Where? Did that mean zhe was going to set tempo high, that zhe expected to see Vanu again? Or did zhe mean something else?

The flyer was now dropping away below the RMV. How would they find it again? They had been incredibly lucky to find it so far, but the search region had been relatively small, guided by what they knew of the flyer's motion. Later, though, the search volume would become many orders of magnitude larger.

As the tension drained out of Vanu, the emotions zhe had been holding in check threatened to engulf hir. <I've lost the connection,> Vanu told Kinla Soffo. <Can you try to lodge it back in again?> Vanu passed the controls back to Kinla Soffo, who reset the RMV's tempo to its original value of 2000.

But Kinla Soffo shook hir head. <It was pure chance that got us there the first time around. Now the flyer is below us, and dropping further. I think it unlikely we could re-establish that same position. I will try, but...> Vanu watched the image sent back by the RMV as Kinla Soffo tried to chase the flyer, but after an indeterminate time, Kinla Soffo declared, <No, it's impossible. And if the RMV drops any lower, we are likely to lose it altogether. I am going to try to bring it back up through the photosphere.>

XLII

SUNSPOT

"Consciousness is only a dream with one's eyes open."

—Gilles Deleuze, *Spinoza: Practical Philosophy*, Accessed from the *All-Human Compendium, Philosophy*, Ido Era 1537

As Vanu sat in a parflot at the Wellhead, watching, while Kinla Soffo piloted the vehicle upward, the light drained out of hir surroundings. Zhe could feel an immense pressure as if located deep below the surface of some vast ocean with all that weight of water above hir, wanting to crush hir or, if that wasn't possible, to seep into hir body by any opening that offered itself. Zhe was reminded of hir experience being trapped inside the shielding water tanks and shuddered. And despite the membrane zhe wore, the bren, which should have protected hir, zhe could sense the rivulets of fluid squeezing inwards. Panic stirred in hir belly.

Indeed, as Vanu stared, the vehicle entered one of the regions of diminished brightness, as viewed in the images on display obtained from orbit. Vanu realized the RMV was inside the sunspot again, a region near the top of the star's photosphere where the magnetic field burst through the surface. Inside this region, the temperature was about a thousand degrees cooler, enough to show up black when viewed from a distance against the hotter and brighter surroundings, but here, still luminous. So the blackness was more within hir than it was outside.

The sunspot was a hole in the sun's surface through which the light and energy poured away, and a deep, moist black gushed in, pushing away the dim remnants of roiling brilliance that had been there moments previous, along with the last remnants of the jonah's music. Vanu now experienced this as if zhe were being smothered by this profound and total black, shockingly wet, the moisture seeping into hir every pore and orifice, filling hir with its otherness, a crooked plenitude that left hir struggling for the oxygen zhe needed to survive. It was the opposite of the wonder in the jonah's song. And yet, while utterly bizarre, the feeling of enclosure was familiar to hir, a consequence of hir earlier vision. Hir body also experienced an unbearable yearning that pulled hir upwards and outwards, away from the successive troughs of despair and loss zhe felt over Joh's descent into destruction a few minutes before. The contrasts were shocking: desire and grief, suffocating heat and wet darkness, sexual connection and emotional despair. Vanu realized that zhe was inside another vision, just as tormented and confusing as had been the earlier one.

What was real and what illusory? Weren't there philosophers who asserted that all of reality was but a dream? Perhaps this was the real reality finally taking hold of hir, banishing the illusory world of Plenum to the fantasy realm from which it arose? But if that was the case, why was hir life in danger in this other realm? Perhaps it had been in danger all along, and this illusion zhe called life was but the last gasps of a dying creature. Or perhaps the real Vanu was an eternally dying beast. After all, if reality was but a sham, there was no reason the true world would follow the same physical laws and rules as the illusory one. Perhaps the liquid world, the submarine world, the submerged world, was the only universe in existence. Something about this idea appealed to Vanu's sense of irony and justice.

Did God still exist in this more real than real place? Perhaps this wasn't the universe itself, but the inside of God, an idea suggested to hir by Joh's statement from moments before. That seemed to make more sense than that hir true self lived in another universe. Was zhe experiencing life inside the impossible paradoxes of a God? How big was God? This God was all-pervasive, and hence, by necessity, all powerful. Omniscient *and* omnipotent. Why, then, did this seem such a depressing environment?

Perhaps it wasn't what it appeared to be, then. A thin contralto, this voice within hir was, the snout of some ancient creature of the deeps, a denizen of the sodden sediment that lined the sea bottom, a fragment from hir obsessions of an earlier time. This was no god, neither a sanctum sanctorum, nor, indeed, some secret pandemonium. No, zhe must be caught up in some unconscious projection of hir tormented inner self. Was this where the loss of Joh led hir? But was Joh really lost, or merely misplaced for some indefinite period of time? If not Joh, then what other trauma could drive hir to feel this way? Nothing in hir past had prepared hir for this. Could it be something in hir future instead? Something that pulled hir forward? What kind of sending could give rise to such an experience?

And with that thought, as if in protest, Vanu rejected the whole experience, and with a snap, found hirself back in the parflot on the observation deck at the Wellhead. Kinla Soffo was still engrossed in the experience of navigating the RMV. Zhe would no doubt soon put the vehicle back into its automated survey mode, where it had been when they took control of it. Meanwhile, however, Vanu was filled with questions.

Not all of these questions concerned hir sibling Joh, whose sense of self had become bound up within currents Vanu couldn't begin to fully comprehend. It was clear to Vanu that Joh's actions expressed a need for moving beyond the expectations imposed by the Kinch upon their members. They were responsible, at least in part, for what had happened. Vanu hirself had struggled to provide an anchor for Joh, but neither of them had gotten much help from the Kinch.

Indeed, the Kinch had failed all the Novices. Joh and Vanu, yes, but also Ranee, who had found hir own way out of the mess. Not to mention Jetsu, Tee'hal, and even Dev, who had been abandoned to hir own torments. Vanu bore some responsibility, as did Joh hirself, but the trouble had started with the Kinship. Who, however, was ultimately to blame? The Caritas Movement and its representative, Dev? The Kinship Council and its leadership? The dissidents? The Kinch all together? DeoFax? The Humanitat?

God?

And yet. And yet...

There was Tee'hal. The jonah had been there, at the very end, when all the others had dropped away. So, didn't that mean the universe wasn't completely a lost cause? Did it mean that God wasn't entirely crooked? Indeed, the jonah's song mattered.

Vanu didn't understand why Tee'hal had chosen that particular means to communicate with Joh, but zhe knew the jonah had wanted to reciprocate their shared sense of loss over Jetsu. The music (music!) had expressed many things, but not the least of these was recognition of the Other, the issue at the heart of Vanu's struggles with the Kinship, and, indeed, of the Prayer of Acceptance zhe had recited earlier.

Vanu was also mystified by the means behind the jonah's communication. How had the jonah actually delivered the music? It wasn't by binup. Instead, it seemed to have arrived out of nowhere, as if it were carried in the mythical ether itself. The matrix? Vanu wondered. The Crucium Matrix, which supported the interactions with the Ido? The matrix was not electromagnetic in nature, but rather consisted of low frequency, low intensity q-fields. Indeed, that was what the work in the Core was designed to do, to enhance the resonance effects of the q-fields. That the jonahs were able to tap into the q-fields offered at least some kind of explanation for the music, although it raised as many questions as it did answers. It seemed to suggest that the jonahs modulated the q-fields themselves. How was that possible? And if so, how was it that that ability wasn't more widely known?

Assuming it was true, however, Vanu still didn't grasp how Tee'hal's music had changed what had ultimately happened to Joh. Had it, indeed, made any difference at all? And what was it, for that matter, that Joh had chosen to do? If Joh had meant simply to put an end to hir life, then why choose such a dramatic means? Kinla Soffo had declared hir actions would result in certain death, but was that really the case? If Joh reset hir tempo to an extremely high value, then even if it took Vanu centuries, or millennia, to find a way to dive inside the sun and bring hir out, zhe might still survive. Was it a lost cause? And even if not, was that what Joh had truly wanted?

Well, yes, Vanu realized. If Joh reset tempo that way, then that was precisely what zhe wanted. At any other tempo setting, zhe would die, sooner or later, before help reached hir. So there was hope. However, if Vanu was to reach Joh, the technical challenges were huge. And even if those could be overcome, the social challenges loomed even larger. Would the Kinch live up to their responsibility in the matter? Would they even listen?

The thought made Vanu's heart quake. The Kinch had turned out to express themselves more as question than as response. So it was likely that Vanu would have to find help elsewhere. The Humanitat was a big place. There would be other resources, other groups. Somewhere there would be people willing to commit the necessary effort—perhaps simply for the sake of the challenge, not necessarily out of altruism, and certainly not for love, in the way that Vanu hirself was driven.

Love? Or was it guilt? Vanu accepted that feelings of guilt might play a part in hir motivation, but it was more that zhe felt a sense of necessity, a need to carry through hir own commitment towards hir sibs. Just as zhe had learned to let go of Ranee, zhe needed to go to the end of the end with Joh.

The world of Vanu's childhood was gone, with its questions, its doubts, and its sense of belonging. In its place there was now only this aching emptiness, and a vast, searching need that poured through hir inner places, driven also by the energy of hir vision. But ultimately, had the Ido been any better? It, too, had failed them, despite its promises. Vanu remembered the flag with the

DeoFax sigil that Joh had carefully draped over the seat in the flyer. Had that not been part of Joh's final words, with its trail of stars seeping beyond the boundaries of the universe? Vanu now realized that was probably what zhe meant by hir final message. "Time to follow the star song beyond the edge."

And, over and beyond both the Ido and the Kinch, and their failings, what about the God they all served? The mystical encounters Vanu had experienced left hir more confused and tormented than zhe had been before. Zhe understood the notion of a suffering God; what zhe couldn't come to terms with was an incomprehensible one, not because It was too big and too powerful to be understandable, but because It acted in arbitrary ways, with no rhyme or reason, sowing destruction in its wake. A Crooked God. Who would want to follow, to serve a God like that?

And yet. And yet.

<Vanu? I'm here.> It was Shosee, who had finally made it back to the Wellhead. <I'm so very sorry!>

Vanu shook hirself free from the layers of murky thoughts that had enveloped hir. How long had zhe been immersed within them? Zhe glanced at Kinla Soffo, who was still controlling the RMV, although zhe appeared to be closing off the connection. Vanu's anger thrummed inside hir still, but it was tempered by the enigmatic image of the jonah, and its remarkable song. What was zhe to make of it all, and how was zhe to find a way forward?

Vanu showed Shosee the exchange of messages, and tried to explain about the jonah's music.

<Yes, I heard some of it,> she said. <What was that about, I wonder? A way of giving meaning where no meaning seems possible? Something like that, I think.>

Vanu heard Shosee's remark at the same time as zhe came to a decision. If there was a way to set Joh free, zhe would find it, however long it took. It seemed likely this quest would take hir away from Plenum, at least for a time. In any case, zhe needed to find answers to hir own visions, and there were none to be found here at Plenum. What were they, what did they mean, and why were they important? They called out for answers.

Zhe remembered then hir conversation with Kinla Eugaine about… was it transformation? No, about grace. 'From fulfillment into grace,' that was the first stage of the process, right? So if Plenum was fulfillment, then the next stage must be grace. But how did one achieve grace from such twisted beginnings? Zhe had no idea, but perhaps zhe needed to meet with the people at the Crucium Institute. They might be able to help hir understand the jonah and its song, as well, so that made good sense. Although hir first order of business should be to talk to the Kinship Council.

XLIII

A NEW LIFE

"It is those who are scarred by the disappearance of irreplaceable others that become individuals."

—Peter Sloterdijk, *Globes*, Accessed from the *All-Human Compendium, Philosophy*, Ido Era 1537

Vanu looked up as someone came through the portal from the docks, but it wasn't Shosee. Zhe was back at the Annex, but probably not for long. Shosee had agreed to join hir to meet with the new Kinship Council, but her ship was overdue. She was coming in from the Yard, where she had gone to work with her father.

The meeting wasn't due for another hour yet. Although Vanu accepted the idea of talking with the newly formed council, zhe still refused to be held waiting for them in an antechamber. Zhe had agreed to meet with them only if they would meet with hir on hir terms and at a time of hir choosing. Zhe was forced to accept that this meant holding hirself in readiness until the time to go and meet the council. The point was, zhe wouldn't have to wait on them. But now zhe was unnerved by the fact that Shosee was late. Although ultimately if it meant the council had to wait for their arrival, maybe that was God's justice.

Zhe had thought that hir fury might have abated by now, but it hadn't. After leaving the Wellhead, and dropping Shosee off at the Yard to rejoin her father, zhe had stopped at the Station for a long stay. It was an environment zhe didn't know well, except for that brief period in transit from the Annex to the Wellhead, chasing after Ranee. As such, it harboured no significant memory traces to entangle hir. Even after zhe had agreed to the meeting, zhe found zhe resisted the steps necessary to returning to the Annex.

Zhe had organized with Kinla Lorca at the Hospitality House on the Station to ferry Tee'hal back to his family near the Annex. Kinla Lorca had been as abrupt as the last time, but had agreed to making the arrangements. There was enough movement between the Annex and the Station that finding someone to accompany the jonah wasn't too difficult. Truth be told, the jonah could probably have handled the journey on his own, but Vanu felt beholden to the creature. Unlike the way zhe felt about the Kinch.

In the aftermath of their abrupt departure from the Annex, as well as the incident involving Dev, there had been a small revolution inside the Kinship. The old leadership had been replaced with members among the dissidents, including several of Vanu's friends and acquaintances. Zhe should be feeling jubilant, but hir frustrations trying to negotiate with Kinch at the Wellhead prevented hir from such a reaction. Kinla Soffo, who had admittedly been extremely helpful in Vanu's efforts to at least connect with Joh after hir descent into the sun, had been firm about opposing any additional efforts on the part of the Wellhead staff to rescue Joh.

<You have to accept that your sib is gone,> Kinla Soffo had said, firmly but kindly. <Once hir flyer dropped down into the photosphere, our ability to find hir diminished dramatically. And even if you found hir, we have no means of extricating hir, barring sinking another elevator to hir exact location, which is beyond our means.> Despite hir evident sympathy, zhe refused to engage additional resources.

Despite their misgivings, however, Kinla Soffo and hir colleagues did allow their sensors to be used in a long, and ultimately fruitless, search for Joh's tempo signature. If Joh had reset tempo, the sun's spectral signature would be redshifted to radio wavelengths of hundreds of meters or more, perhaps even kilometers. The star was largely quiet at those wavelengths, except during periods of solar activity. Which meant that Joh's vehicle should stand out as an intensely bright point against a dark background. Provided they could get enough resolution.

Vanu realized they had been incredibly lucky the first time to have honed in on the vehicle as fast as they had. That luck, however, had been facilitated by the information concerning the flyer's initial trajectory obtained from orbit. Now it was further down, and likely hidden in the turbulent noise kicked up by the star's combustion processes. The search volume had become much larger, and was getting larger with every passing moment. After weeks of effort, with Vanu insisting repeatedly that zhe needed more time, Kinla Soffo finally called a halt to the process.

Vanu, however, had not given up. Zhe was ready to tackle the next stage of the effort, to try to garner more support from the larger Kinship. That was where Shosee had offered to help. <Let me ask my father if we can exert any kind of pressure on the Kinch, or even get wider support within Plenum for an attempt at rescue. And you should try the Ido, as well.> She was right. Indeed, during hir exchange with the Ido on their way to the Wellhead, there had been mention of support for hir efforts to obtain some form of accountability from the Kinch. This had originally been about the events at the Annex during their departure. But Vanu had updated hir query to accommodate the new situation, and the Ido had confirmed that zhe had the right to ask for more. Vanu followed through and lodged hir complaint. There was nothing further they could do there. Eventually, it should be possible to catch up with Ranee, but that would take time.

On the journey back from the Wellhead, when Shosee had asked to be dropped off at the Yard, she had told Vanu that if zhe succeeded in setting up a meeting with the new Kinch leadership, she would be happy to provide support, and even be present for the meeting. Vanu thought having someone else present, especially Shosee, with her history of involvement in the incidents that led up to this moment, and backed by the power and influence of her father's church, could be important.

Finally, Vanu caught sight of Shosee's head passing through the portal and waved her over. <Sorry,> she said. <The ship was late leaving the Yard. There has been an influx of visitors to the system, and it has affected intra-system transport.>

<Really?> There had always been a steady stream of visitors to Plenum, but this rarely fluctuated much. <I wonder what's going on?>

<Actually, it may help your case. Some of them have come because of Joh's descent into the sun. News of the incident went into the forums and it has attracted a certain number of the curious. Are they waiting for us, do you think?>

Vanu shrugged. <We still have a few minutes before our appointed time. And it wouldn't hurt if we arrived late, either. Tell me about your trip, and about your father. Is he well?>

They talked for a while in the waiting area by the docks, and then Vanu steered Shosee up through the Annex towards the Council chamber. Vanu found hirself relaxing in Shosee's presence. All Vanu's encounters with the Kinch had become tense, so zhe felt grateful towards Shosee for her support. They were no longer intimate together, but their relationship had developed into the kind of friendship Vanu had previously experienced only with hir sibs.

Within the Council chamber were the fourteen principal members as well as several observers. It was a full meeting. Vanu noted Kinlas Pater, Eugaine and Val among others. Kinla Truman, the head of Vanu's Disciplinary Committee was still apparently a member of the Council. Vanu was also startled to see Kinla Hayden, hir supervisor during hir time at the Yard. Hayden had been present at hir initial meeting with the authorities of the Hospitality House, although Vanu did not believe zhe had been unsympathetic to hir cause. Sympathy, however, wasn't where the trouble lay, Vanu reminded hirself.

They were in a circle, although there was no gravity here, nor was there a table. Instead, they used tethers to stop themselves from drifting. Vanu touched one of these to still hir own motion, and put out a hand to stop Shosee's forward drift as well. They were all aligned in the same common direction.

<Kinla Vanu, and Maestre Shosee Greatbear, we are glad to meet with you,> said Kinla Eugaine, who seemed to be the new spokesperson for the group. The honorific for Vanu was no doubt intentional. Indeed, in the flurry of activities that followed the events at the Wellhead, Vanu had received word of hir 'promotion' to Kinla status. It just didn't carry the same meaning as it would once have done.

Vanu said nothing in reply. Zhe waited, and Shosee calmly held position beside hir. After an awkward silence, Kinla Eugaine tried again : <You requested this meeting,> zhe said. <While we might make guesses about its subject, it would be inappropriate to do so, young... Kinla Vanu.>

Vanu was not in a rush to fill the second silence, but finally succumbed as the tension built to a satisfactory level. <There are several items we need to discuss,> zhe finally said, each word in its own small silence. Then, more quickly and fluidly, <First of all, I gather this council is in agreement with the decision by the Wellhead staff not to devote more efforts to rescue my sib. We would like to know why, given the complicit role of the Kinship in the unfolding of events that led to hir actions.>

<You seriously believe your sib is still alive down there?> This from Kinla Truman. Several of the others shifted uncomfortably.

<The last exchange we had concerned the suggestion that Joh temp up. If zhe did so, then, yes, I think zhe will still be alive, and likely to remain so for some indeterminate time. However, eventually the active forces in play within the star will finish the job, so the sooner we can reach hir, the better.>

<That may be the case, uh, Kinla, Vanu,> Kinla Eugaine said. <Although Joh's decisions are not within your control. But you must realize the cost in time and resources you are asking us to commit, for an uncertain outcome. I would be the first to support a concerted effort if I thought the chances of success were at all possible. Kinla Pater, you served in the Core for many years. Is what Kinla Vanu outlines even a remote possibility?>

Kinla Pater looked disconcerted. Zhe hadn't, perhaps, expected to be asked so directly such a question. Zhe looked apologetically at Vanu, paused, but finally spoke. <Although Core workers can survive long periods deep in the sun's interior, we do so only partially as a result of high tempo settings. We are also protected by the qube, the degenerate matter cage that surrounds us as we work down there. Without the shielding provided by the qube—> Zhe shrugged, then added, slowly and with clear regret, <None of us would survive down there long.>

<But the Core workers need to be active,> Vanu replied. <Joh does not. The Core workers are prevented from setting tempo arbitrarily high as a result. Joh has no such limitation.>

<But you also have no firm evidence that your sib followed your suggestion, either.> Kinla Truman again. <Taking a flyer down into the interior of a star is an act of madness, of mental or emotional instability. Suicide. The word has to be used here. It may be an unusual method, but the intention was clear.>

<And we generally treat suicide by giving in to the will of the indiv who attempts it?> Vanu asked.

<That's not what I meant,> Kinla Truman replied. <You are twisting my words.>

<We would not abandon anyone to suicide if we could do something to prevent it,> Kinla Hayden said. <But there are limits to our resources to mount a rescue. Among other things, we have a contract with the Crucium that we must respect. If I'm not mistaken, sinking a new elevator would cause significant delays in our ability to meet our contractual engagements.>

<Have you asked the Crucium Institute if they would consider relaxing their requirements? That would seem a logical first step,> Shosee interjected.

<That would be a good idea,> said Kinla Pater. <They are probably already aware of the incident. Let me take care of organizing such a request,> zhe added.

<Good, yes,> said Kinla Eugaine. <We will follow up with the Crucium and continue the discussion then, if that is acceptable, Kinla Vanu. You mentioned that you had several concerns…>

Vanu's frustrations were barely mollified by the discussion. The matter of mounting a rescue for Joh retained its urgency for Vanu. As Kinla Pater's remarks had suggested, hir sib's ability to survive was likely to diminish rapidly with each passing moment. But the Kinship Council was by its nature slow to act, or, at least, had been in all except the incidents involving Ranee's departure from the Annex. Well, perhaps zhe should set the discussion aside for a moment, and come back to it after raising hir second concern.

<While I don't at all agree that we should await the Crucium's response before undertaking efforts to extricate Joh,> zhe said, <I am also concerned about the deeper issues that gave rise to Joh's actions in the first place. Some of these were raised by the Caritas Movement. The Kinship needs to challenge its doctrines

and cultural assumptions, in order to make sure others do not feel compelled towards similar responses.>

There was a stirring of movement across the Council. Eugaine waited for the other Council members to quieten. <As you are no doubt aware, Kinla Vanu,> zhe said, <the Council has been re-organized following the incidents involving the Caritas Movement. Several reforms are being discussed, but it is premature for us to make definitive statements about any of these. While we recognize the validity of your concerns, there are procedures which must be followed for the kind of change you are asking to be carried out. In fact, your participation in these discussions would be welcome. Your unique point of view would be highly valued in our ongoing efforts to, um, modernize Kinship culture.>

Vanu experienced a perplexing wave of... what exactly? Zhe should be pleased, there appeared to be at least some measure of engagement with the idea of change. But instead, zhe experienced a subsurface irritation, perhaps associated with hir doubt about how sincere they really were. Shouldn't zhe at least recognize the positive role played by Kinlas Pater and Val on the Council? True, zhe had expected more cooperation from Kinla Eugaine, but the latter had played against expectations in hir response to Vanu's plea on behalf of Joh. Maybe that was the source of Vanu's sense of annoyance with the Council—even those who should have been hir allies had receded into the common party line. Even Pater.

And ultimately, maybe, the problem wasn't with the Kinship per se, or its Council, but with Vanu's own state of mind. The experiences through which zhe had passed, like those of a convective cell being churned into the sun's envelope, had closed off access to any kind of return to hir former life. Maybe that was part of what the vision had been about, the wet terror inside the sunspot? Zhe needed to move outwards, away from the world of the Kinship. How to reconcile that drive with hir commitment to rescuing Joh, though? Well, maybe zhe didn't have to have all the answers right away!

Vanu shook hir head, and finally sought to give form to the words zhe needed to say. <I'm not coming back to the Annex,> zhe told them, for the first time publicly acknowledging the change zhe felt in hir makeup. <The Kinship no longer feels like it can provide a home to me. In fact, I'm not even going to stay at Plenum. If the Council was willing to commit to a rescue attempt for Joh, I would stay, but I can see that your resistance is substantive. I also have doubts about the ability of the Kinship to deal adequately with the changes that need to happen. I don't want to discourage you from making the effort, but from my perspective, your process doesn't go deep enough. If it did, we would be having a very different conversation.> Zhe paused, and glanced at Shosee, who nodded back, acknowledgement that she, too, understood. <I'm sorry,> zhe finally concluded, <I wish I could do more, but not all portals that have closed can be re-opened.>

Kinla Eugaine nodded. <You will do as you must, Kinla Vanu. As will we. I personally hold onto hope that you may one day find it in your heart to forgive us for our failures. You will remember the intimate heart as the penultimate stage of the mantra we once talked about? There is hope for finding common ground, though perhaps not in the short term.>

Later, after Vanu joined Shosee on the arship going back towards the Station, they had a final chat about the situation. <What did Kinla Eugaine mean about the mantra? It sounds familiar, but I am unable to place the reference.>

<Zhe was referring to the Kinship's motto, which is 'From fulfillment into grace, from the inner heart to divine transformation, we surrender ourselves to God's path of suffering, sacrifice and awakening.' Kinla Eugaine and I talked extensively about 'fulfillment' and a little about 'grace,' but very little about 'the inner heart.' Although I suppose it is relevant, even if I have no interest in doing anything at all with regard to the Kinch at the moment.>

<I understand,> Shosee said. <I really do. For a long time I wanted nothing to do with my father's calling, his relationships with the ECC. But now, I guess, I have changed. My father has asked me to take on more responsibility in the church, and I've accepted. I know I haven't given the impression of someone much committed to spiritual matters. But you've had an effect on me, Vanu. And I may have learned something from my encounters with different faiths. Something I could pass on to others. But I gather from what you said that you will be leaving us. I will miss you. Your questions always led beyond what people think of as normal. Life will be duller without you.>

<My questions? It seems to me you were the one always asking me things!>

<Yes, but that was for clarification purposes. You ask deep questions, ones for which there are no easy answers. I find I have become habituated to that.>

<Well, at least there is still room in life for some small miracles,> said Vanu, smiling.

EPILOGUE

"Cosmos requires the small, not the large… we listen to the foam, its popping, crackling, rustling, slithering, sighing, the way it gathers and disperses; ours is the slowness, the settling in. Space-time itself speaks to us and for us, but to listen we must enter the slowness."

—Ionian Nazari, *Third Testament*, Accessed from the *All-Human Compendium, Theology*, Ido Era 1540

Additional commentary from the working notes of Doric, Co-Scribe of the Sentiat, Ido Era 1540

Beginnings matter. More than endings, perhaps. Furthermore, the only true beginnings are the beginnings of lives. All others are matters of choice, the chronicler's first and foremost. People view history as a succession of events, but, of course, nothing could be less true. Events don't succeed each other; they occur in vast collections that gather together and then pass into other collections, all of them overlapping in time. Separating out what happens first and what happens later is problematic, especially when widely separated in space. Physics tells us that there is an inherent uncertainty in such matters. So picking particular elements out, and calling these "beginnings" is always contingent. But a person's life has a beginning, although admittedly a fuzzy one. When does self-awareness arise? Can a gamete be considered aware? These are deep questions. But even if one cannot determine after the fact when such a beginning occurred, there is no doubt in anyone's mind that it did occur.

Vanu's story is not the only beginning that matters in *The Ido Chronicles*, but it is—how can we say it—more relevant than most. Of the five braided strands that form the *Chronicles*, Vanu's is the most luminous. And yet, with one possible exception, hirs follows the darkest path, the one that drags us through the layers of muck and pain that coat the lowest levels of human existence. But such paradoxes abound in the stories recounted in these *Chronicles*.

Vanu's tale also defies easy understandings. Even in this modest volume, zhe passes through events that break up standard interpretations of hir life story. What are we to make of hir visions? This is possibly the most pressing question. They seem relevant, and yet, fall outside the main scope of the narrative. Each marks a major transition in hir evolution as a person, but their content defies simplistic analysis.

And what of the jonah's song? The jonahs, as we shall see elsewhere, were a force for change within the Humanitat. They were exemplars of the Other that humanity brought along for the ride. Here, of course, the jonah's song also provided entry into the numinous, in unexpected ways.

But there are other questions that also bother us. Is Vanu nothing more than a youth struggling with issues of identity? Or is zhe a harbinger of a different kind of person? A person more attuned to community? How does one track such changes, when they occur? All we have are acts, carried out by individuals, but from these we are to determine when history changes its character?

Furthermore, there are Vanu's sexual leanings. Hir gender, too, but gender, as we all know, is tricky. Seven genders mean seven modes of being. Gender forms the field from which a person shapes their life, or rather, within which a person's life is shaped. But sexuality is the force that carries us forward into the world. There is nothing simple about this. We form relationships out of this impulse, and not just with lovers, or even other people. Our sexuality carries us into our encounters with the light in the world. And also, with its darker veins.

Furthermore, our sexuality comes embedded within enclosures and zones of interdiction. These, too, are built into our emergent natures. No wonder community is complicated, and families are often impossible. Vanu must find hir way out of the impasse recounted here, but reading between the lines, one infers that hir actions will defy history's attempts to contain them.

Indeed, stories are not meant to be hermetically sealed. They escape around the edges. So although later volumes in these *Chronicles* will provide some answers to questions such as these, do not look for closure. History is not about certainty, even if it is primarily concerned with the past. There are gaps in our knowledge. And stories, as distinct from histories, carry their own unravelings.

THE END

AFTERWORD

Vanu's story will be continued in *Gratia: The Second Book of Deo*. In addition, it will be possible to follow the other four strands that make up *The Ido Chronicles*, that is, the *Books of Uma*, the *Books of Eco*, the *Books of Eng* and the *Books of Ido*. Each trilogy recounts events from a different character's perspective.

GLOSSARY

(* indicates terms referenced elsewhere in the Glossary)

arship: artificially constructed starship, in opposition to a jonah*

ball pit: a microgravity*, or null gravity, closed space for playing a variety of ball games

barnak: a co-adapted organism, derived from underwater barnacles on Old Earth, that grows on surfaces in a hard vacuum environment

beamer: a device that constructs and delivers large metallic beams

binach: the ubiquitous bio-nano technology that pervades human environments

binup: a brain-implanted interface for controlling a variety of binach* technologies integrated into the human body; the binup is installed in the lower brain stem and draws on a tiny power supply installed in the upper shoulder just below the neck; the power supply is recharged from human physical activity

Bok globules: dense absorption nebulae where star formation is occurring

bren: body envelope that serves as a covering and as protection or life support, as necessary; the bren includes receptors that will absorb oxygen-carrying motes* from the ambient environment, channel the oxygen to binach*-enhanced skin pores, and collect carbon dioxide released from skin pores; the bren also includes emitters that release motes filled with carbon-dioxide and waste products back into the environment; the bren therefore acts as a sophisticated interface for transfering binach-mediated functions between the environment and the body

cabrali: these are heavily engineered co-adapted* trees derived from a hybrid of a deciduous tree and a cactus

Caritas Principles: historic principles of communal care and active intervention upon which the Kinship* is partially based

ceethree: a perflav bar* that incorporates parflots* for sexual intimacy

co-adapted: the term used to describe organics that have been adapted using binach* to function in contemporary environments with other organisms

code-sign: an indication that a pard* is inhabited; a code-sign is partly a physical sign, partly a virtual sign displayed via the binup

cognome: the part of the binup* responsible for monitoring diverse cognitive functions

Crucium Institute: the organization that manages the Crucium Matrix* and the ongoing functioning of the Ido*

Crucium Matrix: broad q-field* which collects human mental states as input and uses these to compute game moves within the Ido*; the Crucium Matrix spans a sizeable portion of the Milky Way Galaxy

DeoFax: the faction that embraces theistic perspectives towards human development; see also EngFax*, UmaFax*, EcoFax*, IdoFax*, and NarFax*

dindiv: a traditional male gender, also called a do and sometimes do-boy

dotes: airborne binach* particles which carry out cleaning or waste management tasks, and carry waste material away

dresser: unit which contains the materials used to form brens* around people; to acquire a new bren, a person steps through the dresser unit

EcoFax: the faction that embraces ecosystemic approaches to human development; see also DeoFax*, EngFax*, UmaFax*, IdoFax*, and NarFax*

ecos: generic name given to the group of people responsible for the co-adaptation* of ancient Earth species to space-based environments

elpac: liquid pack attached to a bren* and used for food via a straw-like tube near the mouth

EngFax: the faction that embraces primarily technological approaches to promoting human development; see also DeoFax*, EcoFax*, UmaFax*, IdoFax*, and NarFax*

exfolded: children born via genetic input from two parents (i.e., not clones); see also infolded*

exuterus: an external, artificial uterus heavily equipped with binach* to both monitor and oversee the development of the embryo, but also to begin the embryo's adaptation to binach; exuteri are usually individual, but the support of multiple embryos is possible, including twinned or cloned embryos

Fax Courts: the Faxes each maintain a Fax Court, which judges the legality of game moves based on complaints; the Fax Courts operate across all human habitats with representatives, and physically move to different locations

findiv: a traditional female gender, also called fa-gendered, a fa, or sometimes fa-girl

First Exodus: humanity left Sol System in three distinct waves; the first before the emergence of the Ido* but coincident with the development of binach*, resulting in the colonization of habitats in the Solar neighborhood, a region called the Cradle

fitchu: a swear word; swear words based on sex or body wastes no longer have any potency in an era where sex is fully accepted and body wastes are automatically dealt with via binach*; instead, swear words have been passed down from different language sources

flav: flavoured scent

flyer: small airborne or sub-orbital vehicle

fugue: a collection of tiny autonomously motile binach* elements called variously particles, flakes, flies, candles, motes*, or dotes* according to their function

glov: a specialized term used to describe mainstream communities, usually on the surface of a planet—a conflation of the term "global village;" see also mycs* and grat* communities

grat: a specialized term used to describe a clan or family-organized community that exists outside the Ido* civilization and enters into contractual arrangements with the latter, carrying out certain tasks, in exchange for resources

gravimetrics: sensors devoted to gravity measurements (including quantum gravity)

greenbak: part of the Annex's co-adapted* ecosystem, this is a plant that combines a bacterial gel related to a pre-binach* plant called green sulfur bacteria and kelp-like bladders; greenbak harvests oxygen from non-water molecules in the ambient environment and stores the gas inside the bladders; these are then harvested by motes* or diffused directly into the ambient environment

harvester: a free-floating device that collects ambient matter in interstellar space; harvesters are often used to collect oxygen

headpiece: worn on the head as a fashion statement

Humanitat: the region of the galaxy settled by humans

humorn: a contraction of "human normal" that generally refers to the standard physical conditions under which humanity lives, especially the standard tempo*

Ido: the game to end all games, whose goal is the improvement of the human condition; also sometimes treated as an oracle or even a system of governance

Ido Era: modern dating started with the beginning of the Crucium*, in AD 2500; however, Ido Era (IE) dates attempt to average out tempo* changes; as humanity started slowing tempo, the average tempo value changed— during earlier years, average tempo never varied above 50, but as the reach of humanity expanded within the cosmos, average tempo increased

IdoFax: the faction that views human development through the prism of paradox; see also DeoFax*, EcoFax*, EngFax*, UmaFax*, and NarFax*

Ido forums: both synchronous and asynchronous virtual social environments for exchanging ideas and activities; the forums are organized separately for each Fax*, although there are also common areas for all Faxes

idotag: unique identification associated with every binup* unit; serves as an address for messaging individuals

infolded: children born through cloning

jetpac: a pack attached to a bren* that contains a gas under pressure so that a person may move around in null gravity

jonah: a co-adapted organism derived from ancient whales that serves as interstellar transport

Kinch: the mycs* community who proclaim themselves Followers of the Suffering God; also used for an individual of this community; see also Kinship*

Kinla: honorific given to members of the Kinship*; all members at the time of *The Ido Chronicles* are lindivs*, hence the suffix "-la"

Kinship: the mycs* community who proclaim themselves Followers of the Suffering God; see also Kinch*

lindiv: a person of la gender, who possesses a shoud* in place of traditional genitals

magsoles: magnetized boots that act to attract a person to a magnetically active surface

mastodon: an alternate morph to the basic human, involving huge body size, large muscles, large head, body fur, and tusks; mastodons were originally developed to function more effectively on certain planetary surfaces, but they became popular later for reasons that had more to do with fashion and mores

mat ceremony: the party that is traditionally held to celebrate the attainment of maturation status

mat status: status awarded to indicate adulthood upon completion of an evaluation determined individually for each child, based on data provided by their cognome* or cognitive monitor, a part of their binup*; also called maturation status

Messicaven: a globular cluster on the far side of the galaxy

Messioph: a globular cluster near the North Galactic pole

metallofabric: binach*-enhanced fabric with conductive properties

microgravity: a synonym for null gravity or zero gravity

moelen: a motile membrane that replaces both the penis and vagina in the mi-sexed and ti-sexed individual

motes: free-floating binach* particles which carry oxygen and/or carbon dioxide; they shuttle between receptors on the skins of organisms and suppliers usually in the form of teats (oteats*)

mycs: generic term applied to religious communities; see also glov* and grat* communities (note that these are a different type of category than the factions—mycs communities are often, but not always, associated with the DeoFax* faction)

NarFax: a faction that views human development as irrelevant, and proposes instead to focus on hedonistic values; see also DeoFax*, EcoFax*, EngFax*, IdoFax*, and UmaFax*

nemos: a binach*-adapted variant developed from a pre-binach underwater species called anemones; nemos incorporate a net of thin tendrils that capture moisture from the ambient atmosphere, and they can emit small gaseous particles

netterball: a ball game played within a microgravity* ball pit*, which uses netting to catch and fling the ball

neuws: publically shared information concerning current events made available via binup*; the same term is sometimes used for the information stores that can be accessed via binup

obren: a bren* designed to incorporate receptor sites to take up oxygen from scurrying motes* and to return carbon dioxide to these motes

oggies: co-adapted* species originally based on the octopus, adapted for hard space environments

opac: a pack attached to a bren* that carries compressed oxygen to supplement oxygen intake from other sources, such as motes*

oteat: a supply nozzle for allowing motes* to take up oxygen or to release carbon dioxide into storage modules

overbren: a garment worn over the protective bren*

overgame: an immersive, mixed reality game, often based on a historical context, and often designed to enhance cognitive function

pard: general term for the private spaces assigned to individuals to support their activities; pards are distinct from rooms in that they include specialized functions, such as binach* refresh packs adapted to a particular individual

parflot: a fugue* of weight-supporting particles that acts as an enfolding surface for lying down or for sitting

perflav bar: bars which cater to liquid delivery of subtle flavors and airborne microscents

q-fields: the particle fields used to support the Crucium Matrix*, based on the so-called "q particle;" q-fields are a second order quantum gravitic effect

qubes: generic name for habitat boxes used in extreme energy environments, generally constructed from degenerate matter

ramjet: the motor used by a ramscoop*

ramscoop: the main propulsion system used for interstellar travel; the ramscoop requires an initial velocity generated by other means—this allows the electromagnetic capture field to deploy and collect interstellar matter which will be accelerated and released, generating forward motion

sarde: filling a microgravity* room with people, that is, in volumic space

s-bren: a specialized bren* envelope that accommodates several people—primarily reserved for sexual intimacy

sensenet: array of sensors that pervade any human inhabited environment

sleepnet: a net-like arrangement for sleeping in zero gravity

shoud: an additional form of sexual genitalia, distinct from the penis and testicles, the vagina and uterus, and the moelen*; the shoud is a re-engineered full body skin that allows for tunable, diffuse pleasure—one can increase or decrease the sensitivity at will; the overall effect is said to be more global than the other genitalia

spiner: co-adapted* spiders used for constructing habitats

stareye: co-adapted* starfish

teach: artificial intelligence devoted to tutoring

tempo: binach* that allows the rate of time progression to be slowed at the molecular level; tempo can be varied from unity to infinity, that is, to any time rate slower than realtime

tether: a cable-like filament with high tensile strength that is used to stabilize motion in microgravity* environments

Third Testament: a document in wide circulation, purportedly written by Ionian Nazari, that presents itself as the successor of the First and Second Testaments of Christian thought; the Third Testament, however, supports a pan-religious spirituality

thrailpard: dedicated learning space

threader: a point-to-point transport vehicle inside large habitats; a threader typically glides on a specially designed fugue*, and most habitats are equipped with dedicated tubes to facilitate threader movement in areas that are away from the main pedestrian thoroughfares

tindiv: a modified gender for individuals with both the moelen* and the shoud* but no traditional genitalia; also called ti or ti-sexed

UmaFax: the faction that views human development as a creative or artistic process; see also DeoFax*, EcoFax*, EngFax*, IdoFax*, and NarFax*

underbren: a bren* designed as underclothing

vabren: a vacuum-adapted bren*, that is, a bren that incorporates the means to survive in a vacuum

vacsmell: a pseudo-smell sense activated when in a vacuum environment; the vacsmell is programmed to create 'smells' based on particles detected

zoomer: part of the binup*, the zoomer enlarges visual imagery; note that the zoomer is not primarily an optical device—rather it draws on sources of enhanced imagery within the local sensenet*

ACKNOWLEDGEMENTS

Plenum: The First Book of Deo, as the first volume of a work of considerable size, has taken many years to develop. Initially begun over the course of 2012, the publication of this volume marks a significant step forward towards the completion of the whole series, *The Ido Chronicles*. As is the case with novels generally, the work has not reached this stage without the productive participation and critical feedback of many people. As a Novice fiction writer at the beginning of this exercise, I relied on several precious souls to give me the encouragement I needed to labor on. I would like to thank particularly my brother, Cliff Edwards, who has always given me prompt and highly useful feedback even on early drafts of my novels, as was the case with this one. Also, my dear friend Marie Louise Bourbeau allowed me to read much of an early version of the manuscript on our long drive from Quebec City to Boston in June of 2013. Ursula Le Guin claims that the sound of fiction matters, and reading aloud a text is one of the best ways to "hear" it, even when sitting alone later at one's computer, listening via the memory trace of the voice.

I also received significant feedback from a professional editor with whom I worked, Allister Thompson. I found Allister through Reedsy.com. Some writers are disdainful of the services provided through this site, but I got exceptional help from Allister, who was the first professional to let me know that my writing was well constructed overall, but, of course, could still be substantially improved through careful editing, for which he gave me abundant and relevant feedback across two successive readings.

Another inestimable source of feedback has been my writer friend and collaborator Mary Thaler. Mary has probably read this manuscript more than half a dozen times, which is beyond the call for what I could reasonably request from someone, and her support and encouragement have been one of the mainstays of my own growth and development as a writer. Her support has also been of critical importance helping me steward the revisions for this manuscript.

I also am deeply indebted to diverse members of Cosmos Cooperative and the Infinite Conversations discussion forums; the Metapsychosis journal's writers groups; and, especially, the beta reading group that formed in the spring of 2019. Participants in the latter were Mary Thaler, Douglas Duff (who was the first to propose that Untimely Books, the publishing imprint of Cosmos Co-op, might want to publish *Plenum*), and Heather Fester, a wonderful poet and thoughtful collaborator in several other projects. Over the course of eight weekly sessions, I received detailed feedback on the manuscript from this extraordinary group of individuals, each of them talented writers in their own right.

I would also like to thank my classmates at the *Clarion West Workshop on Performance for Writers*, led by the inestimable (and irreverent) Andy Duncan. The class was focused on the practice of reading from one's work in public and was the first time I read aloud in a public setting from the novel, and therefore constituted an important milestone for me.

Finally, it goes without saying that I owe a debt of gratitude to Marco V Morelli, who provided me with careful and thoughtful feedback on the penultimate version of my manuscript and has served as editor and publisher for the present work. Marco's suggestions led to a major revision of the last third of the book, which, in my opinion, bootstrapped the work to a new level of maturity. Thanks also to members of the Untimely Books production and marketing teams, including Brigid Burke, Eduardo Próspero, and Kayla Morelli, in addition to Mary and Marco, already mentioned. Also my thanks to Jonathan Proulx Guimond for the lovely cover art he designed for me, and to my friend Ernesto Morales who developed the five Ido sigils under the challenging constraints that they had to produce interesting and aesthetically pleasing images in any combination.

This volume is smaller than some of the others to come in the series. It might seem a lot of work to put into one volume, but, of course, it is but the first section of the larger work that will form *The Ido Chronicles* as a whole, which is conceived to be what I call a "braided quintet of trilogies," hence fifteen books in total. By spending time and effort on this first volume, I hoped to save time on later books in the series—not by skimping on necessary steps but simply because aspects of the writing, revision, and publishing process that were mysterious to me to begin with have become clearer and the process of producing the finished work more streamlined. My understanding of the steps involved in finishing and publishing novels has deepened dramatically over the course of this effort, and I hope that as a result this understanding will transfer into a more rapid publishing effort that is nonetheless of high quality.

Note that writing always involves compromises at some level, trade-offs between sometimes conflicting goals, and therefore the finished work is by its nature flawed. Those flaws I claim as my own and no one else's; indeed, they are what make the work so engaging to produce. If perfection were the result, the continued investment of time and energy in other projects would be of lower value. One continues, because one expects, one hopes, to do better the next time. Writing is a learning process, and one that changes oneself as one engages with it. I wouldn't have it any other way. I hope my readers enjoy this book as much as I have enjoyed writing it.

Geoffreyjen Edwards
February, 2021—Quebec City, Canada

ABOUT THE AUTHOR

Geoffreyjen Edwards planned to be a full-time writer from an early age. He took a long detour, however, from graduate studies in astronomy and astrophysics, on through a successful career as a scientist, and returned to his aspirations as a fiction writer only a few years before retiring from his university position. Since then, however, he has been writing and publishing steadily. *Plenum: The First Book of Deo* is not only his first published novel, it is the first installment of a 15-book saga currently in development called *The Ido Chronicles*. He lives in Quebec City, Canada.